# BROTHERS IN BLOOD

A brutal game devised by three intelligent, but bored teenagers escalates into murder. Led by the charismatic and cunning Laurence, the trio of 'brothers' meets once a year to carry out untraceable, motiveless murders – for fun. Until, years later, they must murder in order to protect one of their own, leaving themselves vulnerable to discovery. This killing is investigated by Detective Inspector Paul Snow, a complex man with a secret of his own which links him to his murder. As Snow grows closer to unmasking the killers, his professional life begins to unravel in a terrifying fashion.

# BROTHERS IN BLOOD

# BROTHERS IN BLOOD

*by*

David Stuart Davies

**Magna Large Print Books**
Long Preston, North Yorkshire,
BD23 4ND, England.

British Library Cataloguing in Publication Data.

Davies, David Stuart
        Brothers in blood.

        A catalogue record of this book is
        available from the British Library

        ISBN   978-0-7505-4268-5

First published in Great Britain in 2013 by The Mystery Press,
an imprint of The History Press

Published in Large Print 2016 by arrangement with
The History Press

Magna Large Print is an imprint of Library Magna Books Ltd.

Printed and bound in Great Britain by
T.J. (International) Ltd., Cornwall, PL28 8RW

*To Katie, as always, with love.*

# PROLOGUE

## 1970

They waited.

Despite their nervousness and apprehension, they were very patient in those days. Simply because they could afford to wait. Time, eternity, the future and youth were all on their side. For them the whole unfolding nature of life was just beginning. There was no rush; such bright boys could pace themselves. The arrogance of salad days quelled all other dark concerns. Future dangers were unthought of. Here they were: ready for the big adventure. They had made the decision. It was irrevocable. Although there was no going back, equally they were in no hurry. It had to be done properly and so they were content to take their time until everything slotted neatly into place. There must be no mistakes.

It had been agreed between them that once the lucky prize winner had been chosen, the recipient of their beneficence, as Laurence referred to him, they would stick to that decision, no matter what obstacles were thrown in their way. That was part of the appeal, the thrill of the venture. After all, it wouldn't be as much fun if it all went too easily. There had to be some difficulty, some danger to spice things up.

After all, fear was part of the drug.

11

And this was the night.

The first test.

One for the memory bank.

It was Laurence, of course, who had picked out the old guy and the other two had readily agreed that he seemed an ideal candidate. He looked ragged and desperate, hostel based no doubt, and with no real function in the world. A piece of shit on the heel of society. Please feel sorry for me, his grubby demeanour seemed to say to them. I fucked up my life and I just exist from day to day so I need your sympathy and generosity. Please give me money to enable me to get drunk, piss my pants, sleep in a stinking room with a lot of other dead beats and then face another day of degradation and begging. Please feel sorry for me.

There was no debate. He was better off dead.

And so they waited, the three of them, in that dingy, foul smelling boozer with the noisy one-armed bandit, crap music, grim lighting, sticky carpet and with what they regarded as the greatest collection of low life ever seen under one roof. Alex did make a comment about it being a good job P. T. Barnum wasn't still around or he'd sign up the whole lot for a freak show attraction under his big top. These solitary creatures were glimpsed through eddies of cigarette smoke which swirled lazily about the place like swathes of grey ectoplasm, further heightening the unreality of the occasion.

Laurence was aware that they would have looked odd themselves in such an establishment if they'd gone as *themselves*. They would have stuck out like three vicars in a brothel. A trio of young, clean and intelligent faces would have really attracted the attention of the degenerate clientele. However, on Laurence's instructions they had carefully dressed down for the occasion – way down, almost into the realms of fancy dress – and altered their natural appearance with greasy hair, a few fake tattoos and grimy stubble. Laurence, who had a talent for this kind of thing, was almost unrecognisable from his usual debonair and arrogant self. Their theatrical efforts had paid off for they blended in perfectly with the surroundings and no one took any notice of the three scruffy lads huddled in the darkest corner of the bar. They had become invisible men.

The other punters sat, their noses stuck in a glass, considering the ashes of their lives and only acknowledging another human being when they grunted at the barman asking for another drink.

Their chosen prize winner, whom Laurence had christened Alpha Beta, sat at the end of the bar, perched precariously on a rickety stool, nursing a pint of cheap dark beer. Apart from the moments when he took large gulps from the glass, his throat pulsating in a strange reptilian fashion, he could have been a waxwork doll. Surreptitiously they studied this creature whose face was ingrained with the grime of the street, the nose raddled and bulbous with pores like small moist volcanic craters and eyes that were rheumy, lifeless and bleak. He could have been aged anywhere between forty and seventy.

One thing was for sure: he wasn't going to get much older.

God knows what he had been in some other life,

thought Russell. He'd been a son, probably a husband, maybe a father and most likely an employee at some time. What had happened? What had he done or what had been done to him to cause the humanity to seep away? How had he become detached, amputated from mainstream society? What tragedy or what farce had brought him to the gutter? He almost felt sorry for the bastard. Well, he thought, his suffering was almost over.

'You know he's going to stay here until chucking out time,' Russell observed quietly. 'It might be best if we wait for him outside.'

Laurence shook his head. 'That will look far too suspicious: a group of youths hanging about outside a pub late at night. We don't want to have some diligent copper pulling up in his police car to ask us what we're doing. No. We wait in here.'

They had drawn lots to see who was to be in charge of this particular operation and, to the relief of Russell and Alex, Laurence had won and so they were obliged to obey any decision he made. That was part of the rules.

And so they continued to wait. They waited through another two pints that Alpha Beta downed sporadically. It was nearing closing time and the clientele began to leave. Like rusty automatons, they shuffled towards the door individually, dragging their weary limbs out into the winter cold, solitary grey figures, Billy no mates, off to some grim and greasy bed somewhere. Life on the planet Scumball.

Eventually, Alpha Beta slipped off his stool and gave the barman a vague, drunken smile and headed for the door. He swaggered past their

14

table without a glance in their direction, his eyes hooded with inebriation. As he passed through the door, the three of them exchanged nods. This was it.

It was time.

Russell grinned nervously. Fear and excitement throbbed through his body and he suddenly discovered that his hands were clammy and beads of sweat were trickling down his brow. But strangely he found that it was a thoroughly pleasurable sensation, acknowledging possibly for the first time that this was a game no more. This was the real thing.

He glanced across at the other two. Alex seemed to be sharing similar emotions: eager but anxious with a touch of suppressed fear in his fixed expression. Laurence was as cool as ever, his face almost blank apart from a hint of excitement in that feral grin that hovered briefly on his thin, pale lips.

They waited exactly one minute before following their prize winner out into the dark. He hadn't gone far. He was less than thirty yards ahead of them, a shambling silhouette, shuffling aimlessly along the pavement occasionally muttering to himself, his breath escaping in small white clouds into the sharp air. Without a word, they followed him casually at a safe distance.

It was late November and a patina of frost was in the process of icing the pavement. In the distance, to their left, they could see the vague shapes of the town's Christmas decorations: the garish coloured lights, the large illuminated Santas and grinning snowmen. However, the council's Christmas cheer didn't stretch to this benighted part of the town. This was no-man's land, ignored and rejected by the local burghers. No fairy lights here – only the harsh yellow glare of sodium lamps.

As mere foot soldiers, Russell and Alex waited obediently for Laurence's command. He was aware that although the street was quiet with no pedestrians in view, the road was too well lit, too busy with traffic for it to be safe to take action now. They would have to wait until the sad old bastard turned into a quieter thoroughfare, which thankfully he did after about ten minutes of shuffling.

Patiently the three youths followed Alpha Beta as he tottered down a quiet, dingy street where conveniently several of the street lamps were out of order. With suppressed excitement they pulled on their gloves and exchanged knowing glances.

'Get ready,' said Laurence with a tight grin, his eyes glittering eerily in the darkness.

Alpha Beta was now passing a small patch of waste ground which had an electricity substation on it.

'Perfect,' said Laurence. 'All systems go. Game on.'

Extracting the hammer from the inside of his parka jacket he jogged ahead of the other two and caught up with their prize winner.

'Excuse me, sir. Sorry to bother you, but have you got a light?'

Alpha Beta, his brain clouded with alcohol, turned slowly and awkwardly to respond to this request.

As he did so, Laurence raised the hammer high

16

and brought it down on the fellow's skull with great force. There was a sharp crack similar to the snapping of a stick of firewood and Alpha Beta, eyes wide with shock and confusion, made a brief gagging sound as though he had a piece of food stuck in his throat. Laurence hit him again with more ferocity this time. Alpha Beta fell silent and dropped to the ground like an old pile of clothes. Alex and Russell rushed forward and bending over the body stuck their knives repeatedly deep into the fellow's chest and stomach. The soft flesh offered no resistance to the sharp blades.

They grinned and chuckled. It felt good.

Really good.

Alpha Beta grunted quietly while his body shuddered as it received the wounds. Blood spilled out, splattering his coat and running on to the pavement. His killers stepped back to avoid it contaminating their shoes. He rolled over on to his face and they watched for a moment while life oozed out of his body. Eventually he lay still, one glittering eye visible, staring sightlessly at a small stream of his own blood.

'Mission accomplished chaps. Game over,' grinned Laurence. 'Well done.' For a moment they gazed down at their handiwork, capturing the image in their minds.

*One for the memory bank.*

Then, with a quick shake of hands, the group dispersed with some speed, each making their separate way home.

# PART ONE

# ONE

## 1984

Detective Inspector Paul Snow gazed at his face in the shaving mirror. He didn't like what he saw. He rarely did, but on this occasion his natural revulsion was stronger than usual. His skin was blotchy and dark circles shadowed his eyes. He looked unhealthy and haggard. He wasn't sleeping well and he wasn't thinking straight most of the time. Of course he knew why. His past was coming back to haunt him in spades; closing around him like some invisible straitjacket, clamping itself around him, suffocating him, and he had no idea what to do.

His dark cupboard of secrets was about to be opened.

He parked in his usual space in the Huddersfield police station car park and sat in the car for a while. It was still early. He could see in the distance that the sun was only just rising above the stark silhouette of Castle Hill, making the ancient tower sitting there seem as though it was on fire. Snow wasn't ready to interact with other humans just yet and so he decided to have a walk about the quiet streets before going into the office. A peaceful stroll might help him relax – and then again it might give him pause to dwell on his troubles.

Nevertheless there was something comforting about walking about the old town when it was so quiet: shops closed, traffic sporadic and only the occasional pedestrian, usually walking briskly on their way to work. He breathed in the early morning air and felt his body relax a little.

He passed a coffee shop which was open and went inside. The coffee was thin and bland but at least it was hot. As he sat hunched up on one of the plastic stools, the coffee mug inches away from his face, he gazed at the other early morning customers and wondered what terrible secrets they harboured. Were they as terrible as his?

By the time he arrived at his office, Snow had managed to stow away his dark thoughts temporarily, and to begin thinking about the case – the case that could be his undoing. He found a package waiting for him on his desk, sent by the internal police mail. With his usual measured precision, he opened it and extracted the contents: a cardboard bound note book. What had old Daniels said? 'Here, lad, I'll let you deal with this. You'll think Christmas has come early.'

Snow placed the note book on his desk, opened it and then began reading.

# TWO

# JOURNAL OF RUSSELL BLAKE
## 1968–1970

I want to make some sense of it before I forget. I'm already aware how memory can play tricks on you. And, I suppose, I want to capture that fascinating rush of excitement from those early days. In writing it down, I hope I can in some strange vicarious way, re-live that time. I know now it will never be as good again. There seemed so many possibilities then but now they've all drifted away. But those early days with Laurence... Oh, yes...

Where did it all begin? Where does anything really begin? In the womb, I guess, while you're soaking up your parents' genes as your little body begins to take shape and you are influenced by all the crap your mother puts into her body, including, of course, your father's penis, along with the booze and the pills and such like.

But then that doesn't really make you a murderer, does it?

Or does it? How can you be sure?

To be honest, my parents were fairly docile, fairly nondescript, fairly boring individuals, who brought me up and cared for me in a desultory fashion and failed to influence me in any way about anything. They also had the decency to die

23

young, allowing me to get on with my life in my own way. Looking back, I think of them as rather shadowy black and white creatures in the background of my Technicolor life. It seemed to me that they lacked any real passions or strong desires and I often wonder how they ever managed to summon enough enthusiasm to create me in the first place. Perhaps the stork really did deliver me and it's all his fault.

No, the greatest influence in my life was Laurence. And it still is. Laurence Barker. Well, Barker as he was then. God bless him – although I doubt if He would.

I was just seventeen when we met at Sixth Form College. The year was 1968 and my parents had moved from Hayward's Heath because of my father's boring, nerdy but fairly lucrative job and landed up in Huddersfield, the sort of gritty northern town that was very popular in the British cinema round about that time. Think *Billy Liar, A Taste of Honey, Room at the Top* and you've got it. Then the town seemed to be full of old men in flat caps and long raincoats – Lowry's stick men fleshed out, dumpy women with tight perms squeezed into garish headscarves, sad, fat teenage boys with lank hair wearing Terylene suits from Burtons and cheap imitation Carnaby Street flowered shirts, noisy Asians who thought they were cool mimicking tabloid oafs and silly nubile girls whose main ambition in life was to get themselves in the family way and have a squawking brat to play dolls with. No A Levels or degrees for these ladies – just a pram and a stack of damp nappies. And of course a nice house on a nice estate and,

24

most importantly, no job.

The cobbled streets, smoking chimneys and the factories were disappearing fast but there was still enough of the town's pre-war industrial past in evidence to keep it parochial and old fashioned despite the creeping cheap plastic veneer of Sixties sophistication which was gradually invading the place. It was a small-minded, insular dump – and I hated it. But then I hated most things. Hating things made me happy. It was my hobby.

That's what helped me to bond with Laurence. He felt like I did about Huddersfield and life. Both were a pain in the arse. Laurence had a lanky arrogance that attracted me from the start. He had what Huddersfield folk would call 'a posh voice' and looked like a young Peter Cook, his hair carefully combed so that it fell across his forehead, cresting his brow. His parents had been wealthy but some dodgy business deal had caused them to lose a fortune. Not only a fortune but a palatial house with grounds in the ethereal environs of Harrogate. And so like precious driftwood they had washed up on the shores of Huddersfield. Financially Laurence's family might have been shadows of their former selves but in Huddersfield they were still rich Bentley-driving, champagne-swilling, indoor swimming-pool splashing bastards.

I knew he was a kindred soul when I first saw him at that God-awful 'Freshers Party' organised at Greenbank Sixth Form College to help us academic virgins bond with our fellow students. Held in what was laughingly called the common room ('Because everyone was common in there,' observed Laurence), the party consisted of bowls of crisps, salted peanuts, jugs of cheap non-branded cola and a boring DJ playing naff music. The other freshers, desperately trying to prove they were part of the swinging sixties, pranced about like prats, while I stood on the sidelines, bored and depressed. I was going to be sharing my life with this load of wankers for the next two years.

Laurence was standing close to the door as though ready to make a quick getaway. He was smoking, which was strictly forbidden on the college premises, and wore an expression of the highest disdain as he watched the dancers gyrating in the centre of the room. Their efforts seemed to amuse Laurence. His lips curled delicately at the edges and his large pale blue eyes flickered with contempt. He was dressed in an expensive dark suit with a white shirt and a slim black tie dangling from a loose collar. He was terribly thin, with high cheekbones and a bloodless complexion and looked rather like a young vampire. But to me he seemed glamorous and elegant and I envied his appearance.

I wandered over to him. 'Simply spiffing party,' I observed putting on my jokey Bertie Wooster voice.

Laurence gazed at me lazily; smoke obscuring his features for a moment. 'Have we been introduced?' His expression was haughty and the voice arrogant, but there were traces of humour in those clear blue eyes.

''Fraid not,' I replied, still using my Wooster

voice, but now uncertain whether this tall boy with the penetrating gaze was being serious or playing along with my charade. I didn't have to wait long.

'You're not Gladys Upme, the defrocked house-wife and black pudding hurler from Hampton Wick are you?' he said with a kind of camp nasal tone used by Kenneth Williams in *Round the Horne*.

I took the outstretched baton and ran with it. 'That's my brother. He's in Rampton for sheep rustling.'

'Good job, too. Damned noisy occupation.'

I laughed and he gave me a slow grin.

'Would you like a little ciggy?' He offered me the packet. I didn't smoke but I knew it would be inappropriate to refuse. Besides he looked so good holding the little white cancer stick in his forefingers up by the side of his face that I wanted to look like that as well.

He flicked a lighter and soon I was puffing in-expertly on the 'little ciggy'.

'I'm Russell,' I said.

He raised an arched eyebrow. 'Not related to the sheep, I hope?'

I grinned and shook my head.

'Laurence,' he announced grandly. 'Good to meet you, a fellow castaway in this shit hole.' His face hardened, his features were taut with anger. 'Do you think if we closed our eyes, all this would disappear and we'd find ourselves in hall at Ox-ford or Cambridge...?' He stopped suddenly and placed his face close to mine. 'Are you very bright?'

'Brighter than most of the losers in this dreary dump but no more.'

'Ah, well, we're members of the same club then.'

He smiled and the warmth from that smile charmed me, thrilled me, and soothed me more than I am able to say.

With casual disdain, he dropped his cigarette on to the floor and pressed it into the carpet with his foot. 'Come on, life is too fucking short to stand here watching a load of spastics trying to dance. There must be a pub around here that'll sell beer to two bright seventeen year olds.'

Indeed we did find a pub not more than a few streets away: The Sportsman, which became our haunt, our bolt-hole, for the next two dreary years at college. It was a scruffy little place mainly inhabited by pensioners and grey-faced unemployed loners. The landlord, a thin, pale chap called Alf knew how old we were and where we were from but it didn't bother him. He was happy to add to his meagre profits by supplying us with alcohol. Often was the afternoon we'd bunk off lessons and escape to Alf's where Laurence and I would talk and talk.

That first evening in the pub Laurence and I bonded a life-long friendship and in some strange way we knew it. We forged a link that would only be broken by death.

We hated the college; we hated the teachers – second rate losers; and we hated most of the other students – unambitious dullards more interested in the minutiae of their barren lives than in developing their brains. We were good at hating. Despite all that, we both did well in our studies. This was not due to hard work on our part but merely a combination of our natural brilliance and the low expectations of the staff. Well, let's face it, they were used to dealing with intellectual dwarfs.

We gained a reputation for being aloof – which we were – and that we were gay – which we were not. The trouble with these northern no-brains is that anyone they encounter who is not a clone of their own stupid selves is labelled as a queer, a poofter, a nancy-boy. They can't bear the idea of anyone being different and, indeed, better than they are; and if you are, you must be some kind of pervert. Laurence and I fancied girls and indeed we talked about sex a lot but I don't think our libidos had quite kicked in yet. We ogled tarts in magazines like *Fiesta* and *Bounce* and one or two of the girls at the college took our fancy in a purely physical way, but at that time we were more concerned about sorting ourselves out, trying to come to terms with life and what we wanted out of it and what it could offer us. There was plenty of time for sex later.

Neither of us wanted to follow the route that our fathers had taken into boring business or stultifying corporate life and the idea of marriage, a 'nice' house and two point four children, filled us with dread and loathing. Our boredom threshold was low; we needed some kind of excitement to keep us awake and alert. It was a discussion about this very topic that formed our first watershed moment. We were in Alf's one Friday afternoon finishing our week's labours with a drink or two.

The pale sunlight struggled through the grimy windows throwing beams of dusty light into the room while we sat at our usual corner more than normally disconsolate with our lot.

'I want to do something this weekend that will make a mark on the world,' Laurence suddenly announced grandly. 'I'm fed up with mooching around on Saturday and Sunday. We do nothing of any consequence. Nothing memorable.'

'We could indecently expose ourselves in the market place,' I suggested lightly.

Laurence wrinkled his nose. 'My dear Russell, I have no desire to have my manly member placed on a police file. Besides it's a bit nippy for that kind of activity.'

'Well, it would be memorable.'

'Steady, big boy! I think you miss my point ... or perhaps I didn't explain myself clearly enough. I'm happy do something outrageous and shocking as long as...' He paused for dramatic effect and leaned closer to me, a broad grin on his face. 'As long we are not identified. We have to be the invisible perpetrators. It must be something secret. It's like farting behind the bushes. We produce the noise and the smell but no one knows who did it. That gives the joke an added frisson. Get it? We can crouch behind the hedge laughing our socks off and no accusing finger can be pointed at us.'

'I don't think I'm up for farting behind hedges this weekend.'

'I had something a little more adventurous in mind. Something more elegant and vicious.' He positively beamed.

'You sneaky bastard,' I grinned. 'You've already got something in mind, haven't you? You've got a plan.'

'Excellent deduction, *mon ami.*' He tugged at his imaginary moustache, slipping into his Hercule Poirot impersonation. 'The little grey cells are on fine form today. You are quite correct. I have devised a ... how shall I say ...? a little *divertissement* for us this weekend.'

'Tell me more.'

'Let's have another drink and I'll explain.'

Our glasses replenished, Laurence set to his task. 'Tell me, Russ, who is the most irritating, most pathetic and most despicable member of what is laughingly known as the teaching staff at the Dotheboys Hall we attend...'

'Which we attend when Alf's is not open.'

'Point taken, but answer the bloody question.'

'Most irritating...?'

'Despicable, pathetic ... loathsome.'

'There are so many.'

'The worst. Come on there is only one fucking candidate.'

'Ooh, oh I don't know,' I said, playing with him.

'Ha ha. Now give me her name.'

'Oh, *her* name. It's a woman is it?'

'Don't be a prick.'

'You couldn't possibly be referring to Miss Irene Black, could you?'

Laurence's eyes lit up with triumph. 'The very same. Old Mother Black, she of the floral dresses and curly wig.'

It was true, Old Mother Black, as she was generally known by all the students, wore her

31

hair in the scrunchiest perm I'd ever seen, so tight that the hair did not move, not even on the windiest day. Not only that but its unnatural colour contrasted with the pale, ancient wrinkled features beneath it. If it wasn't a wig, it looked like one. Granny Black was a dinosaur. She should have given up teaching years ago. She was fussy, incompetent and had no understanding or tolerance of young people. As a relic of a bygone age it was appropriate that she taught history. Laurence and I had a particular dislike for the old bag. We didn't think she was up to the job. She was easily flustered, ill-prepared and unable to move from her notes. Laurence had a particular talent for bowling her a question from left field just for the pleasure of unsettling her, which he did frequently. She'd flush and dither and shuffle her papers. 'Not now, Barker,' she would announce distractedly. 'We'll come to that later.' More shuffling of papers.

Laurence took a sip of his beer before continuing. 'Wouldn't you like to upset the old cow? I mean *really* upset her. Wouldn't it give you great pleasure to see Old Mother Black reduced to a nervous wreck?'

I laughed out loud. 'I'd pay for the privilege,' I said, an image forming in my head of Old Mother Black, wig askew, on her hands and knees, blubbing for all she was worth.

'I'll arrange it for free.'

'Go on then.'

'Right. Tell me, Russ, what is Old Mother Black's pwide and joy?'

'Her knitting bag.'

32

Laurence raised his eyes in mock frustration. 'And...'

'Ah, you mean Caesar.'

'Hail Caesar. Indeed.'

Caesar was an ageing, arthritic West Highland Terrier that old spinster Black brought to college every day. It would sleep in the back of her Mini for most of the time, but she took it for walks around the grounds at lunchtimes and in her free periods. On some occasions she even brought the smelly mutt into the classroom where it would curl up by her desk and fall asleep. She treated the creature like the child she never had, talking to it in cutesy woo-woo language like stupid women do when leaning over prams. The girls quite liked Caesar, while the boys in the class would have taken great delight in booting the dog in the bollocks.

'What about Caesar?' I asked.

'We kidnap the beast. Snatch it from its hearth and home.'

I laughed. I didn't know whether Laurence was serious or not but the idea tickled me greatly.

'Can you imagine the histrionics, the floods of tears? The old bag would be reduced to a quivering wreck.' Laurence now adopted the fluttery, whining voice that closely approximated the tones of Old Mother Black. 'Oh my Ceasar-weasar has gone. He's been taken from his mummy. I can't go on. I just can't go on.' With a little shriek, he threw his head down on the table in a comic display of mock sobbing.

One or two of the aged boozers whiling away their afternoon with a glass of mild gave us a puzzled glance before turning back to their geriatric reveries.

I giggled and joined in the improvised drama of Old Mother Black's kidnapped pooch. I pulled out a handkerchief and dabbed it to my eyes. 'He was my whole life,' I sniffled. 'I loved him like a first born, my little Ceasary – weasary.'

More looks from the pensioners as we collapsed in laughter. Silly, giddy young lads, their disapproving glances seemed to say; they've no idea how to behave in a pub.

'See how much fun the idea is,' said Laurence suddenly becoming serious. 'But how much better when we actually do it.'

'You're not joking, are you?'

'Of course not. There's no real cleverness or thrill in just thinking these things up unless ... unless you do them. Put them into practice. That's where the real enjoyment comes.'

'Kidnap Old Mother Black's dog?'

Laurence nodded. 'Precisely. However, if you're frightened, a little chicken maybe ... then I'll have to do it on my own.'

'I'm not chicken.'

'Well, then, mon brave, are you up for it?' His eyes sparkled brightly with humour and excitement.

I couldn't resist such a look. 'I'm in.'

'Good man,' he said with a grin and laughed out loud. 'Then the game's on.'

# THREE

# JOURNAL OF RUSSELL BLAKE
## 1968–1970

Laurence had done his detective homework in preparation for our adventure. By slipping into the college secretary's office when she had popped out to the loo, he had rifled through the staff files and located Old Mother Black's address. So on Saturday morning we caught a bus out to Woodcroft, a twee-ville suburb of town where she lived ... in a thirties bungalow called The Haven. When we saw the name on the gatepost, Laurence put his fingers down his throat and produced a gagging sound.

'Well at least it's not DunRoamin,' I said.

'DunTeachin would be better.'

There were frilly net curtains at the windows, a neat, boring lawn and a shiny brass letter box. It was just as we had imagined.

We stood across the road from The Haven, partially shielded from view by the bus shelter. Old Mother Black's light blue Mini was parked in the drive at the side of the bungalow, but there was no sign of the old biddy herself. Suddenly I began to feel very stupid. What on earth was I doing here wasting my time on this fruitless exploit? How could we grab the bloody dog without being seen? And what would we do if we got it? It all was rather silly.

'So now we are here, what on earth do we do?' I said, unable to keep the note of irritation from my voice.

Laurence shrugged. 'Haven't got that far. It's not going to be easy, is it? We have to get the dog away from Old Mother Black without her knowing.'

'Well, that's going to be impossible. She has the thing with her where ever she goes. Probably takes the beast to bed with her.'

'That's an avenue of thought down which I have no wish to travel... Ah, talk of the devil...' whispered Laurence, pulling his woolly cap down as far as he could and pointing.

Old Mother Black had emerged from the side door of the bungalow with her precious Caesar on a lead. She unlocked her car and let the creature clamber into the back seat. She said something to the dog. We could not hear the words, but we recognised the simpering tone. Then she got in the car herself and after some moments while she adjusted her seat belt, checked her mirror and turned around to mouth some further soppy comments to the dog, she reversed out of the driveway slowly and set off down the road.

'That's our kidnapping plans up the spout,' I observed pithily.

'Oh, Brother Russell, you do give up rather too easily. I never said this was going to be a piece of cake. But everything comes to he who waits. It's Saturday morning. No doubt she's gone shopping. There are all those doggy biscuits to buy and cans of Woofy meaty chunks.'

'Or she could have gone off for the day.'

Laurence shook his head. 'She'd have taken stuff for the dog if she was going to be away that long. Water and its bowl and probably a tin of dog food. Nah, she'll be back in an hour. You mark my words.'

'I'd like to mark a part of your anatomy instead. This is a crazy plan.'

'Of course it's a fucking crazy plan! Is there any other type you'd like to be involved with? Something safe and predictable perhaps? Nicking Mars bars from Woolworth's?'

'Well at least I'd have some Mars bars to show for my efforts.'

Laurence grinned and I couldn't resist him when he grinned. 'So you don't want to be in my gang now then, is that it?' he said with mock dismay. 'I'm not keeping you here under duress, y'know. You can bog off anytime you like. But you wait until Monday morning when the news of Old Mother Black's tragedy is the talk of the college – oh, how you'll wish you'd been part of it then.'

'I am still part of it – for the moment.'

'Right, well I suggest that we're safe to go now and we can come back in say an hour when I predict Old Mother Black will have returned from her shopping trip.'

'What then?'

'We play it by ear. We wait and watch.'

'And I thought you said this was going to be exciting.'

'Come on, misery guts, I'll buy you a cup of tea if we can find a café somewhere round here.'

We did find a café about a mile away in a dilapidated row of shops which had once been the hub of the little suburb of Woodcroft. Now the green grocers and shoe shop had closed down and the other premises had clearly seen better days. Obviously the inhabitants were catching buses into town to get cheaper goods in the one stop supermarket there.

Laurence did buy me a cup of tea in the quaint little tea shop which was inhabited solely by visitors from the old lady planet. The place was full of them, as though the café owner had bought a job lot. The whiff of moth balls nearly knocked us out as we entered. Even the waitress was wheel-chair fodder and she seemed shocked to have customers of our tender years on the premises. She treated us with suspicion as though we'd escaped from some penal institution. No doubt to her any male under twenty five was a thug.

Eventually, we were served our tea and Laurence lit a cigarette. On witnessing this exhibition of youthful decadence there was a lot of tut-tutting from the throng of geriatric ladies, not unlike the clucking of hens at feeding time. 'Perhaps I should have lit a moth ball instead,' grinned my companion before blowing a glorious mouthful of smoke into the air with dramatic aplomb.

As he did so, my attention was caught by a figure passing the window. It was Old Mother Black. 'Bloody hell!' I exclaimed rather louder than I intended, confirming again to the aged jury that young people were the work of the devil. In a hurried whisper I relayed the news to Laurence.

'Let's scarper,' he said, stubbing out his cigarette in the saucer.

Within seconds were out on the street again. 'Which way was she going?'

I pointed down the street and lo and behold there she was, emerging from the newsagents and heading towards us like a galleon in full sail. Luckily she was too wrapped up in her own thoughts to take any note of her surroundings. We did an about face and began strolling at a steady pace away from her.

'I don't think she recognised us.'

'Nah,' agreed Laurence as he cast a glance over his shoulder. 'Hey, slow down, boy. Our luck is in. She's going into the café.'

And so she was, but even better, she had tied up Caesar to the rail outside.

We didn't need to discuss matters. We knew exactly what we had to do. And we proceeded to do it. Casually we strolled back towards the café where we knelt down apparently making a fuss of the dog while Laurence untied its lead and then, just as casually, we walked off trailing little Caesar behind us. The dog offered no resistance. He was probably glad to get away from his simpering mistress.

'Pity we can't stay around to see Old Mother Black's face when she comes out,' I said.

'That is a pleasure we shall have to forgo. Come on.' Snatching the dog up and carrying it under his arm, Laurence set off at a trot. I followed.

'Now we've got the stinking mutt, what do we do with him?' I asked, some five minutes later as we continued to jog along a series of side roads, the thrill and excitement of snatching the creature having already dissipated.

'The whole purpose of this exercise was to upset Old Mother Black, to bring the black cloud of doom to hover over – no not to hover over, to envelop her head. Agreed?'

'Agreed.'

'We're not in the business of sending ransom notes and trying to extract some financial reward for our efforts.'

'Certainly not. That involves the police and investigations which may well lead to discovery.'

'Yup. It's our job just to make little Caesar dog disappear.'

'And how do we do that?'

Laurence grinned his chilling grin. 'We bury it, of course.'

And we did bury the dog. We did it that night in a strange ceremony which involved drinking several cans of beer and digging a deep hole in some woodland near where Laurence lived. He'd taken the dog home and locked it in the garden shed until nightfall when we met up again.

Armed with a large stone each, we took turns in beating the dog's brains out. He whelped and wriggled after the first two blows but then he soon lay still as we turned his head into the consistency of raspberry jam. At first I had been nervous, well frightened really, about actually doing the deed. It had been a fun exercise up to now but actually killing the dog was perhaps taking things a bit too far. Or so I thought; but I would never have admitted these feelings to Laurence. I just followed his lead. Buoyed up by the beer, I suppressed my reluctance and joined in the ritual killing with some relish. Strangely, I found it a rather satisfying experience.

We dumped the creature into the hole we'd dug and then filled it in. 'I come not to praise Caesar, but to bury him,' intoned Laurence, stamping down the earth with his foot. After scattering a pile of dead leaves over the grave, Laurence uttered some words of gobbledy gook, poured a splash of beer over the dog's resting place and then with silly satisfied grins on our faces and arms around each other's shoulders we wandered back to the road and our own individual beds.

# FOUR

## JOURNAL OF RUSSELL BLAKE
### 1968–1970

I didn't see Laurence on the Sunday. We thought it best not to meet. We needed time to come down from our exhilarating experience; time to savour it a little. As usual, I had Sunday lunch with my parents while they bickered and then read the papers, virtually oblivious of my presence. They could never raise their game to a full blown argument, which I would have admired and enjoyed; it was all just gentle sniping and muttered undertones. I longed to lean over the

41

table and tell them what I'd been doing the day before, giving them a graphic account and taking great delight in seeing their shocked and outraged faces. But I didn't. Instead I sat quietly by while they snapped and moaned. Apart from that elegant bit of socialising I stayed in my room reading and doing some essay work, but after a while I allowed my mind to wander back to the events of the previous day, particularly the killing of the dog. I remember feeling a tingle of excitement as I recalled the image of the creature's shiny red skull and its dead sightless eyes staring up at me. It's odd that I felt no guilt or regret about our actions. In fact quite the reverse. The whole thing had made me feel alive and vibrant, interacting with the world for once in a vital fashion, instead of just being a spectator. And I had Laurence to thank for that.

I couldn't wait to get to college on Monday morning to find out if there was any news regarding Old Mother Black and her missing pooch. I encountered Laurence in the common room before morning assembly, his face split with an enormous smile.

'Have you heard the news?' he said, barely able to contain his glee. 'Old Mother Black will not be in today. Apparently she's ... sick.'

I raised my eyebrows. 'Poor old thing. Wonder what can be the matter.'

'Let's hope it's something serious.'

'Let's hope for that, certainly.'

Old Mother Black did not return to college. Ever. The distress she felt at the loss of her dog, its inexplicable disappearance, brought about a nervous breakdown and so the old dear retired due to ill health. We had, as Laurence had predicted, made our mark on the world.

We didn't talk about the matter in any depth until some months later. Ensconced as usual in Alf's one Friday afternoon, we came to it again. There is something about a large, quiet decrepit pub in those funereal post lunchtime hours with muted daylight just squeezing in through the grimy stained glass windows, and the place peopled with only a few punters, pensioners with dominoes and the odd out of work alkie, which gives it an air of the confessional. We had been discussing Old Mother Black's replacement, a fit piece of stuff in her early thirties, and congratulating ourselves that it was through our efforts that we now had the pleasure of Miss Cornwall, with her tight jumpers, buttock hugging pencil skirts and flashing brown eyes, for our history studies.

Laurence leaned back in his seat apparently staring at the smoke-tarred ceiling with a beatific smile upon his face. 'Poor Old Mother Black. We really did for her didn't we?'

'And that bloody dog of hers. We did for them both.'

We chuckled.

'You are quite right, *mon ami*,' continued Laurence. 'We made the difference. We altered the course of history – only a teeny weeny bit, I grant you, but nevertheless... Through our little efforts we managed to change things. Surely that's what we're here for. That's what makes life bearable, to shape things to our own ends ... and in particular to affect the lives of others. We're not like those dumbbells at college who just let life happen to them. We make it happen to us.'

I grinned and made a kind of roaring noise emulating the sound of an appreciative crowd. '*Sieg Heil, sieg Heil*,' I added with a grin.

Laurence flashed me an angry glance. 'I'm not bloody joking, Russ. What we did was the best thing we've ever done in our fucking miserable lives. There's a dog out there rotting in its grave and a stupid, insipid old woman dribbling into her cocoa because of us – because of what we did. That's power. It gives life a purpose.'

I stopped grinning. I hadn't thought of what we had done in this way. I hadn't really thought about it in any way. It had been a kind of exciting diversion from the dull routine – a bit of lark – but now I began to see what Laurence meant. It had allowed us to become the puppet masters. Through our actions we could control or at least affect destinies. We pulled the bloody strings for a change! As always Laurence was the perceptive one, the one who showed the way.

He bent low over the small table until his chin was on a level with the top of his glass, his face eager with enthusiasm. 'You realise that what we did bonded us together – forever. On your bloody deathbed when you're a gummy old bastard pissing on the mattress and farting uncontrollably, you'll think back to what we did and grin a toothless grin in remembrance. We shed blood together. We are blood brothers now.'

He held out his hand to me, eyes shining brightly. I took it and shook it firmly.

'Brothers,' he said.

'Brothers,' I said.

We didn't speak for some time. We just sat there enjoying our new established closeness. For this words were not necessary.

It was an unspoken understanding between us that we both knew that we would have to do something again before long. Something startling. Something forbidden. Something to make a difference once more. It was the start of the addiction. The satisfaction and adrenalin rush of the Old Mother Black episode had long gone, and dull, stultifying life was once more starting to overwhelm us. Similarly, we both knew – although we never discussed it – that we'd recognise the challenge, the fresh opportunity when it arose.

At the beginning of our second year at college, sex reared its seductive head and we both had a few flings with several nubile girls. Because of our aloofness and self sufficiency, we had become something of a challenge for a number of our fellow students. Some of the lads wanted entry to our exclusive two man club to find out what made us tick and some of the girls fancied us because we didn't walk around all day ogling them, touching them up with our tongues hanging out as though we were gagging for it. We intrigued them. We had become a mystery duo.

The novelty of sex was pleasing at first, although I can't say that in the end it was that much better than a good wank. The dreaded routine one had to go through before you reaped your reward soon put me off. The chatting up, the boring, empty conversations in pubs and discos, the pre-coital perambulations seemed too much like hard work for just a few moments of pleasure. Laurence was luckier than I. He never really had to exert himself in getting a girl. A flash of his smile and the allure of his eyes soon had the birds eating out of his flies. We'd be at a party and he'd start chatting up some leggy creature and the next minute, he'd be in one of the toilets giving her what for. But he got bored, too. 'When you've been in the sweetshop a while all that sugar palls,' he observed. 'What we need is another endeavour. Something stimulating to stop our brains rotting.'

He was right. What we didn't realise at the time was that we had taken the first step on the ladder with the Old Mother Black affair and now we would never be content until we made our way to the next rung. However, we knew that it couldn't be rushed and it had to have the same conditions established by our first 'experiment': we must act anonymously so that our involvement would never be suspected. That was part of the fun.

Fate provided us with an ideal opportunity.

# FIVE

# JOURNAL OF RUSSELL BLAKE
## 1968–1970

It was the Christmas season of our second year at college. Ho fucking ho ho and all that. And our last Christmas before university. With some cunning, a little hard work and a certain amount of luck Laurence and I had both been offered good places. If we got the grades – and there seemed little doubt of that – he was going to York to study English and Drama and I was off to Durham to do languages. We hadn't wanted to go the same university; we both felt that it was important to spread our wings and we were sensible and objective enough to realise that our close friendship might interfere with our studies. Getting through A levels was a doddle but degree work, we suspected, might be a little harder to cope with. However we vowed to stay in touch and remain close. After all we were blood brothers now. Neither of us knew what we wanted to do after that. We just planned for that flash of lightning to inform us.

Taking the next step on our special ladder came about one Saturday night a few weeks before Christmas Day when Alex came into our lives. We'd been to see some crap film at the ABC and after leaving the cinema had decided to go for a drink to compensate for the two hours of boredom.

We favoured rough old pubs like Alf's establishment rather than the tarted up bars, designed to attract the untamed youth of Huddersfield on a Saturday night, where they would cram themselves in, sardine style, drink themselves more stupid than they already were and then try to cop off with some sweaty inebriate of the opposite sex. 'The vomit and ripped knicker places' we called them, because that was all that was left when the dump closed down in the early hours.

Laurence said that he'd heard of a pub called the Dog and Gun down by the canal, about half a mile from the town centre, which was almost like a museum. 'Lots of doddery fellers in flat caps and real old fashioned prostitutes – you know, rouged faces, fish net tights and a pension book.'

'Worth a look,' I agreed. And so we strolled down there in the frosty night air, our breath escaping in pearly wisps as we chatted.

The Dog and Gun didn't quite live up to Laurence's description. There certainly were no obvious prostitutes in there and no flat caps either. However, it was quiet with just a few gloomy middle aged couples sitting around like waxworks: women with peroxide perms and men with hangdog expressions, married so long they had run out of anything to say to each other so they stared into space while slowly revolving their drinks. There was a group of young rugby types having a go on the one armed bandit, cave men in jeans and jumpers, and a lad about our age sitting on his own reading *Private Eye*. Most of them were regulars, no doubt, for when we entered, all eyes focused on us with suspicion. It was as though we had just landed in our alien space ship outside and invaded their private domain. You could cut the atmosphere with a rusty bread knife and Laurence always overreacted to such mean-spirited parochial attitudes.

'I say, landlord,' he announced in a posh effeminate voice that could be heard above the din of the one-armed bandit, 'two pints of your very best foaming ale.'

The cavemen turned to look at us with scowls of disdain and muttered to each other.

'Steady boy,' I whispered to Laurence.

'Steady yourself,' he snapped back.

The wizened barman plonked two pints on the counter without a word.

'How much do I owe you, landlord?' Laurence continued his mincing charade.

'Four and six,' came the gruff reply.

Laurence shelled out a series of coins and dropped them casually on the counter in a pool of spilled beer.

'Keep the change, my good man,' he said grandly, and gave a wave of his hand to emphasise his benevolent gesture.

The barman glared at him, picked up the coins, counted them and replaced a sixpence on the counter in the same pool of beer.

I dragged Laurence over to a corner table. All eyes still remained on us as though we were the unexpected cabaret. The cave men were obviously discussing us in less than positive terms.

'You'll have us lynched before we can get out of

here,' I whispered to Laurence.

'Well, that might be more interesting than that film we saw tonight. Whose idea was it to see that?'

At least he had resorted to his normal voice.

'Just drink your beer,' I said, trying to hide my smile.

After a few moments one of the cave men came over. He was big, beefy and blond with eyes like two small currants in a large white loaf.

'One of you gentlemen got a light?' he asked with sarcastic politeness.

'No, I'm sorry,' I chimed in quickly, before Laurence had chance to start his performance again. 'We don't smoke.'

Our caveman grinned and turned back to his mates. 'They don't smoke,' he said, as though announcing the death of a friend.

The other three men guffawed at the news.

'Too manly for you is it, smoking?'

This time I was not quick enough, Laurence came in with a sibilant retort: 'It gives you cancer, old boy. And it makes you impotent ... if you know what that means. But by the look of you that's already happened...'

The smile faded from the caveman's face and without warning his hand snaked out and grabbed Laurence's coat by the lapels. 'Why, you fucking queer,' he snarled, his face so contorted with anger that his currant eyes had all but disappeared into the folds of his flesh.

Laurence was not fazed at all. 'Now, now, temper, temper. Thumping me won't bring back your manhood.'

But thumping Laurence was what he intended to do. Uttering a Neanderthal growl he drew back his fist.

'Craig! That'll do,' came a voice to the rescue. It was the barmaid who seemed to have materialised out of thin air. 'We don't want any trouble … again,' she added more firmly. 'Just get back to your mates.'

'Aye c'mon Craig. Leave the poofters alone. They're not worth it,' cried one of his burly companions in support of the barmaid.

Reluctantly Craig released his grip on Laurence's jacket, but he leaned forward until his brutish mug was only inches away from my friend's face. 'I've not finished with you yet,' he grunted in a harsh whisper before returning to his cronies.

'That's great,' I said. 'Not only have you got us labelled as queers, but I doubt if we'll get out of this pub alive.'

Laurence turned to me and smiled. 'Relax. You take things too seriously. At least that little encounter was more exciting than the movie tonight.'

I rolled my eyes. 'That was entertainment. This is real life.'

'And so much better.'

I lingered over my drink, hoping the rugby lads would depart but I hoped in vain. They replenished their glasses and stayed. From time to time they broke off from their conversation to turn and stare at us. Like poachers eyeing up their prey.

'You realise that we're going to get bollocked as

soon as we leave this pub, don't you? Genghis Khan over there is just waiting for us to walk through the door and then he and his mini-horde'll be after us like a shot,' I murmured.

'Yes. It's a nice little problem. What are we going to do about it? You got your running shoes with you?'

I knew Laurence well enough by now to know that he was enjoying himself. He thrived on such danger and discomfort. The fact that he would probably get his head kicked in for his efforts didn't seem to matter to him. I had to admire his nerve.

'Look,' I said, trying to be practical, 'some of them are bound to go to the loo sooner or later. I suggest when at least one of them goes, we make a quick exit, belt it to the end of the street and then spilt up and make our own way home. You go left and I'll go right.'

'And I'll be in Scotland afore ye. All right, Einstein. You are in charge of Operation Scarper. I'll abide by your decision.'

'That'll be a first.'

We waited and waited but our bruising trio seemed to have infinitely expandable bladders. I was getting really worried as closing time neared and then eventually two of the lads went off 'to the bog for a slash' as one of them announced loudly. That left just one of the bruisers still standing by the one armed bandit.

'Let's make our move now,' I whispered. 'You go to the bar as though you're ordering another round and I'll make for the door. Once I'm out, you follow quickly.'

Laurence grinned and hummed the theme music from *The Great Escape*.

'Ready,' I said.

He nodded, still humming.

Operation Scarper was all systems go. As planned Laurence went up to the bar and then I walked as casually as I could to the exit and slipped outside. I waited in the freezing night air for him. He didn't come. For what seemed ages, he didn't come.

And then all of a sudden the pub door slammed open and Laurence emerged at full pelt. 'Run!' he roared. 'Run!' On seeing the three cavemen close behind him, I needed no further telling.

But it was futile.

We hadn't gone twenty yards when two of the brutes brought Laurence down to the ground in a rough tackle while another had grabbed me by my coat collar and I had the cartoon experience of my legs swinging backwards and forwards furiously and yet I wasn't going anywhere. This comic sensation was superseded by a sharp pain in the gut from the delivery of a heavy blow. I crumpled to the frosted pavement and curled up knees into my chest, hands around my head in an attempt to protect myself from further harm.

On the periphery of my dazed, wild and whirling sensations, I was conscious of the muted cries of pain from Laurence who was being roughly manhandled by two of the cowardly brutes.

And then suddenly another voice was added to the melee. It was clear and strong. 'Leave them alone,' it cried. 'Leave them alone, you morons.'

For a moment the three stooges froze puzzled,

as I was, by this intervention. Painfully, I lifted myself on my elbow and saw that it was the youth from the pub, the one who had been reading *Private Eye*. He was a tall stringy kind of lad – but now he was wielding a stout piece of wood about the size of a cricket bat.

'It's the bloody Lone Ranger,' groaned Laurence, scrabbling to his feet. As he did so, the lad swung the piece of wood wildly, catching one of our assailants around the side of the head, knocking him clear off his feet. With a sharp cry he fell backwards and I saw blood gush down the side of his face. The two remaining attackers now turned their attention on our ally. But he was nimble and side stepped quickly, easily avoiding their drunken advance. Again he clouted one of them around the head. The brute staggered, his knees buckling, but he managed to remain upright. Clamping his hand to his wounded head with a moan, he turned on his heel and ran off. Laurence and I now rose to our feet and launched ourselves on the remaining musketeer. I pulled his legs from under him, while Laurence kicked him in the balls and the Lone Ranger bashed him on the head with his weapon. The street was alive with the sound of music.

Laurence gazed down at our victim. It was old currant eyes. 'And a good evening to you, sir,' he smirked, kicking him in the balls again.

'Time to head for the hills, partner,' I cried, grabbing Laurence's sleeve. 'And I think you'd better join us,' I added with a nod to our new friend.

He needed no encouragement and so without any further words, the three of us ran off at speed in the direction of the centre of town.

Fifteen minutes later we were sitting in a scruffy little café which stayed open late, it seemed, to provide sobering black coffee to the wandering drunks who had missed their last bus home and had no money for taxi fare or had forgotten where they lived. It was fairly full of bleary-eyed silent types slumped in the squeaky plastic seats waiting for death or the thin coffee to cool down, whichever came first. In the far corner a young couple were having a muted argument. She was pulling at his jacket and crying and both were mouthing unintelligible insults at each other.

We sat down at a small table by the door and Laurence bought us three coffees from the smiling Greek owner.

'Here you go,' he grinned placing the tray down on the table. He raised his coffee in a toast. 'Here's to the Lone Ranger.'

'Hear, hear,' I responded clinking my cup against his. 'What's your name? Who are you? And why did you do it?'

'Those are just a few questions to be getting on with,' smirked Laurence. 'We'll come to your in-side leg measurement and your choice of the five best movies of all time a little later.' Our friend looked apprehensive for a moment, not sure whether we were joking or not and then he too began to smile.

'I'm Alex. Good to meet you.'

We nodded in agreement.

'I've seen those fuckers before. They haven't got a brain cell to rub between them and they are notorious queer-bashers in the area. There's nothing I hate worse.'

Laurence raised an eyebrow and cast me a glance. 'Because...?'

'Why do you think?'

Laurence pursed his lips and shrugged his shoulder. 'We've no problem with that, have we?'

I was not so sure but I wasn't about to upset the Lone Ranger. Without him we might be in a casualty ward rather than sitting in this greasy spoon supping watery coffee which I suspect had never seen a coffee bean in its life. I shook my head and uttered a fairly indistinct 'Nah'.

Alex looked confused. 'Why the fuck should you... I thought you...?'

Laurence laughed. 'Ah you mean my queen-like performance in the pub.' He laughed again. 'What a compliment. I didn't know it was so convincing.'

'It was convincing enough for Grendel and his two ugly brothers to want to kick the shit out of us,' I observed.

'You mean you two are ... straight then?' Alex seemed surprised.

'Well not so much straight as rather curved. I would never regard myself as straight. Straight is boring, predicable ... safe. Don't worry we have no prejudices against gay people – unless they are stupid and irritating and get in our way. But that applies to the rest of mankind. I'm Laurence, by the way, and this shifty individual here is my best friend Russell.'

With a strange kind of mechanical formality, we shook hands.

'What on earth prompted you to come to our rescue tonight?' I asked.

'Hi ho, Silver,' Laurence brayed.

A ghost of a smile touched Alex's lips. He was, I had to admit, a good looking chap: fluffy blond hair, dark brown expressive eyes and finely chiselled features. He was not feminine or girlish like some queers are but one could see that he was a gentle creature – except when wielding a piece of wood in anger. 'If the truth be known, I've been waiting for an excuse to have a go at that lot. Some time ago they beat up a friend of mine – well, ex-friend now.'

'Why ex-friend?' I asked.

'They scared him off, didn't they? They'd scare you off, too, if you'd ended up in the infirmary with several broken ribs and a fractured wrist. They pride themselves in having inbuilt gay-sensors. They really must have thought their luck was in tonight when you sashayed in the pub, camping it up.'

'So they never sussed *you* out then. They ignored you in the pub tonight', I said.

'Nah, they just think I'm Billy No Mates. I go in there and just read.'

'So you *are* Billy No Mates,' observed Laurence.

'Not exactly...'

'Certainly not now, anyway. Laurence and me'll be your Tonto,' I said.

'Sure,' agreed Laurence. 'We'll take it in turns to wear the headdress and the buckskin jerkin.'

'Ooh, get you ducky,' exclaimed Alex in an

outrageously camp voice.

We all laughed and that was the beginning of our enduring friendship.

# SIX

# JOURNAL OF RUSSELL BLAKE
## 1968–1970

'You realise that time is running out. We haven't got long before we depart these grubby shores for the groves of academe and we must have one final adventure before we go. One that is planned and will warm the cockles of our hearts when the winter winds start to blow.'

Laurence was in an expansive mood. He sprawled back on the leatherette seat in Alf's, puffing wildly on a little cigar, a new affectation of his which he had taken up on his eighteenth birthday. It was late May and all our exams were over and we had loads of time on our hands until the results came out in August.

'Do you have anything in mind?'

Laurence screwed up his face dramatically and pointed the tip of the cigar in my direction. 'I think it's your call this time, Russ. Old Mother Black was my party. Now it's your turn. Time to get the old brain box ticking over. Come up with something juicy and surprising.'

'I'll give it some thought ... but there's one thing ... are we going to let Alex in on it?'

'You know, I think we should. He's part of the team now. In a way. I mean he'll never be a close as you and I, the founder members of this grand and glorious association, but he's a good guy and I reckon he'll run with us.'

I agreed. In many ways Alex had very quickly become 'part of the team'. I had thought that Laurence and I were unique in our ways but Alex seemed to share the same ideas and views, 'our nihilist philosophy' as Laurence called it. He detested the dullness of mankind, the acceptance of routine and the reluctance to look beyond the norm.

We didn't see him as often as the two of us saw each other. Well, we were at college every day and Alex was working. It turned out that he was a couple of years older than us, his fey angelic looks belying his maturity, and he worked as a designer for a printing company. He seemed to like his work but disliked the people he worked with.

We would meet up one night a week and on Saturdays and talk and drink and slag off humanity. Sometime we'd go to the flicks or take a trip to Leeds to visit the theatre, but generally we'd just talk and drink and slag off humanity. However, we hadn't yet told him about the Old Mother Black incident. We would, when the time was right – and that time was fast approaching.

'So,' I said, 'you're throwing down the gauntlet. You challenge me to come up with a little fun adventure before we leave for university.'

'You have hit the nail on the head, *mon ami.*' Laurence waved the cigar around dramatically as a sign of approbation.

'Very well, your wish is my command,' I replied, grinning. The prospect filled me with glee.

In the end inspiration came by way of the local paper, the *Huddersfield Examiner*. This is not the kind of literature that I read normally, but I'd gone to the barbers – they were still called barbers then, hairdressers came later – and while I was waiting to be shorn by Brian the Barber there was nothing else to read but an old edition of the *News of the World* and the local paper. As I skimmed it, full of boring accounts of dog shows, retiring teachers, reviews of crappy amateur dramatics, traffic accidents and tales of woe concerning the council's mismanagement, a picture caught my eye. It was of a convicted drug addict who had just been released from prison after serving a term of two years. Apparently local boy Darren Rhodes (aged 32) had robbed an old lady of two hundred pounds to pay for his habit and she had suffered a heart attack and died the following day. This had happened a couple of years ago and now, incredibly, he was out of the clink after having served only half his sentence. To add insult to injury, he had just won five thousand pounds on the football pools. This fat-bellied nauseous creature was beaming out of the photograph giving two fingers to the camera and, indirectly, to the rest of us. It seemed to me that here was an ideal candidate for the brotherhood's next adventure.

I was determined to work out a scenario all by myself and present it to Laurence as a *fait accompli* and see what he said. I had a sneaking feeling he thought I wasn't quite up to the careful planning of such a caper. I intended to prove him wrong. I set to it with joyful determination. Using the basic facts I'd gleaned from the paper, after a little investigation I soon discovered where this tosser lived. Darren had a terrace house in Sheepton, one of the run down districts on the outskirts of town.

The next Sunday I cycled to the area to find out exactly where he lived. It wasn't very difficult. Terrace houses were few in this part of town, the bulk of the properties were dilapidated semis built by the local authority after the war. They were still known as 'corporation houses', a dreadful epithet for dreadful dwellings. Most of them had now been bought by the current occupants, who in a desperate attempt to individualise their little squat boxes had carried out all kinds of horrendous cosmetic alterations to them. Either that or they'd ignored the fact that they were supposed to be respectable homes altogether and allowed them to degenerate into slum properties. Along one road you would see neat frontages filled with gnomes and plastic windmills, houses painted in vivid, eye-searing colours rubbing shoulders with properties displaying boarded up windows and gardens that replicated overgrown wildernesses, often filled with rubbish and/or old sofas or rusting prams. Darren, however, lived in the older part of Sheepton in a short row of blackened stone-built terrace houses erected sometime in the nineteenth century. His was the end house: a grim pile with a warped, paint-peeling door and a garden that

Tarzan would have felt at home in. I visited the spot several times and always the curtains were drawn across the dirt ingrained windows so no one could see inside. In a way I was rather glad of this. I really didn't want to see inside. I wasn't sure my stomach would stand it. Two hundred yards away from his house stood the equally doubtful and inappropriately named public house, The Royal George. It was a shabby, disreputable looking boozer where Darren did his drinking and no doubt purchased his drugs.

You'd think that a scumbag like Darren, a drug addict and a murderer of an old woman, would be treated like a pariah once he had returned home from the nick, but it appeared that the opposite was the case in this neck of the woods. He was regarded as a tarnished hero, the local Jack the Lad returning in triumph.

On my second visit to the area I ventured into The Royal George and saw for myself. It was a gloomy establishment, pungent with an unpleasant but unidentifiable odour. The air was thick with cigarette smoke and chatter. At one end of the bar was the man himself, local celebrity, Darren Rhodes, a bulky individual with a beer gut straining at his black T-shirt. He was surrounded by a motley group, mainly men of a similar appearance with a few heavily made up women in possession of lurid peroxide hair, loud uncouth voices and smoke-aged faces. He was holding court and expounding on some subject or other which required him to use the words 'fucking' and 'cunt' at regular intervals.

The barman served me a half a bitter without a

glance in my direction. His attention seemed to be fixed on his star punter. I took a seat opposite Rhodes and his fan club so that I could observe the man at close quarters. He was an ugly, unshaven fellow with two very small shifty eyes, receding black wiry hair which sprang from his large head in an unkempt fashion and was already turning grey at the temples. He had a large mouth with flabby lips which he moistened with his tongue constantly. Rhodes was recounting an anecdote from his prison days. It concerned some incident where he had got one over on 'the screws'. It was clear to me, but not to his enraptured audience, that it was a made up piece, a lie to make him look good, to make him look tough, to make him look sharp. He was not merely embellishing the truth, he was manufacturing it.

'And then I held his head down the fucking toilet until he pissed himself,' he announced with a rasping declaration, bringing the story to a close. There was general laughter and patting on the back.

The psychology of this reaction puzzled and fascinated me. It would seem the onlookers, damaged by poverty and a poor education, felt so alienated by society and authority figures that their main source of entertainment was to revel in stories of anarchy related by an unrepentant drug addict/murderer. As someone once said, 'How different from the home life of our dear Queen.'

I became determined to damage this errant star, this jumped up piece of human garbage. With the help of Laurence and Alex we would delete his arrogant leer forever. As he began another tale of prison life, I drank up quickly and left. Now, I thought, was the time to take a closer look at Rhodes' house. He would be rattling on with his concocted tales of self glory and basking in the sunshine of the mob's approval for some time. Long enough for me to have a shufty at his gaff.

It was dusk when I walked up the garden path. Well, not so much a garden path as a short track through the long grass and rampant weeds leading to the front door. The curtains, as usual, were drawn across. I went around to the back. There was a yard here with the remnants of what had been an outside lavatory and a motorbike covered by a tarpaulin.

I pulled back the cover to reveal a shiny new mean machine. It was an impressive piece, purchased no doubt with part of his pools win. Unlike the house and the tiny garden it was obviously cared for with meticulous devotion. It gleamed and shimmered in the fading light. As I gazed at it, bells started ringing in my head.

I've never been attracted to motorbikes, they are too vulnerable on the road for my liking, but I had to admit that this piece of machinery looked very cool. I noted down the make and model which meant nothing to me – a Kawasaki 750 – a plan already forming in my mind.

There were no curtains up at the kitchen window and I was able to peer inside. It was a tip. I could see the sink piled high with unwashed crockery and discarded boxes from some take away establishment, the left over congealed food already furring with a green mould. Miss Havisham would have felt at home here.

Before I left, I looked again at the motorbike. This time I pulled the tarpaulin cover off completely and straddled the machine, leaning low over the handlebars and emitting a soft brum brum noise, smiling as I did so. I toned my noise up an octave as I took an imaginary bend at incredibly high speed and then with great glee I manufactured a loud crashing sound at the back of my throat. And then there was silence and I grinned broadly.

## SEVEN

## JOURNAL OF RUSSELL BLAKE
### 1968–1970

I took great delight in working on the Darren Rhodes project on my own. I saw it as my special baby and I wanted to present the whole scheme to Laurence carefully planned down to the finest detail – pre-packed and ready to go.

I wanted to impress him.

I haunted the reference library reading up on motorbikes and even visited a couple of garages in the role of an eager teenager ready to buy his first machine, (a rich eager teenager) wearing the cocky salesmen down with my questions. In the meantime I made the odd visit to The Royal George to keep my eye on Darren. I learned a little more about him. In truth, there really wasn't very much to learn. He was a simplistic, shallow creature, small of brain and big of ego. He lived off benefit and his pools win, with apparently no intention of seeking work. Lying in late and spending most lunch times and evenings in the boozer, his horizons were low and narrow. Occasionally he would take the bike out for a run in the afternoon. 'I likes doing a ton on Lakely Moor Road, a nice stretch that, with no fucking coppers around,' he was fond of repeating to his cronies. Even having a splendid bike like the Kawasaki 750 – through my researches I now knew this to be the *crème de la crème* of roaraway engines – he had no greater ambition than to speed at a hundred miles an hour on a quiet country road just five miles away from where he lived. His life like his ambitions was small with limited vision. It was my intention to make it much smaller and more limited.

Laurence chuckled and then took a drag on his cheroot. 'You have been busy, Russo. Quite the worker ant.'

'I trust you approve, sir,' I said in my Jeeves voice, after I had explained my plan in detail.

'Indeed I do, my man. I shall raise your wages by a penny per annum and allow you to sodomise the gardener once a week on his day off.'

'You are too kind, but I do that already.'

Suddenly Laurence dropped the silly voice and looked serious. 'So, we need to tell Alex. Rope him in. What d'you say?'

I nodded. 'I think he'll be all for it.'

'So do I. But if he isn't we'll have to dump the plan and pretend it was some kind of wishful joke thing.'

'And then dump him.'

Laurence nodded rather glumly. 'Yeah. It will be a pity but we can't have a wimp queering our pitch – if you'll pardon the expression.'

I giggled.

As it turned out, any doubts we'd harboured about Alex becoming a fully fledged member of the Brotherhood proved to be ill-founded. He knew of Rhodes through the local press and TV reports and jumped at the chance of being involved in some scheme to bring 'the oiky bastard down a peg or two'.

In reality, the plan was destined to do more than that, but we didn't quibble over the sentiment.

'This calls for pints all round,' smirked Laurence. 'And as I managed to half-inch a fiver from my dad's wallet this morning, the round is on me.'

It was the same night, after several pints, that we told Alex the Old Mother Black story. He listened in wide-eyed fascination. I could see that at first he didn't quite know how to react.

'Is this really true?' he asked after we had finished, suspicious that we were sending him up.

'Not if you don't want it to be?' said Laurence mysteriously.

Alex looked blankly at us for a moment and then, as the truth dawned on him, he smiled gently. 'You bastards. You terrible bastards.' He was laughing now. 'You really did it, didn't you? You killed the mutt. Poor old Caesary-waesary.' His laugh had grown into a splutter and his eyes bulged in merriment as he tried to control himself.

Laurence and I exchanged glances and joined in the laughter with pleasant relief.

And so the triumvirate was formed and sealed with a pint of Tetley's bitter. It was an historic moment which was to affect the rest of our lives.

It was very early on Sunday morning two weeks later. The month was June and even at six o'clock in the morning you could already tell it was going to be a beautiful summer's day. The pale blue sky was clear of clouds and there was a thick, gentle warmth in the air that promised a hot day to follow. Laurence had managed to borrow his mother's car and we had transported all our gear up to Lakely Moor Road. It was a wild whipcord of a highway which ran across the expansive moorland, rising up into the hills and cutting across into Lancashire. And it was deserted. There was no traffic at all, which suited us perfectly.

First of all we set up our tent and changed our clothes and then began adopting our disguises. For three young lads to appear much older than we were and to play figures of authority was one of the dodgier aspects of the plan. If we couldn't fool our victim about this we were lost. Laurence was a born actor and he volunteered himself for the role of police officer. He had secured a fairly authentic looking uniform from the local amateur dramatics group costume department and even before he began applying other parts of his disguise he looked pretty impressive. He whitened the temples of his hair and applied a false moustache which he'd also obtained from the drama group wardrobe. He was, he'd told them, going to a fancy dress party in aid of the Samaritans. The jammy devil had managed to get a reduction in the hire fee, as a result. Once he'd doctored the moustache and put the peaked cap on, he looked very much the part. As long as Darren Rhodes didn't peer too closely, the illusion should work.

I'd borrowed a tweed jacket from my dad's wardrobe and bought a corduroy flat cap to shade my face and hide my youth. Laurence applied some rouge to my cheeks to give me a ruddy aged appearance and tested me in lowering the tone of my voice until it sounded older and resonated with gravitas.

From the point of view of appearance, Alex had the easy task. No real disguise for him really, just jeans and a T-shirt, although he wore a baseball cap to hide part of his face. However, he had a pivotal role to play. Failure to carry out his duties meant a total failure for the whole scheme.

Once we were ready, Alex pinned the sign to the side of the tent, 'Speed Bike Trials – Check In'.

And then we waited.

It was at this point that I began to panic. I began to see all the potential holes in my supposedly water tight plan. There suddenly seemed to be so many links in the chain that could lead the authorities to us. The leaflet for example. Could they trace it back to Alex's printer at work? Anyone passing could stop to ask us what was going on and then we became evidence. Even at six thirty in the morning that was possible. What if someone had noted down the number of Laurence's mum's car on our way here? That was highly unlikely, I knew, and we had now driven it off the road behind some trees out of sight, but it was possible. And worst of all, what if Darren Rhodes had smelt a rat and turned up with a gang of his mates. I began to feel sick to my stomach.

I felt sweat begin to dampen my armpits. This was a crazy, shit scheme. I should never have suggested it.

Laurence sensed my unease and gave me a little punch on the arm. 'Come on, *mon ami*, no long faces,' he murmured in his Poirot voice. 'Today we shall triumph. No other outcome is acceptable.'

'I hope so. I don't fancy prison food.'

Then just before seven we heard a faint droning in the air. The sound of a distant motorbike. It seemed to resonate in the pale sky and the skeletal trees all around us.

'I spy Muggins,' cried Alex pointing at a little red dot on the horizon. He was right. As the vehicle drew nearer, I could clearly identify the Kawasaki and its brutish driver.

'Action stations,' I snapped, although in truth there was nothing we could do until Darren Rhodes arrived.

Less than a minute later, he skidded to a halt beside the tent. 'What's this all about?' he growled brusquely by way of an opening gambit, as he clambered off the bike. From one of the zipped pockets in his leathers, he extracted the flyer we had sent him and held it aloft. 'I mean this?'

70

I stepped forward with my clipboard. 'Mr Rhodes,' I ventured, low of voice.

'Yeah.'

'Good man. You have come to take part in the speed trial.'

'Maybe. What's it all about?'

'It explains it all on the leaflet,' I said simply, taking it from him, retrieving the evidence. It was that easy.

I smiled indulgently. 'This is a speed competition to see how fast you can drive in a ten mile stretch. As you can see,' I nodded at Laurence, 'we have the co-operation of the local constabulary in this venture...'

Laurence saluted.

'We are testing six Kawasaki owners in the area who have bought the 750 within the last six months. Three today and three next Sunday and the rider who records the fastest time will win a thousand pounds.'

'Why?'

'Publicity for Kawasaki of course. The best bikes on the road.'

Darren Rhodes sniffed and looked about him. 'Where are the others?'

Laurence stepped forward. 'We can't have more than one bike on the route at a time, sir. That would be far too dangerous. You're in our 7 a.m. slot. The next rider is due at 7.30. So ... er, we'd better get a move on, eh?'

'What do I do?'

Our fish was nibbling at the hook.

'We time you when you set off. You drive ten miles along this road and there you will see the

71

Bike Trials finishing line. Our officials there at the other end will note down the time of arrival. Out of the six riders, the one with the fastest time will win a thousand pounds. As simple as that. That's all there is to it.'

Rhodes sniffed again. 'OK.' He made a move to return to his bike, but I waved my clipboard at him. 'Oh, sir, just before you set off, we need you to sign a few forms – an entry form and an accident waiver form. If you'll just step into the tent, it won't take a moment.'

Without a word Rhodes followed me into the tent. Bless his simple little brain. He'd taken everything in. Greed had overridden any other thoughts he may have had. But then again, our Darren was not a man for thoughts anyway. Laurence stepped smartly forward and held open the flap to the tent. I followed behind, giving Alex the nod. On the instant, he made a beeline for the Kawasaki.

Sadly my pen wouldn't work and I had to leave Mr Rhodes in the tent while I went to see if the police officer would lend me his. As I returned to the tent with Laurence's Biro, Alex gave me the thumbs up.

The forms duly signed, Darren returned to his bike. Alex took a photograph of him astride the machine, 'for publicity purposes, sir.' Rhodes liked being called 'sir'.

'Good luck,' I cried as he revved the engine. I retrieved a stop watch from my pocket and Alex raised his arm in readiness. I shouted 'Go!' and Alex dropped his arm. With a screech of tyres, Darren and his mean machine shot off down the deserted road which led into the soft fold of the hills.

As soon as he was out of sight, we galvanised ourselves into action. Alex sprinted off to get the car, while Laurence and I dashed into the tent and removed our disguises. We were just taking the tent down, when Alex drove up. Within five minutes of Darren Rhodes speeding out of our lives, we were driving back into Huddersfield all singing a snatch of some pop song of the day. I can't remember what it was now, but I do recall that I felt wonderful. I glowed with a vibrant inner warmth of pleasure.

I closed my eyes and imagined the scene: Darren Rhodes zooming along that winding stretch of open road, the bike at full throttle, the speedo well over a hundred miles an hour. I wasn't sure what would come next: the strange noise or the slight juddering motion, a juddering motion that would grow in intensity. I tried to visualise Rhodes' fat stupid face and his changing expression which would slide from uncertainty to concern to real terror. He would wet himself with horror, I hoped, as the wheel came off at great speed and as the bike faltered he would fly through the air like a great ugly black spastic fairy and land awkwardly, with immense bone crushing force on the tarmac. I trusted that he would scream.

That was the only flaw with my plan. We couldn't be there to witness the wonderful climax. Still you can't have everything, I suppose.

# EIGHT

## JOURNAL OF RUSSELL BLAKE
### 1968–1970

We didn't have to wait long to discover the fruits of our labours. The following night I met up with Laurence and Alex in Alf's. They were already waiting for me. Bright evening sunlight streamed in all around them so that they had turned into ethereal haloed shadows. As I approached their table I raised the local paper triumphantly. In response, they matched my action, shaking their copies of the *Huddersfield Examiner* in joyful greeting. We collapsed in wild laughter.

At length Alex had spread his newspaper out on the table for us all to see. We had made the front page:

## DARREN RHODES IN BIKE CRASH

'They could have called it a "Rhodes Accident",' said Laurence, lighting up a cheroot.

The report informed readers that:

*Darren Rhodes, 32, who had only been released from prison three months ago after serving a term for robbery, was found yesterday morning on Lakely Moor Road besides his damaged motorbike in a critical condition. Detective Sergeant Michael Ripley of the West*

*Yorkshire Constabulary told our reporter that the front wheel of the motorbike, a Kawasaki 750, had broken free and this was the cause of the accident. It had been determined that Mr Rhodes had been travelling at 120 miles per hour because the speedometer had jammed on impact. There were no other vehicles involved.*

*Rhodes is now in intensive care. He has suffered serious injuries to his head and legs. Surgeon Majid Lopal said that they could not rule out brain damage at this stage. They were making all efforts to save Mr Rhodes' left leg from amputation.*

'Let's hope they fail,' I said, running my forefinger along the statement about Rhodes' leg.

'I'll drink to that,' said Alex, clinking my glass with his.

'What puzzles me,' said Laurence, languidly blowing smoke away from us, 'is how a brain that small can be damaged.'

We laughed again and then fell into a satisfied silence.

It was Alex who broke into our private thoughts a few minutes later. 'You know,' he said quietly, 'I can't help thinking, it might have been even better if we'd have killed the bastard.'

Laurence gave us both a sharp glance. He leaned forward, his eyes wide with suppressed excitement.

'Next time we will, boys. Next time we will.'

# NINE

## JOURNAL OF RUSSELL BLAKE
### 1968–1970

The euphoria we felt after the Darren Rhodes project lasted for many weeks. It was partly supported by the continuing reports in the local paper concerning his progress or lack of it. As it turned out, he wasn't brain damaged, but he suffered memory loss and had no recollection of why he was racing along Lakely Moor Road early on a Sunday morning. However, poor Mr Rhodes did lose his leg which was a kind of compensatory bonus to us. The situation helped to buoy up Laurence and me particularly during this period, as we waited for our exam results. When they came, they were extra icing on our cakes. We got the grades we wanted and, to be honest, what we expected.

Our futures were mapped out for us. As planned, he was headed for York and I was off to Durham. Our paths, which had run in close parallel furrows for two years, were about to diverge. The sadness of this was, to some extent, modified by the growing sense of excitement at leaving home and facing new challenges and wider horizons. 'Leaving Huddersfield is a transportation devoutly to be wished,' noted Laurence grandly.

Alex however grew less communicative during the late summer months. It hadn't quite struck us that while Laurence and I were moving on in all sorts of ways, we were, in a sense, leaving Alex behind. There was no change of circumstances for him. He was to be abandoned in the dull town of his birth in the same old job with no prospect of career or life development. He never voiced these feelings but we were close enough to gradually realise what our departure would mean to him.

A week before we were due to go off to University, we had a farewell party. Laurence's parents were off somewhere on a cruise and he had been left to look after the house. He invited Alex and me one evening for what he termed an extra special meeting of the Brotherhood. We were instructed to turn up in evening dress. Admission was by a bottle of champagne.

Strangely, at first we felt awkward with each other. We were not used to sitting around in domestic surroundings together. The house was big and impersonal and lacked the salty conspiratorial air of Alf's place. This was Laurence's parents' gaff and somehow I felt as though I was trespassing. At first the atmosphere seemed to restrict our normal natural behaviour, not to mention the funereal formality of the dinner suits and bow ties. The unfamiliarity of it all seemed to place some invisible barrier between the three of us. However after a few glasses of champagne, it became easier to shrug off this feeling. As usual, alcohol released what inhibitions we had.

Laurence had provided some nibble type food and we sat around the candlelit dining table and chatted, dipping into the various bowls of nuts, crisps and prawn crackers.

We relived the Darren Rhodes episode in pleasing detail, giggling as we did so.

Suddenly Laurence leapt from his seat and opened one of the drawers in the sideboard. He extracted a large carving knife and placed it on the table. 'Gentlemen,' he said grandly, 'I thought tonight we should formalise our friendship. Despite the fact that Russell and I are off to the groves of academe, while Alex stays behind to caress the cobbles of 'Uddersfield we still remain a team. We will rendezvous in the holidays and we shall triumph again. We are brothers after all. Closer than brothers really. I thought we needed some physical act to signify this. To bind us in mind and spirit forever. We should swear to be true to each other and never, never reveal any of our secrets.'

'What exactly do you mean?' asked Alex.

'I mean ... I mean that we should shed our own blood as evidence of our dedication and allegiance to the Brotherhood. This friendship should neither die nor fade away. This should survive throughout our lives wherever that strumpet Mistress Fate takes us. Let's celebrate this unique union in deed as well as thought.'

He took a gulp of champagne, slipped off his jacket and then rolled up the left sleeve of his shirt. With calm deliberation he cut the pale flesh on his forearm with the knife. He dragged the blade across the skin leaving a fine red line which blossomed and spread, the blood oozing forth down his arm and then it started to trickle on to the table. He pressed the forefinger of his right hand into the blood and smeared his cheek with it. He dipped his finger again and anointed my cheek. 'You have been blooded, my brother,' he intoned in all seriousness.

He repeated the process and then anointed Alex in the same manner.

For a moment I was tempted to laugh because this 'ceremony' seemed to me to possess all the risible characteristics of a scene from a Hammer horror film but Laurence's solemn features in the candlelight stifled this urge at birth. He was deadly serious. His mood and attitude affected me and I found myself caught up in the spirit of the occasion.

Laurence handed me the knife. 'Now it is your turn,' he said.

It was only for a second that I hesitated. I knew in my heart that this was not only the right thing to do, but necessary. It was Laurence's wish and I would obey. It was the great unifier. I spilt my own blood, anointed myself before smearing the faces of my two brothers. I cannot explain to this day the overwhelming feeling of spiritual satisfaction and rightness I felt on that occasion. The memory has stayed with me all my life. Not just the images but the whole sense of the occasion from the smell of the candles to the feel and taint of the warm red blood on my cheek.

I handed the knife to Alex who was eager to follow suit. Within moments he had shed his own blood and shared it with us.

Laurence lifted his glass and indicated that we should do likewise while he made a toast. 'We are now brothers in life and brothers in blood. Nothing but death shall separate us.' He looked directly at me and smiled.

Instinctively, Alex and I responded in identical fashion: 'Brothers in blood.'

Laurence beamed. 'Good men. And the next time we organise a caper, we shall spill someone else's blood.'

And that's what happened. When Laurence and I came home for the Christmas holidays, the Brotherhood set out for Wakefield with one purpose in mind: to kill. And we did. We murdered an old tramp: our Alpha Beta as Laurence called him. We followed him from a scruffy old pub and did for him on the street. We took our first life. It was the real beginning.

And I suppose that's where my youth and my uncertain innocence ends. What follows will never equal that time. In the beginning is the joy, the excitement, the freshness. One can repeat, of course, but with each repetition comes a wearing away of the pleasure. This journal is my insubstantial aide-memoire of that time. I am so glad I have caught it, however inadequately. I need write no more...

# TEN

## 1984

Detective Inspector Paul Snow stared at the final page for some time, his vision blurring as all kinds of disparate thoughts and images tumbled through his mind. My God, how many people had this unholy trio murdered in the intervening years! It was like some nasty horror film. And his disquiet increased as he realised that he was now a member of the cast – he too had become part of the drama.

With a groan, he closed the book and placed his hand firmly on the cover and shivered involuntarily.

# PART TWO

PART TWO

# ELEVEN

## 1983

The old excitement returned. It never failed to do so. As the date of their annual excursion neared, Russell felt an actual ache in his stomach, the anticipation developing like some growth within him. He knew that it was a measure of how, by contrast, the rest of his life was dull, mundane, a great disappointment. Indeed, he was a great disappointment to himself. Despite his early aspirations and ambitions, he had achieved nothing special in his life. Gradually, he had morphed into one of those dull sods he had sneered at in his youth. Without Laurence's influence, inspiring him to dare, to reach, to grasp the challenging and the unknown, he had made the obvious choices. Out of laziness and a lack of passion for anything else, he had simply taken the easy options. He had not even moved away from his university base. He was still in Durham and for all he knew would remain there until the end. He was trapped in his own web of incompetence. He had allowed himself to fall onto the predictable middle class conveyor belt that chugged its way through all the conventionalities he despised so much.

On leaving university, he had settled for teacher training because it required no thinking or effort.

85

He'd got his Cert Ed and sank with ease into the swamp of the teaching profession. Here he was in his early thirties with a wife and mortgage neatly chained around his neck. All other avenues had effectively been sealed off. Or so it seemed to him. He had made his rather unadventurous bed and now he would have to lie on it. The only bright spot in his life was the Brotherhood.

The annual excursion of delight.

And here they were together again. Older, wiser and keener. This year it was Bristol. Another first. Long ago they had let Laurence arrange the details. He had the flair, the knack and the ingenuity. He always provided the novelty. And this year was to be particularly special.

They were breaking new ground.

They'd never killed a woman before.

'A prostitute, of course,' Laurence had assured them. 'A raddled, drug-taking tattooed slag who is of no use to man nor beast.'

As usual they had met up for drinks and dinner in a restaurant chosen by Laurence, each staying in a different hotel in the city. Over the meal they chatted in a desultory fashion, mainly about the past, rarely commenting on their other lives, their real lives. Russell was grateful for that.

They were all in their thirties now and Russell noted that the youthful bloom had faded from their faces, his included. But in discussing the night's business their eyes blazed with the enthusiastic exuberance of old.

Laurence had planned the event in his usual meticulous fashion. Sitting back in his chair, a little cheroot dangling from his mouth and a glass of brandy in his hand he explained the arrangements for the evening's entertainment.

'The red light district is heaving with tarts on Friday night, but there's a narrow street on the edge of this area which attracts the rougher types – the older, less tasty doxies, if you get my meaning. I'll do the initial picking up. The car I've hired is pretty big. You two hide in the back until the slag's inside and I've driven off. She'll no doubt give me a location where we can park up and do the business – but I'll suggest we go back to my hotel.' He grinned. 'We won't of course. You crack her on the head, Russ. Try to do it without spilling any blood, eh? Don't want any stains on the upholstery. And then we'll take her to a nice quiet spot by the river that I've picked out and we can complete the deed there. OK?'

Russell and Alex nodded greedily.

It went like clockwork – to begin with. When Laurence drove up the narrow cobbled street, there were just two girls on show. He pulled up by the kerb and wound the window down.

This was the signal for the girls to saunter over.

They were both past their prime but, given their profession, Laurence was unsure when that would have been. They certainly looked over forty but may well have been much younger.

'You after business?' said one, a peroxide blonde in a shiny plastic mac.

Laurence adopted a Brummy accent to respond. 'How much?' he said in a brusque, charmless way. He knew these women would be used to this kind of treatment. There was no room for niceties in such a transaction.

'Forty quid.'

'What about you?' Laurence said, glancing at the other woman. She seemed a little older and less confident. Behind that awfully heavily made up visage was a tired, timid woman.

'I'll do it for thirty-five,' she said, softly, moving forward.

Laurence nodded. 'Get in,' he snapped, pushing open the passenger door. He grinned to himself. Little did the poor cow know, in cutting her price she was effectively cutting her own throat. He couldn't help but give a little chuckle.

They laid her out on the river bank. She was concussed but breathing heavily. Alex was the first to strike a blow. He stabbed the knife deep into her abdomen. The woman gasped and gurgled. For a few fleeting seconds her eyes opened wide in shock and then clamped shut. Russell stabbed her in the chest, but she was already dying now and the body gave no reaction. Finally, with a flourish, Laurence slit her throat, taking great delight in seeing the blood spurt like a series of mini-fountains and trickle down towards her flaccid cleavage.

The three of them stood by the corpse for some moments, their eyes gleaming, tight smiles on their lips. Instinctively they held hands, affirming their brotherhood. Their quiet moment of reflection was disturbed by stirrings in the darkness at the far side of the pathway by the river. There was a sharp rustle and the sound of inarticulate grunting.

And then, suddenly, out of the shadows, a dark form emerged. 'Here, what you doing?' came a voice, harsh and accusative. In shock, the three of them turned to face the stranger, a tall broad-shouldered man with grizzled features and a mop of tousled hair who was fast approaching them. His gait was a little ungainly and he carried a half empty whisky bottle in one hand. 'You've killed her. I saw you, you bastards ... you've killed her,' he cried, as he lunged at Laurence, with surprising speed and agility, wrapping his arm around his neck. So swift had been his movements that Laurence had no time to defend himself and in an instant he was yanked off his feet and flung to the ground as though he were the discarded toy of an angry child. The stranger then brought the bottle down on his head. The blow was not entirely accurate and only caught Laurence's left temple. Nevertheless, the skin split and blood began to seep from the wound. Laurence groaned loudly and sank back onto the grass beside the path.

Laurence's cry of pain seemed to waken Russell and Alex from their frozen state of shock at the sudden violent intrusion of this stranger. Alex leapt forward and stabbed his knife into the back of stranger's neck. The man gave a gruff cry and turned in fury on his attacker, punching him to the ground. Now his eyes lit upon Russell who stood before him, knife in hand. With a roar, he lunged forward, but Russell sidestepped him and his assailant staggered close to the water's edge, but with a nimbleness that belied his size and sobriety, he spun round and grabbed Russell by the neck, his brutish fingers sinking hard into the soft flesh. He brought his face close to Russell's so that even in the fading evening light, he could see the flashing rheumy eyes and the snarling rotten teeth. Terrier-like the man shook his victim violently as he began to throttle him. Russell started to choke and he knew he was in danger of losing consciousness. As his vision began to fade, he summoned up all his energy to thrust his knife hard into his assailant's stomach.

This action had an instant effect. The man gave a roar, a strange mixture of pain and fury, and releasing his hold of Russell's throat, he staggered backwards. As he did so, Russell snatched up the discarded whisky bottle and brought it down with great force on the back of the man's head. He crumpled to the ground and lay still.

Russell and Alex stared down at the derelict, their bodies heaving and their minds awhirl. They were joined by Laurence who was dabbing his forehead with his handkerchief. Suddenly he began laughing, a rich, natural fulsome laugh. The other two stared at him in surprise.

'Well,' said Laurence, containing his merriment, 'that was an interesting *divertissement,* was it not? Two for the price of one.'

Neither Russell nor Alex seemed to share Laurence's amusement. They saw the incident for what it was: a very dangerous close call.

'Now let's get the hell out of here,' said Alex, looking around nervously, wondering if there were any other strangers lurking in the shadows ready to pounce.

Laurence nodded. 'Good idea, but first we must commit our friends to their watery grave.'

Without speaking, they tipped the bodies of their victims into the dark silent waters of the river and watched them sink slowly below the murky surface and then flung their knives after them.

'And now a drink, I think, gentlemen. We have earned it,' announced Laurence with a grin, still using his Brummy accent.

## TWELVE

### 1984

Russell took a sip of the ice cold gin and tonic and then relaxed back into the inadequate folds of the garden lounger, closing his eyes and surrendering himself to the warm summer sun. His mind wandered back to the incident on the river bank a year ago. At this distance the panic and sense of danger had subsided completely and he viewed it merely as an exciting adventure. He remembered it now with affection and amusement, an unexpected bonus to their night's activities. The thought that one of them could have been injured or worse no longer crossed his mind. Instead he focused on the killing of the girl, the tart, the sack of flesh in a dress. He ran the images in slow motion in his mind. In particular, he focused on the blood spurting from her throat. It was an erotic image and as it rippled in his brain, he felt stirrings at his crotch. The sensation pleased him, but he banished the image before it roused him further.

Oh, but it had been good. It was the last time he had really smiled.

He tried to turn his mind to other things. It was Friday again, the end of another fraught and tedious week, and the freedom of two whole days away from the hell hole where he worked beckoned. For him it was just a brief, occasional respite from the reality of his dull, tense existence. He'd been warned by many, not least Laurence, that he would regret going into teaching. Forget the long holidays and the supposedly short hours, he had been told. Think about the pressure, the constant battle with young savages, the preparation and marking and the increasing burden of paperwork, he had been told. But he had ignored the warnings.

With a sudden movement he drained his glass. The surge of cold alcohol pleased him. Its anaesthetic properties were beginning to work. With this prospect in mind, he padded back into the kitchen and poured himself another double and returned to the lounger determined to fill his mind with pleasant thoughts. It would not be an easy task, he accepted, as he sipped his gin greedily. Much of life bored him or filled him with disdain. It always had, of course. He really believed that he had a limited capacity to be happy. To a large extent this was due to his inability to form close relationships. He could get so close but then some inner force, prompted by insecurity, laziness or, more usually, a complete lack of curiosity about other people held him back. He only felt anything approaching happiness when he was with Laurence and Alex, particularly Laurence. Then the protective shell fell away. He could be himself – or as much as he was ever able to be. It was a truth he accepted: Laurence had spoiled him for others.

Of course he cared for Sandra – in his own reserved fashion. She was a sweet, intelligent woman and, perhaps more importantly, made very few demands on him. She didn't try to mould him to her tastes and outlook as he'd seen so many wives of his acquaintance do. Sandra accepted him – loved him – for what he was. Well, he assumed that she loved him. She behaved as though she did and he didn't question the matter further. It was, he supposed, a marriage of convenience. They rarely argued. If she didn't agree with him, she just left him alone. He knew that in this respect he was lucky; he also knew that if something happened to her – if she disappeared from his life – he would survive. Quite easily. He would continue in his own stoical way.

With this observation floating around his brain, he drifted into sleep. The gin and the sun, combined with the natural fatigue following a week teaching bore him away into a dreamless slumber.

He was awakened some twenty minutes later by a cool hand on his brow and a warm kiss on his lips. He opened his eyes to find Sandra smiling down at him. 'Getting pissed before the evening meal is a bit desperate, darling, even for you,' she said brightly.

'I am not pissed,' he responded with mock grumpiness, shaking off the rags of sleep. He pulled himself up in the lounger and reached for his glass on the lawn. It lay on its side, having

93

fallen over when it had slipped from his grasp as he had dropped off to sleep. He studied the empty glass as though it were some prize exhibit in the empty glass museum. 'I'm just tired. If a couple of gins make me pissed, there's no hope.'

He grinned and Sandra kissed him again.

'Would you like another?' she asked.

He nodded. 'Is the Pope Catholic?'

'I think I'll join you.'

'Good girl.'

She returned minutes later with a tray containing two fresh glasses and a bowl of peanuts.

'Had a good day, darling?' he asked sarcastically.

'So, so,' she said, plonking herself down in the other lounger. 'Frantic morning but, y'know, appointments dry up on a Friday afternoon.'

'People are too busy preparing for the weekend to be ill, eh?'

Sandra gave a tired grin. 'Something like that.'

'Have we treated anything really nasty today? Any bubonic plague around?'

'You know, people around here are not that adventurous. The odd case of impotence and slipped disc was the best on offer. Apart from that it's summer sniffles, hay fever and piles.'

'Piles of what.'

She grinned. 'Exactly. And what about you? Did you have a good day?'

'Yes. It was a Tuesday in 1973. I remember it well.'

'Hey, that was before you met me.'

'Oops.'

Exhausting the empty banter, they lapsed into a

comfortable silence. Sandra was content. That's all she wanted out of marriage: a relaxed and undemanding partnership. That's all she wanted out of life: smooth sailing – drifting casually on the mill pond – and not being tossed and blown on the unpredictable ocean. Despite choosing medicine as a career and being one of the best students in her year at medical school, she had no desire to specialise or face the cut and thrust of hospital life. She just wanted to be a common or garden GP. Like her father. Steady and unremarkable. Like Russell. They were well matched.

Sometimes he felt that she had chosen him because he was apparently unambitious and posed no challenge. She knew that he wasn't going to drag her from her own comfort zone. It also struck him that this is why he had chosen her.

They made love that night. It was Friday and they usually made love on Friday. After five years of marriage, it had become a somewhat mechanical routine but in its own way fulfilling. Usually after the climax, they each turned over on their side and slipped into contented sleep. However, on this occasion they lay close on their backs, staring at the ceiling, still pleasantly vague from the alcohol and savouring the moments of intimacy.

'I suppose we should be smoking a cigarette now?' he said at length.

'Smoking is bad for you. I am a doctor and I know.'

'Everything pleasurable is bad for you.'

'Except sex.'

'Ah, the one thing God forgot about.'

She reached for his hand beneath the covers

and pulled herself closer to him until she could feel his body heat.

'Russ, I have news.'

'News?' He was puzzled but not concerned.

She leaned over and whispered in his ear. 'You're going to be a daddy.'

'What...?'

'I'm having a baby. *We're* having a baby.'

Russell lay very still for a moment, assimilating this information, digesting it as quickly as he could and working out how he felt about the matter.

'You are certain?' he asked quietly.

She smiled in spite of her apprehension. 'As I've already said, I am a doctor, darling. I think I should know.'

Deep within him, Russell was disappointed. A baby changed so much. The dynamics of their life would never be the same. Inconvenience and responsibility came with all that baby baggage. He was angry, too. They hadn't discussed this in detail; it had always been a case of someday, yes, but perhaps not now. It seemed that Sandra had made up her own mind on the matter. He had been removed from the decision making process.

However, as he looked across at his wife, her face almost luminous in the dimness of the bedroom, touched by the moonlight falling through the window, he could see the pleasure in her eyes and the tenseness of her expression. She wanted the baby. Possibly she needed the baby. And she needed him to be happy about it.

He hugged her tightly, kissing her forehead as he did so. 'That's absolutely wonderful, darling,' he said, his voice warm and reassuring, while his face remained an expressionless mask.

He felt her relax into his embrace and her arms tightened around him. 'Are you sure you're happy, Russ? I hoped you would be.'

'Of course. Of course I'm happy. I'm just a little surprised that's all.'

'Well, I am, too. Just a couple of missed pills. I really didn't think it would make any difference.'

'Not deliberate?'

'Oh, Russ, no. You don't think...'

'No, no, of course not. Hey, mummy, this is great news.'

She hugged him tighter. She believed him.

Great news! Now there really was no escape from this life. He'd have to stay in the job now until his legs or his mind went. He was to be a FATHER with all the financial and social responsibilities that came with the role. Middle age, penury and parental responsibility loomed. My God, he was turning into his own father. How on earth had he allowed this to happen to him? He had never meant to end up here: a teacher married to a doctor in a neat and tidy semi in suburbia with nothing to look forward to but grey hair, school fees and a pension. He had become the epitome of all that he and Laurence had sneered at in their youth. Dull little men whose lives were set on fixed rails with no diversions. They just chugged along the ordained course until they hit the buffers in their sixties or seventies with a heart attack, cancer or sheer boredom. It was a nightmare.

Sandra fell asleep in his arms, a smile of contentment on her face. Gently he disentangled himself and laid her on her side. She stirred momentarily but slipped back into deep sleep, the soft smile still touching her lips.

He lay back staring at the ceiling feebly fighting off the mood of despair that was overwhelming him. What, he pondered, would Laurence do in this situation? The question afforded him a bleak smile. Laurence would never have got himself into this situation in the first place. He wasn't fool enough to get married for a start. Oh, if he could have been more like Laurence. But he wasn't and never could be.

After a while, realising that sleep would not come to him, his mind full of disparate and desperate thoughts, he slipped out of bed and made his way down to the kitchen. Here he poured himself a generous measure of whisky and then went into the small downstairs room which he used as an office. The desk was littered with papers connected with school and a pile of pale green exercise books waiting to be marked were perched precariously on the top. Russell had a sudden urge to send them flying but he resisted it. Common sense told him that he'd only have to pick the buggers up afterwards.

He sat down and switched on the desk light. Its bright beam hurt his eyes at first and he swivelled the head away from him, spilling light up the wall. He slid open one of the little drawers and extracted an envelope which contained a key. This unlocked another drawer from which he took a long foolscap envelope. It was addressed to him in elegant flowing handwriting with vivid purple ink.

The envelope contained the last letter that he had received from Laurence about a month earlier. He knew he should have burned it. That was the agreed arrangement. There should never be any evidence that they had kept in touch. He would destroy the missive soon, but he always kept Laurence's wild and witty letters for a month or so. He liked to re-read them for pleasure and for comfort. There was a kind of warm vicarious enjoyment to be had from these letters. Laurence certainly hadn't set his life down on staid, pre-dictable middle class rails as he had. After university he had entered the acting profession – or blagged his way into it, as he was fond of ad-mitting. His endeavours had taken him all over the country, playing farces at the seaside, Shakespeare in schools, and the occasional season with reput-able theatres in York and Salisbury. He only just scraped a living but it had been a living and not just an existence.

Russell had not seen Laurence perform on stage since their university days. That was another rule of their pact. They should never meet unless it was for their annual project. Once a year, every year, the three of them met up in some location unrelated to their normal lives to reconstitute the Brotherhood. To spill blood. That was all.

Russell had been tempted to go and see Lau-rence incognito as it were when he'd been in York for a season the previous year but he knew that he must be true to the pact above all things. Their lives depended on it.

As he sat there, sipping the whisky and reading

the letter, Russell felt immeasurably sad. He hated himself for feeling so maudlin; sentimentality was abhorrent to him, but he couldn't help himself. The letter allowed him to glimpse a richer, grander, more exciting existence. It permitted him to press his nose against the window pane of Laurence's life and in doing so he ached to be inside.

When he'd re-read the letter, he took it through to the kitchen and set fire to it. He held the envelope aloft above the sink and watched it flame itself into flaky black ashes. At last, as it shrivelled down towards the tips of his fingers he dropped the burning remains into the sink and doused them with cold water. It was gone now. The words already a fading memory, apart from the post script which he had memorised. It was a date, a time and a location for the next meeting of The Brotherhood: August 27th, 10.30 a.m., the café of the art gallery in Manchester.

## THIRTEEN

'Are you ready? I'm bored out of my skull.' John elongated his face and yawned to add weight to his statement.

Alex frowned. 'You're always bored these days. What's up with you, man? Time you chilled out.'

'Here? How can you fuckin' chill out here in this dump? You must be jokin'. The music's rubbish and it's the same old faces every week. It stinks.'

'You go then, eh? Get a taxi ... I'll see you later at home. I just want to hang around a bit longer.'

'Hopin' to cop off are you?'

'What the hell does that mean?'

'I've seen you eyein' up Leather Man over there. Mr I Fancy Myself.'

Alex didn't know whether to grin or get angry. 'I'll pretend I didn't hear that. I'm with you aren't I? What sort of bloke do you think I am?'

'Sometimes I'm not sure, actually. Especially when your eyes come out on stalks and your tongue hangs down like a dog on heat whenever Leather Man passes by.'

'Oh, go get lost, will you.'

Alex rose and pushed his way across the crowded room to the bar. He bought himself a rum and coke and downed it in two gulps. He'd just had enough of John's whining ways and his selfishness for one night. He had become a jealous bore. He just wasn't grown up enough to realise that gay people can be as dedicated to their partners, just as monogamous as straight people. It wasn't always about jumping into bed and getting your end away. There was commitment and love as well. But John, who was five years younger than Alex, was riddled with insecurity and while this had a kind of quaint charm in the early days of their relationship, it was now beginning to pall. He was no longer a fun guy to be with and that was why, yes, Alex had been eyeing up Leather Man because he seemed to be just that: a fun guy. You slave away all week with a bunch of intellectual dwarves and so on a Saturday night you need a bit of fun.

101

Alex ordered another drink and while the barman was getting it, he glanced across the room to where they had been sitting. John had gone. Well, bollocks to him, Alex thought. The puff in a huff. If that's the way he wants to play it, let him. Alex hadn't got the patience or the inclination to put up with his petulance any longer. John's disappearance brought into focus the growing doubts Alex had concerning their relationship. Until recently he had been prepared to commit himself fully to it. That's why he had asked John to move in with him. He wasn't by nature promiscuous but in the last few months things had started to turn sour. John had become moody, more jealous and fractious. He was turning into a bloody fishwife, Alex mused. It wouldn't be long now before they parted company. He didn't want to give John his marching orders but he reckoned the relationship had come to the end of its natural life. Oh well, let the bugger storm off home. I'm better off without him. The night is young and I'm so beautiful. He grinned at his own squiffy conceit and finished his drink.

As he turned to the bar to order another one, he felt a presence by his side, a presence that carried with it a powerful cologne. He turned and came face-to-face with Leather Man. He was smiling that smile. The smile that all gay men recognise immediately. One that cuts through all the verbal crap of tentative introductions and small talk. The smile that says I want you – are you up for it?

'Let me get you a drink,' he said, eyes twinkling. His voice was low and sweet and not the least bit effeminate. His features were tanned and his mop of dark hair was carefully gelled and it glistened under the lights of the bar. He wore tight leather trousers and a dark shiny shirt which was open down to the waist.

He was a dish.

Alex nodded. 'That's kind. Rum and coke. Ta.'

Leather Man ordered drinks for both of them. He was on some sort of poncy cocktail.

'You on your own...?' asked Leather Man.

Instinctively, Alex glanced over to where John had been sitting. 'I am now,' he said with a wan smile.

Leather Man nodded. 'I thought so. I saw you with someone else earlier.'

'It's past his bedtime now.'

'So you are on your own then?'

'Certainly am.'

Leather Man grinned and passed Alex his drink. It was a pleasant smile and very alluring. 'I'm Matt.'

'Alex.'

They exchanged chaste kisses on the cheek.

'Fancy a dance then?' Matt took Alex's hand without waiting for an answer and led him onto the crowded floor.

If Alex had a weakness where handsome men were concerned, it was that he was easily smitten. And with Matt he was easily smitten. Initially they indulged in a little gentle bopping but as the tempo of the music slipped down into the smooch gear, they followed the trend and draped their bodies over each other and shuffled around the floor. Alex could feel Matt's firm muscles through the thin material of his shirt.

'God, you must really work out,' he whispered, giving his pecs a squeeze.

'Every day. Twice a day. It's my religion.'

'I think I've got a prayer mat at home.'

They both grinned and hugged each other tighter. It was as though a bargain had been struck.

The club was closing when Alex and Matt emerged with several other couples into the sultry night air. Alex was excited and happy. It had been ages since he'd been involved in a pick up like this. It was fun, stimulating – and dangerous. Which made it all the more exciting.

'Come back to mine, eh?' Matt said in that smooth way of his, eyes twinkling and teeth flashing. 'It's still too early to call it a night.'

Alex was too tipsy to sense the performance, the practised charade in Matt's manner. He just nodded. 'Sure.'

It was that easy. For Matt it always was.

They sauntered down the street hand in hand and then Matt motioned towards a large black 4x4.

'Yours?' Alex pointed at the vehicle, impressed.

'Mine. Hop in.'

Matt told him that he lived at Ravensfield, a rural spot some six miles from the centre of town. He drove like a maniac along the quiet roads, pushing the 4x4 well above the speed limit and taking risks with corners and traffic lights as though he was trying to impress his new friend. Shooting through the little village of Outlane, Matt was now taking roads that were foreign to Alex. And as the normal street lights petered out, he had no idea where the hell they were. But he felt comfortable and strangely secure in the warm, wildly swaying vehicle. He was cocooned in the motor with the best looking guy in the world. He gazed across at Matt's face illuminated by the dashboard, his strong even features bathed in eerie green light. He felt good. He also hoped that he could sober up a little. He didn't want to miss a minute of this adventure. And he didn't want to disappoint.

Eventually, the 4x4 screeched to a halt outside a small detached house on a narrow country lane. There appeared to be no other properties nearby, just darkness.

Matt jumped out into the velvet black night and, racing down the little path, opened the door and beckoned Alex inside. The lights were already on and, stepping inside, Alex was surprised how quaint it was – very chintzy and old maidish. There were horrible porcelain knick-knacks on the mantelpiece, a very inadequate and toe-curlingly garish representation of The Hay Wain over the fireplace and the sofa was covered in some kind of pastoral moquette resembling, John thought, an unpleasant vegetarian pizza.

This did not seem Matt's style at all. Or perhaps he was more than the sum of his parts – a mystery man.

'Plonk down somewhere and I'll grab us a drink. And then I'll give you the grand tour. It'll take all of five minutes.' Without waiting for a response, Matt slipped off into the kitchen. He seemed very businesslike. Very sober.

'Just a soft drink for me,' Alex called after him.

'I think I've had enough alcohol for one night.'

'Yer big sissy,' came the reply.

'Well, you don't want me collapsing on you, do you?' Alex realised that he had an idiotic grin on his face.

'It's the best offer I've had all night.'

Alex thought he heard Matt giggling to himself in the kitchen and then all went quiet. He reappeared moments later with two identical glasses, a slice of lemon floating in each.

'A little gin never hurt a girl, did it?' he grinned passing one of the glasses to Alex.

'Are you trying to get me pissed?'

'I've been rumbled. Cheers.'

They clinked glassed and grinned at each other.

'Come on, let me show you upstairs.'

Matt held out his hand and Alex took it and was led up a narrow curved staircase.

The upper floor was a complete contrast to the granny aura of downstairs. Gone was the chintz in favour of stark minimalist. The bathroom was sleek and modern; there were splashes of chrome with black and white tiles, red towels and shelves filled with various grooming products. One of the bedrooms had been turned into a gym. There were weights, a rowing machine and a punch bag.

'So this is where you turn flab into hard muscle.'

'Yeah, this is my temple.' Matt gave the punch bag a hard bang with his free hand. 'Do you do any of this stuff yourself?'

Alex shook his head. 'Nah, I'm the seven stone weakling type. The one with the incipient beer gut. If you've got any sand around the place, you can kick some in my face.'

'Later, maybe.'

Matt then showed Alex the master bedroom. In here the lighting was muted and discreet. Chocolate hessian adorned the walls and there were silky black sheets on the bed. Alex thought it was bordering on the tacky but strangely macho.

Matt sat on the bed and patted the covers by his side as an invitation for Alex to join him. He did so; and within seconds they were kissing and fondling each other. Despite the amount of alcohol Alex had consumed and that cotton wool feeling in his head, he was quickly aroused.

Soon they were rolling on the bed, snatching each other's clothes off. Matt slipped out of his leather trousers revealing a large penis pressing fiercely against the sheer material of his thong. Alex's body pulsed with excitement and anticipated pleasure and, pulling the thong aside, he went down, slipping his mouth around the erect member. Matt groaned with pleasure and fell back on the bed.

Alex was just about to bring his new lover to a climax when, to his surprise, Matt suddenly pulled back and jumped off the bed.

'You're a good boy, but I don't want to come just yet,' he said in a strange matter-of-fact manner. 'Not on a blowjob anyway. I like it nice and snug up the arse.'

Alex found himself saying, 'That can be arranged' – but he was a little puzzled by Matt's calculating behaviour. It was though he was playing some game by his own rules. Somewhere deep within the recesses of his foggy mind faint alarm bells started ringing. He began to sense that all was not right here. But it was too late now.

'Certainly it can be arranged,' Matt was saying as he moved to the bedroom door and threw it open. 'And, in fact it has been. All arranged. OK fellas,' he cried.

Two men entered the room. One was shaven-headed, plump with a beer gut visible below the line of his black T-shirt; the other was of a more athletic build, blond-haired with cruel, mean eyes.

'Boys, this is Alex,' announced Matt as though he was some night club compere. 'And Alex, these are the boys.'

'What the fuck is this?' snapped Alex, fear rapidly sobering him up.

'This, my friend, is what is known as a gang bang. So brace yourself, Sheila. It's gonna be a bumpy night. OK, boys, let's take him back into the gym.'

When Alex eventually opened his eyes he found himself lying on his back staring up at a grey overcast sky. It was morning. His body was stiff and his head throbbed with a kind of dull bass disco beat. It took him sometime to recollect his thoughts and when he did, he cried out in pain and disgust. Had it really happened? Had he really been treated like a sexual puppet by those three men? Man handled and raped. Buggered until it hurt. Until he'd bled. The ache he felt told him without doubt that it had *really* happened.

He lay there – wherever he was – gazing at the

early morning sky – and began to weep gently.

Slowly the events of the previous night came back to him in fragments. The pickup at the club, the strange house with the chintzy downstairs and the modish, masculine upstairs. He pictured Matt, Leather Man, and their initial embraces on the bed and their wonderful promise. Black sheets, he thought. He remembered the black sheets. Now things were getting hazy. Part of his brain had blocked out the most unbearable moments, but he remembered the animal-like pleasure of the three men, Matt and his cronies, as they had taken turns to ... to use him. His own cries of pain and distress reverberated in his ears. They had taken no notice. They had used him like a rag doll. It wasn't just the sex that inflamed them, it was the power, the brute force, the notion of inflicting pain, while they received pleasure. His stomach lurched at the thought of it and with some urgency he pulled himself up into a sitting position. He wiped his eyes and he noted his surroundings – he was on a bench in Greenhead Park, half a mile from the centre of town. And then with a sudden lurch, he leaned over sideways and was violently sick.

There was a brief respite and then his stomach heaved again, expelling its contents in a foul gush. He remained still, hanging over the side of the bench, for some minutes staring down at the ground and the pool of his own vomit – wondering if there was any more to come and more vaguely what the hell was he to do now.

He heard the sharp staccato clip-clip of female footsteps coming his way. Glancing up he saw a young woman walking down the main avenue of the park. With some effort, Alex pulled himself up into a sitting position and waited for her to pass by. She did so quickly with her head averted from him. He didn't blame her: he must look a sight. In fact, he thought, if he looked like he felt, it's a wonder she hadn't screamed and run off in the opposite direction.

He knew he ought to move; he wanted to move; but he really didn't know if he was capable of moving. His legs felt weak and his body ached. He started to cry again. These sort of things happened to other people, he told himself. It was the stuff of scurrilous Sunday newspapers. His shoulders heaved as he gave in to the wave of emotion that swept over him. Tears rolled down his cheeks and he bent over until his face was almost touching his knees and just sobbed.

At length as the tears subsided, he scrabbled in the pocket of his jeans and found a handkerchief. With a kind of self-punishing roughness, he rubbed his eyes dry and blew his nose. 'You'll live,' he told himself with a sneer. Now he was angry with himself for being too naïve. Too fucking gullible. And too fucking greedy. He'd wanted sex and by hell he had got it. In spades!

Suddenly he thought to look at his watch. It was six thirty in the morning. Then he checked that his wallet was still there and the cash and credit cards had remained untouched. Everything was as it should be. Well it would be, wouldn't it? They hadn't been after cash or property; they'd been after his body.

As his sense or anger and self loathing rose

within him, it seemed to give him enough energy to stand up. He did so for a moment but then his legs gave way and he crashed back down on the bench, his feet skidding in his own vomit.

'Fuck,' he cried. The word echoed around the empty park like a lost bird.

Gripping his knees, he tried again. He stood but did not try to move for at least a minute and then like a metal robot that had not been oiled for some months he began walking towards the park gates. I must look like a fucking old veteran returning from the trenches, he told himself, as he started to make his way down into the centre of town. Every step was a painful experience but he gritted his teeth and his grim determination mixed with that strange strand of guilt that had started to develop with in him, helped to keep him moving.

The sun had appeared now and the early morning chill had begun to dissipate, but this did nothing to cheer his spirits. He felt wretched and, worse than that, he hated himself. He tried hard to switch his brain off, to stop thinking altogether and to prevent the bright searing images from his ordeal returning to haunt him. But he failed. If anything they came back with greater clarity. The three sweaty bodies; their tight grip on him as two of them held him forward while the third forced an entry. Again and again. The excruciating pain mixed with a wild fear and disgust. He felt his stomach retch once more, but this time it was in vain. There was nothing left for him to spew forth.

On reaching the centre of town he headed for

the railway station and got a taxi to take him home.

'Where the hell have you been?' John, still in his dressing gown clasping a mug of tea, rose from his armchair as Alex entered. John was angry and had barely looked at Alex as he walked through the door, but when he did so, he recoiled in shock at his friend's appearance. 'Bloody hell, what happened to you?'

Alex staggered forward and slumped down on the sofa, his eyes filled with tears. 'I don't want to talk about it. I won't talk about it. *Ever!*'

John sat down by him. 'Come on, man. Something terrible's happened. What is it? For Christ's sake you can tell me.'

John moved forward to put a comforting arm around Alex but he flinched and pulled back.

'No, don't ... don't touch me. Don't ... touch me.'

John backed off. 'OK. OK. I won't. But surely you can tell me where you've been. I mean ... what's made you like this?'

Words wouldn't come and so Alex just shook his head.

'Maybe later, eh? Man, you look rough. Have you been attacked or something? Should I ring the police?'

'No! No police. Nothing ... just ... nothing. Just leave it will you!' Alex's voice was hoarse but filled with anger.

John shook his head confused and concerned.

'Well, I can get you a cup of tea, can't I? Surely you'll let me do that.'

'Yeah. A cup of tea ... that would be ... yeah a cup of tea.' He nodded without looking at his friend. The universal panacea. That will cure all ills – won't it?

Twenty minutes later Alex was submersed in a bathful of soapy water scrubbing himself red raw. Attempting to scrub the pain, the shame and the humiliation away. The harder he rubbed, the more he realised the mark on his soul was indelible.

## FOURTEEN

Laurence was on his way to getting drunk. Again. Well, it was Friday night. That was his excuse. There was always an excuse: he was feeling rather low; he was in a good mood; the play had gone badly; the play had gone well; he was bored; he was elated; he was out of work; he was in work; he was thirsty. In truth, it was always for the same reason: he wanted to place the real world at a distance, to soften its edges, to escape dull reality.

Indeed it was Friday night, and the play had gone reasonably well and the reviews earlier in the week from the Salisbury Bugle or whatever the local rag was called had made some fleetingly complimentary remarks about his performance but despite this he was feeling down in the mouth. He was sitting in the theatre bar with some members of the cast and stage crew having a boozy wind down after the performance. Sue Ling, the

113

little prop girl, had squeezed herself in beside him and was paying him a great deal of attention. While he was enjoying this, his mind was not fully concentrating on her animated conversation. He was thinking about the letter he'd received that morning from Alex. It had been most unpleasant, shocking even, full of painful revelations and unsettling images. He thought he had been made of sterner stuff to react as he had done. And the letter presented him with a dilemma. What disturbed him the most was his own response to the contents. They moved him; they angered him; they disgusted him; and somehow they had driven a red hot poker into his soul. But he did not know why. He prided himself on keeping his cool at all times. Never get too close to anything or anyone was not only his motto but his natural, unforced reaction to life. He liked to think he proved John Donne wrong – this man *was* an island. He had killed a number of sad souls in vicious cold blood without the batting of the proverbial eyelid – so why then, why fucking then, had he become so perturbed by Alex's plight? Certainly he was one of the triumvirate. One of the Brotherhood. But that wasn't it. He had no answer and that increased his irritation and discomfort. It was a weakness and Laurence had no truck with weakness. This dilemma had played on his mind all day, only being thrust aside temporarily when he went on stage.

Sue Ling leaned closer to him and whispered in his ear: 'The bar will be closing soon. You could come back to my place if you like. I got some beer in the fridge ... and some wine.' Laurence

114

knew there was more on offer than alcohol in Sue Ling's invitation. She beamed, bright-eyed, wriggling in anticipation of his reply.

Laurence looked down at her. She was a pretty thing. And eager with it. She was alluring too, with her dark shiny hair and engaging smile. Her small frame was shoe-horned into tight jeans and a white T-shirt which emphasised her tiny breasts, her button nipples pressing against the cotton fabric. She squeezed his knee. Sex, in capital letters, was being offered on a plate and Laurence could never resist such offers. The poor girl had a crush on him – how could he disappoint her? She was, he knew, fresh to the world of theatre and in her naïve way still saw it as a magical fairy land and Laurence as the dashing star. She'd learn, he thought sourly, but nevertheless her enthusiasm was flattering. He shouldn't disappoint her. Laurence reckoned that he would just have to put his thoughts of Alex on hold one more time. After all, if he could do it while prancing up and down on stage as Andrew Aguecheek, he certainly could do it for a more energetic, exciting and sensually rewarding performance with Sue Ling.

'Sounds like a good idea to me,' he said with a smile, rolling his eyes and pursing his lips in a comic fashion.

Sue Ling stroked his thigh with enthusiasm.

'Hey, what are you two up to?' Harry Boswell, the company's leading man, could hardly keep the irritation out of his supposedly light-hearted enquiry. Laurence assumed that he was annoyed because he'd got his eyes on the little Chinese cracker for himself. Boswell regarded himself as a something of a catch. He was a bit of a name having done a fair amount of work on the telly, including a stint in *Coronation Street*. Boswell assumed that because of his 'star status', as he saw it, the ladies would flock unbidden to his crotch. But not this time, Harry, old boy, thought Laurence with great satisfaction. He'd take up Sue Ling's offer if only to spike Boswell's guns. A double hit, in fact.

'We were discussing Andrew Aguecheek's sexuality, considering the possibility that he was subjugating latent homosexual tendencies in order to make himself more acceptable in the eyes of Sir Toby Belch,' said Laurence smoothly.

'Bollocks!' retorted Boswell with a sneer.

'Yes, they certainly came into the discussion.'

There was general laughter and with a glare Boswell returned to his pint.

Sue Ling lived in a tiny bedsit in student-land about a ten minute walk from the theatre. She talked all the way there, her conversation punctuated with nervous giggles. She was hyper with alcohol and anticipation. Away from the theatre, she had taken Laurence's hand and hung on to him as though he were a newly acquired possession. She was probably in her early twenties, thought Laurence, but looked much younger. He imagined that she saw this night and its forthcoming events as the start of a wonderful friendship between the two of them, the bud of a passionate romance which would blossom over the coming weeks. Instead of what it really was, for Laurence at least, a convenient fuck handed to

116

him on a plate.

'Would you like some wine?' Sue Ling asked, after she had turned on two table lamps and the electric glow fire.

'I'd prefer to kiss your breasts,' Laurence replied casually, tossing his jacket on to a wicker chair.

Without a word, she pulled off her T-shirt. 'Your wish is my command, Sir Andrew.'

Laurence grinned. 'You are quite beautiful, aren't you?'

He meant it. There was something very attractive about her small frame and smooth features with that broad smile and ingenuous almond-shaped eyes. He kissed her firmly on the lips while his hands cupped her breasts and gently massaged them. She responded with a sigh, moulding herself into his tall frame.

As she slipped out of her jeans revealing her smooth, pert backside, Laurence experienced a strange stabbing pain in his head and he suddenly felt nauseous. He closed his eyes and a violent flashing image filled his vision. An image torn from Alex's letter; vivid, graphic, greatly unsettling. Violent male sex – brutal bestiality. It was like a fierce light being shone in his eyes. He winced and found himself shuddering involuntarily.

Sue Ling noticed his odd behaviour. She ran her cool hand over his brow. 'You OK, Laurence?' she asked.

He nodded and added a weak smile as an afterthought. Despite her naked presence, he felt his ardour waning. His mind had been overtaken

117

by the image, like a scrap of film on a loop juddering uncompromisingly in his head. This was so unlike him and anger mixed with his concern, further diluting his passion.

'Come to bed. Make love to me,' Sue Ling said, leading him to the tiny single bed in the far corner of the room. A sandy-haired teddy bear with a red bow-tie sat on the pillows, its glassy eyes gazing out at them with enigmatic stillness. Carefully Sue Ling lifted the bear from the bed and placed him on the laundry basket.

As soon as Laurence was on the bed, kissing and caressing Sue Ling, he knew the adventure was doomed. That image with its ferocity and blood had stayed with him and dominated his emotions. Nothing stirred below. Even when she gently massaged his penis it refused to respond. She kissed the head gently before placing her mouth over it. But nothing happened. Laurence's emotions shifted from dismay to annoyance and then to humiliation. This had never happened before. He had never even contemplated such a situation. As a rule he could achieve an erection as quickly and as easily as snapping his fingers.

But not tonight.

'I'm sorry, I must have had too much to drink,' he mumbled softly, well aware that this was a pathetic excuse.

Sue Ling was obviously disappointed. 'Maybe later, eh? Perhaps you are too tense. Shall we have coffee?'

Laurence shook his head. 'Some other time. I think I'd better go.' He had got up from the bed and began scrabbling about for his clothes. My

118

God, he thought, I've become a character in some cheap farce. A fucking vicar will come in at any moment without any trousers.

'Oh, don't leave, Laurence. We can just sleep together. It doesn't matter. You might feel better in the morning.'

Feel better. It sounded like he had a bloody illness. A disease. He had been affected with the can't-get-it-up virus. He glanced at the narrow single bed. He didn't fancy spending the night on that and anyway he wanted to escape, to be alone to wallow in his own shame. He was terrified. He had experienced the ultimate male failure. He knew that he may well have started a cycle of impotence that might be difficult to break. He had read all about this in various magazines. Once you fail to perform, the fear and apprehension prevents you the next time and the next time … forever.

He came out in a sweat. He must get away. He needed to leave the scene of his crime. By getting out, he hoped he could disassociate himself from the ignominy of it. He gazed at the still naked Sue Ling. She was eminently desirable. What on earth was wrong with him?

With unseemly haste, he bundled himself out of Sue Ling's flat and staggered into the cool night air. For some moments he leaned against the wall of the building, his chest heaving. It was a nightmare. A bloody nightmare. As soon as this thought came to him, the same violent image flashed back in his mind.

'Fuck off, will you,' he cried to it. Why on earth did this affect him so much? Why was it there and why had it castrated him? He fumbled in his pocket for his pack of small cigars. He lit one and breathed deeply allowing the tobacco to seep into his lungs. At that moment he felt as low as he could ever remember. He was gripped by a sudden fear that true emotion had found a way into his system. Real turmoil inducing feelings had finally broken through the once impregnable barrier.

With a snarl, he threw the cigar into the gutter and made his way home.

Home was a small guest house which in reality was only one notch up from Sue Ling's bedsit; such was the lot of the provincial actor in rep. At least he had en-suite facilities in the room so when he got back, he stripped off and had a shower, attempting to sluice away the growing sense of his despair. Then he lay on the bed and re-read Alex's letter. The last sentence seemed to radiate from the page: 'So you see Laurence, that's why I want this man dead.'

Laurence closed his eyes, a thin veil of perspiration still covering his face from the heat of the shower. It was against all they had agreed, all they had promised to do. They would not leave a mess in their own back yard. It was too dangerous. Connections could be made. They must remain separate entities at all times. And yet they hadn't reckoned on this. One of their own being damaged. They hadn't contemplated Leather Man.

Impulsively, Laurence dragged on his clothes again and ventured out into the cold night air. At the end of the street, he found a phone box. It smelt of urine and stale beer. He dialled a number he had memorised. It rang for quite a time until eventually a sleepy voice answered: 'Yes?'

'Russell, it's Laurence. Are you free to talk?'

'What...' Russell was still dragging himself awake and not quite believing what he was hearing.

'It's Laurence. Are you alone?'

'Yes, yes. Sandra's out at some medical bash. What's this all about?'

'We need to meet up,' Laurence said, his old authoritarian tone reasserting itself.

'Meet up?' There was a faint note of panic in Russell's voice.

'Have you heard from Alex?'

'No. Why? Should I have? Is something wrong?'

'Don't want to go into that now. But I reckon we're going to have to change our plans for the next project.'

'What do you mean? What's up?'

'Not over the phone. Can you get to London next Sunday?'

'Next Sunday! Are you mad?'

'It's important. Vital. You must.'

There was a pause while Russell came to terms with this passionate injunction.

'It'll be bloody difficult,' he said at length, knowing that he'd have to comply with Laurence's wishes. 'On what excuse?'

'Oh, come now, I'm sure you can come up with something. The two of us need to have a board meeting urgently. I'm down in Salisbury and I can't get away during the week because of the play I'm in.'

'This is to do with Alex?'

'Yeah, yeah. Something needs sorting out – rather urgently. It is important.'

There was a pause and a heavy sigh. 'OK. I'll wangle it some way.'

'You are an ace wangler, Russ.'

'I wish you'd tell me what it's all about.'

'Next Sunday. 12.30 in the Spice of Life pub at Cambridge Circus.'

Laurence replaced the receiver before Russell could reply.

So, he thought, Alex didn't send a letter to Russell detailing his ordeal. Only to me. I suppose that makes me chairman of the board. Which I am and always have been, of course.

Once again the image of his friend being savagely buggered flew into his mind and he felt his stomach turn yet again. What am I going to do to exorcise that demon? he pondered, as he stepped out of the phone box. Standing alone in the silent street, he suddenly felt very vulnerable.


## FIFTEEN

Russell was early. It was just after twelve when he walked into the dingy bar parlour of the Spice of Life, the atmosphere heavy with the aroma of strong bleach and stale beer. There were only two other customers. One was a scruff in a decaying track suit that was fooling no one. Its owner, pint in one hand and half smoked cigarette in the other, was coughing heartily. He would have trouble sprinting to the gents let alone doing any serious running. The other punter was Laurence, who was lounging at a corner table with a pint glass, smoking one of his little cigars which he waved in a camp fashion as a way of greeting. Russell bought a pint and joined him.

'This had better be important,' Russell said tersely, without ceremony, slumping down on a seat. A four hour train journey had made him crotchety.

Laurence did not reply. He just withdrew some sheets of paper from his jacket pocket and held them out to Russell. It was Alex's letter.

'What's this?'

'Read it.' It was an order, not a request.

Russell took a long drink of beer and read the letter. While he was doing so, Laurence observed his friend's countenance closely. The stern irritation which had been etched on his features slowly evaporated to be replaced at first by a look of concerned surprised which evolved, as Laurence knew it would, into a look of horror. When he had finished reading, Russell glanced over at his friend, his eyes wide with shock, but he said nothing for a time. Laurence retrieved the letter from his limp hand and replaced it in his jacket pocket.

'Christ almighty,' said Russell at last and then took a large gulp of his beer.

'Indeed,' said Laurence. 'Christ-all-fucking-mighty.'

'I'm having difficulty getting my head around this. Why ... why did he just write to you and not me? I think I had a right to know.'

Laurence shrugged. 'I suppose putting it down on paper once was about as much as he could take. To recount it again, well that would have been too painful. And anyway, he'd know that I'd tell you.'

That sounded a reasonable explanation but Russell couldn't help feeling a small pang of jealousy at not being confided in as well as Laurence and just hearing the matter second-hand. Yet again he was the lieutenant not the captain. He knew this was the case, of course, but it still did not prevent him from wishing otherwise. In all other departments of his life he was an also ran. He had believed that he had at least equal status in the Brotherhood. Apparently not. With another drink of beer he attempted to wipe these selfish thoughts from his mind and return to Alex's horrendous ordeal.

'What are we going to do?'

Laurence stubbed out the small cigar in the tiny glass ashtray. 'There is only one thing we can do. We must kill the bastard. Now how about an Italian?'

Twenty minutes later they were sitting in Pizza Express on Dean Street going through the motions of eating their chosen pizzas. Neither was really hungry and the thought of Alex's experience as recorded in his letter had robbed them of any real appetite they might have had. However, they had consumed most of a bottle of red wine before the food had arrived and Laurence ordered a second.

'Are you serious?' said Russell toying with a

portion of his American Hot.

Laurence knew that he was picking up on the conversation they'd left hanging in the air back in the pub.

'I am. It's our duty.'

'But we've always chosen anonymous victims before – those that had no connection with us. This is really dangerous. There is a link. We could be traced.'

'It is a tenuous link. We're experienced fellows. If we plan. If we take the usual precautions, we'll be fine. Besides ... if we do nothing... Then it's all over. Us. The game. The Brotherhood. If we can't kill for our own, then we can't do it again ... ever.'

Russell stared into Laurence's eyes. The usual jaunty sparkle was missing. His face was grey, serious and strangely sad. 'To be honest, Russell, old chap,' he said, 'I can't get the thing out of my head. It's haunting me. I feel tainted and soiled. It's as though I've been buggered too. Revenge is the only solution. It'll be like a kind of exorcism for Alex and for both of us. It will be like a purge – scrubbing the deed away. I saw your face when you read the letter. You feel like me. Don't you?'

Russell nodded. Laurence was right. It was strange but true. 'It was horrible,' he said softly. 'Far worse than anything that we've... Poor sod.'

Laurence's hand reached across the table and touched Russell's briefly. 'I knew you'd feel the same,' he said.

The two men held their gaze for some time.

'How do we go about it?' asked Russell.

Russell cocooned himself in his own thoughts as the train rattled back to Durham early that evening. The carriage was noisy and crowded and a child was screeching loudly a few seats away, but he was able to shut out all the extraneous sensations and concentrate on his thoughts as he stared out of the window at the rapidly darkening landscape. Trees, houses, farm buildings were gradually merging with the blackness of the sky and houselights, like inferior stars, speckled the inky night.

He went over the conversation that he'd had with Laurence in London and the plan that his friend had presented to him. The mechanics seemed fine – as all Laurence's plans were – but he couldn't help feeling that it was wrong, a mistake to take this particular route. It was a dramatic and a dangerous departure for them. And yet he realised that really this was their only option. There was no choice in the matter. They could not ignore what had happened to Alex, their brother. To retaliate, to take revenge was the only honourable thing to do. He knew that things would never be the same if they did nothing about it. However, Russell was equally sure that nothing would be the same if they did. It was a no win situation. Nevertheless, there was no going back. The time for withdrawal had long since passed. Since he and Laurence had killed old Mother Black's dog they had formed a bloody bond that would bind them until their own death.

'Tea. Coffee. Refreshments.'

The trolley service had arrived at his seat. He waited until the other passengers had ordered and then asked for a black coffee and a couple of whiskies.

By the time the train pulled into his station, tiredness and the whisky had relaxed Russell enough for his mood to have shifted to one of bleak acceptance of the situation as planned by Laurence. He didn't like it, he feared it, but it had to be done. He afforded himself a wry grin as he made his way wearily to the taxi rank. As always, he mused, following Laurence was better than doing nothing.

## SIXTEEN

Sandra lay on her back staring at the ceiling unable to sleep. As usual she had gone to bed early on Sunday evening, extra hours under the covers in readiness for Monday and the week ahead. She had contemplated waiting up for Russell, but in the end she ditched that idea. It was so unlike him to go off suddenly for the day. He was such a meticulous person who planned his activities with great care well in advance. Spontaneous he was not. So this excursion to visit an old friend who was very ill seemed so out of character and, to be honest, suspicious. As he explained it to her without much conviction, she knew that it was a lie. She'd never heard him mention this friend before – Russell didn't really have friends – and he failed to explain why it was so important for him to go so quickly to see this man. As always, she refrained from asking him too many questions but she couldn't help thinking that there was something more to this sudden trip than she was being told. However, this was nothing new. She was well aware when she agreed to marry Russell that she would never know him fully, would never reach that special intimate oneness with him, would never own him as some wives owned their husbands. She thought of Russell as 'iceberg man' – so much unseen below the surface. Even when they made love, she was conscious that he was not giving fully of himself, that he was keeping part of something back, hiding a secret self which he would never reveal. She accepted this. It failed to rouse her curiosity to any great extent. She was content that she had a reliable and respectable husband.

At the thought of their lovemaking, Sandra instinctively stroked her stomach. There was as yet only a gentle swell, but she was conscious of the child growing inside her. The child that would make her whole. The child that would be hers completely, someone she could own and love unconditionally. There would be no reserve, no secrets with her child. They would bond and be inseparable. She acknowledged that in helping to create this baby, Russell had performed his ultimate function. From now on, she knew that they would grow apart – grow further apart. As a married couple with a child they would function in a clichéd fashion without the true warmth and passion of closeness of real partners and parents. As she contemplated these thoughts, the fact that Russell was not yet back suddenly ceased to worry her. Suddenly, it did not matter. She had the baby. That was all that really did matter.

With an incipient smile on her face, Sandra finally slipped away into peaceful sleep and failed to hear Russell return to the house and get into bed beside her just before midnight.

In its own way, Russell's trip had changed both their lives.

Earlier that evening Alex had received a telephone call from Laurence.

'Can you talk?' asked Laurence without ceremony.

'Yes. I'm on my own again. John left about a week ago. I'm a bit difficult to live with at the moment.'

'I will be brief,' said Laurence. 'The Lone Ranger and Tonto are coming to your rescue. We need to meet, form a plan and then proceed with its execution. We rendezvous at the Guardsman in Leeds at noon a week on Saturday. Do not mention this to anyone. Is that clear?'

'Yes.'

The telephone went dead.

Alex stared at himself in the hall mirror. He looked tired, he thought. Tired and something else. What? Tired and ... haunted. He was not sure what Laurence and Russell had in mind, but he didn't think that anything they did would exorcise the dark shadow which had fallen over his life. He doubted if he ever would feel whole and clean again.

When the meeting took place in the Guardsman,

it did not surprise either Russell or Alex that Laurence arrived full of enthusiasm with a fully formed plan of action. It was daring and shocking and all three were aware that that it was taking them into new territory.

'I know there is more danger in this enterprise,' Laurence observed, casually as though discussing the weather, 'but there is a purpose, a focus to our deed – other than our own pleasure – which adds extra spice to the venture. Remember that. Cherish it as an add-on feature. We mustn't get timid now.'

Russell grimaced. 'There's always been danger, but this time it seems as though we are taking too much of a risk. We've never had a reason to act before. Our actions have been random and motiveless and therefore to outsiders, i.e. the police, unfathomable. There has been nothing to connect us with the victim. That's been our success. Tenuous though it might be, in this case there is a link between us and the victim.'

Alex nodded. 'That's me. I am the link. Russell's right, it does seem a bit rash. I'm not sure about this. I really shouldn't have got you involved. I don't want you to take risks on my behalf. I know that you're only doing this because of me...'

'Not just you, old lad,' said Laurence leaning in close. 'But for all the others – past and possible future. This is a bloody social service we are about to perform. As always. And don't tell me that you won't feel more than a frisson of pleasure when we do the bastards in.'

Alex's features softened to allow the ghost of a smile to register there. In truth, he didn't know how he would feel. At first the idea of revenge was sweet, but then he realised that whatever was done to the men who had raped him, it wouldn't alter the fact. The dirty, sordid, unforgettable fact. You cannot wipe out the past by future actions. Now he wondered if anything at all, other than death, his own death, would bring him peace. But he saw the fire in Laurence's eyes and was aware that this was just as important to him.

'If you're sure...' he said quietly, at length, holding back his reluctance.

Laurence raised a questioning eyebrow at Russell who, after the briefest pause, nodded firmly. 'It's the least we can do,' he said evenly.

Laurence gave a little guffaw of satisfaction and ordered another round of drinks. 'Now that's settled, I need some information from you, Alex, so I can set this plan into operation. Don't look so worried, *mon ami*. I assure you, it will go like clockwork.'

## SEVENTEEN

Laurence was thorough. Doing his 'homework', as he called it, was almost as pleasing to him as the actual job itself. The run of *Twelfth Night* had now finished and he had happily said farewell to his fellow actors and, with some relief, to Sue Ling also. After his disappointing performance in her flat, he had avoided her. He didn't want to be reminded of his failure and had no intention of making a second attempt – although she still seemed keen – in case the same thing happened again. That, he couldn't live with.

So he now entered a period of 'resting', allowing him time to devote to his 'homework'. He travelled up to Huddersfield wearing a light disguise, his old favourite: a false moustache and glasses, with hair greying at the temples and a shabby blazer and flannels which, normally, he wouldn't have been seen dead wearing. In this persona he booked in at the George Hotel by the station giving his name as Tom Harris and began his recce. Using Alex's directions, he hired a car and drove out into the country to locate the isolated house owned by the man called Matt. He did it with ease. He parked the car fifty yards away on the opposite side of the road and gazed at the property for some time. There wasn't another house for nearly a mile. There was no sign of life. No doubt Matt was at work – which allowed Laurence the opportunity to scout around. He made his way up the path and pressed the bell. As expected there was no reply. He walked around the perimeter familiarising himself with the geography of the place. He gazed in through the windows; what he could see through the smeared glass matched Alex's description of the ground floor. Very chintzy.

Satisfied with his reconnaissance, Laurence drove back to town calling at a pub on the outskirts for a pint and time to ponder. As he sat in the gloomy snug, he sifted through the elements of his plan, tying them in with the evidence he had gleaned from his excursion and from Alex's account of that terrible evening. One thing was clear. It was not going to be easy. Taking on one man had always been fairly straight forward – but in this case there were going to be three and these fellows knew how to handle themselves. The only real advantage that Laurence and Co. would have was the element of surprise. That needed to be great. Greater than even his comrades in arms realised. A trip to Leeds on the train was next. Apparently Matt worked in an estate agent's office just off the Headrow – Alex had also done some homework.

Tom Harris had suddenly developed an interest in a nice little semi in Headingley. He sauntered into the brightly lit show room and, while pretending to look at the array of properties on display, he surreptitiously cast a glance at the various employees sitting at their desks who appeared to be busily doing nothing in particular. What was really engaging their attention Laurence could not determine but they created an air of studied industry which prevented them from taking note of the silent customers scanning the range of properties on display. There were five worker ants in all: two young girls, blonde totty, if he'd ever seen any, easy on the eye, dim of brain; a matronly grey-haired lady who looked as though they'd built the office around her; and two men. One of these was a sleek, pale faced creature with cadaverous features who snatched eager gasps on a home-rolled cigarette as he scribbled away with his pen. The other was Matt Wilkinson. Matt the bastard. He was big but well honed with hair that looked like a slick Brillo pad. His face was broad and glistened with fake tan and moisturiser. Whatever he was doing at his desk, he was doing it slowly and almost absent-mindedly. Briefly, he broke off to retrieve a mint from his waistcoat pocket. The procedure of popping it into his mouth was a performance, carried out with delicacy, style and flair. Briefly his eyes closed as he sucked on the mint and then he returned slowly to his task.

What an amusing pillock, thought Laurence as he pulled one of the leaflets from the rack and walked over to Matt's desk.

'Excuse me,' he barked in a broad Leeds accent, 'is this semi freehold?' He shook the leaflet in front of Matt's face, so close that the man had to pull back. The frown of annoyance lasted for only a few seconds but Laurence took great delight in observing it. Soon the mask of professional caring was back in place, but that ill-guarded moment had revealed so much of the real Matt, the man behind the suntan sheen. Taking the leaflet from Laurence, with great deliberation he turned it over and ran his fingers down a column of print, stopping at the sentence: 'This property is Freehold.'

Laurence bent over and peered at it, catching a strong whiff of Matt's cologne.

'Oh, I see. I hadn't noticed that. Silly me,' he said, grinning inanely.

Matt did not reply. He turned over the sheet and looked at the picture of the semi-detached house. 'Are you interested in this property?' he asked.

'Possibly. Would you recommend it?'

Matt's eyes narrowed momentarily, deciding

134

which approach to take. He gave a quick glance at Laurence before continuing. 'It's a nice little place but if you are interested in the area and can stretch your budget by five thou or so, I'd recommend 'Rushholme', it has a larger more secluded garden and the road is quieter. Let me show you.'

Smooth bastard. Empty and soulless as a paper bag. That's our friend Matt, thought Laurence as he journeyed back to Huddersfield on the train. He gazed unseeingly out of the window at the crowded hillsides near Dewsbury, dotted with new townhouses, cheek-by-jowl executive rabbit hutches with paper-thin walls and tiny gardens. He was glad he'd got some kind of measure of the man. Laurence could gauge that he was a cold calculating kind of beast. What he had experienced was the shell of the man, his professional persona, not the perverted bully. Strangely, there had been little evidence of homosexuality in his demeanour. Certainly, he was sleek and moisturised, but his beefy build and macho movements were deceptive.

Laurence smiled. Yes, he would take great pleasure in giving the cruel bastard what for. The thought of this lightened his mood and he was still smiling as the train pulled into Huddersfield station.

That night he visited the gay nightclub where Alex had first encountered Matt Wilkinson. He wanted to check it out for himself. For this occasion he wore a long blond wig, a black T-shirt and very tight cord jeans. He fitted in beautifully with

135

the clientele. Being a week night, the punters were thin on the ground and a sad lot they seemed: lonely singletons adrift in a macho world seeking solace in the sweaty gloom of a gay club. Indeed, Laurence hadn't been in the place for more than fifteen minutes before he was being chatted up by a fat perspiring fellow with thinning sandy hair. This pleased him for it confirmed that his assumed persona was convincing, or convincing enough in the dim lighting of the club at least, although he had hoped to engage the attention of a more attractive fellow. He played along with his would be paramour for a while before gently giving him the brush off. After another twenty minutes, during which he carried out a full survey of the premises, even running the gauntlet of visiting the toilets, he was satisfied that he'd seen enough. He high-tailed it back to his hotel and lay on the bed with a large glass of whisky.

Well, he thought, as he swirled the drink around in the glass, I think I'm ready now.

## EIGHTEEN

Matt Wilkinson returned for the third time to the bathroom mirror to appraise his appearance. He gave himself a false grin and adjusted a few strands of hair over his forehead. Satisfied with the result, he stood back from the mirror and turned sideways scrutinising his profile. The face was fine, the jaw line reasonably tight, but he was dismayed to observe that his shirt bulged rather unpleasantly at the front. He was getting a tummy. Blasted Mars bars. He would have to knock that habit on the head before he turned into a fat slob. Still, he looked all right. Quite the catch in fact, although, he mused, he wasn't the one who was going to get caught. This thought brought a genuine smile to his lips.

'Right guys, are we ready to rock and roll?' he said as he breezed into the sitting room. His cohorts, Ronnie Fraser and Dave Johnson, who were lazing on the sofa sipping gin and tonics, nodded in unison. Whatever Matt said was OK with them. They were more than happy to acknowledge that he was the leader of their pack.

'As ever,' said Dave before downing the dregs of his drink. 'Come on darling,' he added ruffling Ronnie's blond thatch, 'rouse yourself.'

Ronnie giggled. 'Later, sweetie, later.'

It was always the same in the Starlight on Saturday night: a heaving dimly illuminated sweatbox with sudden flashing coloured lights spraying the faces of the punters with rich rainbow hues. It was a kind of discothèque version of hell: bodies writhed, music boomed, hands groped and squeezed, eyes scrutinized and liaisons made.

As usual Matt, Ronnie and Dave split up as soon as they entered, each seeking his own little adventure to begin with, a frisson of pleasure, an appetiser, before the main course later. While Ronnie and Dave skirted the dancing area, Matt made for the bar. He grabbed the last available stool and ordered a ginger ale from the slim youth who served there all on his own. Usually on these occasions he rejected alcohol, not wanting his sensibilities to be impaired in any way. Booze would help him relax later but for now he wanted everything to be pin sharp and real.

As he turned on his stool to face the dance floor, some lanky goon with shoulder length blond hair stumbled into him, knocking the glass from his hand.

'Ooh, I am sorry,' he said, throwing his hands up to his face like a camp version of Edward Munch's The Scream.

'Bloody idiot,' growled Matt.

'I am, aren't I,' said the blond in a disarming fashion. 'Let me buy you another. What was it?'

For the first time Matt looked at the interloper. He was tall and slender with pointed features, and remarkably bright blue eyes. He had to admit that clumsy though he may be, this bloke was quite attractive. Could be that he'd hit upon the jackpot very early on this week.

'Ginger ale,' he said and managed a smile.

The blond raised an eyebrow. 'How exotic. Can't I press you to a short or something?' The voice was camp, sibilant and pure Huddersfield.

'Ginger ale is fine.'

'Well, I suppose it is appropriate.' He giggled. 'I'm Barry by the way.'

Matt nodded. 'Matt.'

And so it began.

In another part of the club, Russell lurked, keeping an eye on Matt while trying hard not to catch anyone else's eye. He wasn't very comfortable in this environment. He knew he did not have the flamboyant skills to carry out any charade if he were to be approached by one of the prancing fellows who seemed to press in on him from all directions. It was all very surreal and unpleasant. The claustrophobic dark made him feel very vulnerable. For the first time ever he wished he was not involved. Not involved in this crazy game that had now grown personal and much more dangerous. It really was too close for comfort. But he was trapped. He was part of the team − the bonded brotherhood − and there was no getting out. The journey had been started and one must follow the road to the end.

Russell glanced at his watch. God it was only nine o'clock. It was going to be a long night. He envied Alex waiting outside in the car.

Russell felt a hand on his thigh and he brushed it off with a brisk motion.

'Sorry I'm sure,' said a voice in his ear.

Without looking at the owner of the voice, Russell moved away to another part of the room. He wondered how many times he'd have to do that before the evening was over.

Matt and his new blond friend were dancing now and seemed to be getting on famously. Ronnie and Dave who had gravitated to the bar watched the pair's gyrations on the floor with great pleasure.

'He's got a lively one there,' said Ronnie. 'Ooh, I do like a lively one.'

'He reels them in, doesn't he,' observed Dave. 'He's just got the knack.'

'Lucky for us, eh?'

Grinning lewdly they clinked their glasses in a mock celebratory toast.

Around ten thirty, Russell saw Laurence head for the toilets. He followed him. Luckily they were empty, allowing them time for a brief conversation.

'How goes it?'

'Thumbs up, I should say. I'm rather good bait. Keep an eye out for his mates: the blond haired guy in the check shirt and the baldy in black. I reckon they'll be leaving soon.'

The door thumped open and two other fellows staggered in, noisy and tipsy and so the conversation was at brought to a halt.

Matt eyed his new conquest as he made his way from the toilets, circumnavigating the dance floor and its throng of gyrating bodies to join him at a small table in a dimly lit alcove.

'Are we having another drink or what?' asked Barry as he resumed his seat, his hand stroking Matt's.

Matt pulled a face, 'It's a bit dull here tonight. And a bit restricting. How about coming back to my place?'

'Your place?' Barry seemed hesitant.

Matt nodded. 'I've got a cosy bijou pad in the country. Nice and quiet. No neighbours to hear the moans of ecstasy. Clean sheets and all mod cons. The lot.' He grinned.

'That's some invitation.'

'You'd better believe it. Well, are you on?'

'I trust you make a mean breakfast.'

'Just you wait.'

Barry grinned and nodded. 'OK then. Lead on, Macduff.'

'I'll just get some fags and then we'll make tracks.'

Matt wandered to the bar and seemed to indulge in a brief conversation with two men there before making his purchase. They moved away from the counter before he'd paid for his cigarettes. Russell clocked them as they headed for the door in a far from casual manner.

With some relief, he followed them.

Outside, Alex waited. He was sharing similar thoughts to Russell. He now wished that they'd never started this project. He had been carried along by Laurence's enthusiasm and zeal and his own desire to exact revenge. But this desire had cooled considerably. There really could be no effective vengeance. That awful night was branded on his consciousness and would stay with him for the rest of his life. A childish getting your own back wouldn't lessen the hurt. He was also aware, like Russell, that the thing was too personal. The enjoyment and indeed the safety of their previous ventures was in ending the life of a stranger, someone with whom there was no connection whatsoever.

Was it too late to turn back? he wondered, while already knowing the answer.

It was nearing eleven and one or two punters were starting to leave. His stomach churned menacingly when he saw Matt's mates emerge from the club. There they were: the two men who had helped to rape him. He would never forget their faces or their voices. Unlike the others leaving the premises, they did not saunter, but moved quickly and with a purpose to a black Corsa and drove off at great speed. Moments later Russell emerged and headed for Alex's car.

'All systems go,' he said as he slid into the passenger seat.

'Are you sure we should go ahead with this?'

Russell glanced at Alex, his face ghoulishly green, illuminated by the lights on the dashboard. 'What on earth do you mean?'

'I ... I don't think it's right. I've got bad vibes...'

'Now's a fine time to start having second thoughts...'

'And you haven't?'

Russell turned away and gazed out of the window. 'Yeah, of course I have... But then I always do when we have a project on the go.'

'But this isn't the usual.'

'It isn't... Don't you think I know that but I think it's too late for this conversation now. Look.'

Standing on the steps of the Starlight Club were Matt and Laurence. As he swaggered forward Matt slipped his arm through Laurence's and gripped it tightly as though he was announcing to the world that this fellow was his.

'The show has begun,' said Russell quietly, almost to himself. Even as he spoke, his mouth suddenly felt very dry.

Matt and Laurence walked down the street and turned the corner.

Automatically, Alex started up the engine and drove slowly, following them at a distance. On a nearby side street, they saw Matt opening up his large 4x4. When Alex caught sight of vehicle, his stomach retched. It was the very same one that he had travelled in. The same one that had transported him to his nightmare. The sight of the 4x4 suddenly brought horrid images welling up before him. Things that happened to him that night. 'My God,' he cried faintly, shocked at his own reactions. He should have been expecting this, to be disturbed and unnerved by what he saw and what memories it would regurgitate, but strangely he hadn't considered it. Not given it a thought. Perhaps, subconsciously his brain had blanked such things from his mind. But now, seeing that bloody vehicle again, he was shaken to the core.

'What is it?' asked Russell.

Alex shook his head. He didn't want to explain. To verbalise his thoughts would make it so much worse. Instead he concentrated on trying to bring his turbulent stomach into check and banish all images from his mind.

Both men saw Laurence clamber aboard the vehicle and within seconds the beast roared forward into the night, the exhaust booming. With gritted teeth, Alex slipped his car into gear and followed.

The streets were empty and Matt took advantage of this, racing the car through the centre of Huddersfield at high speed, soon reaching the long stretches of country roads. Alex had great difficulty in keeping up with him. He knew that he couldn't hang too closely on Matt's tail for fear of giving the game away but no way could he afford to lose him just in case they weren't headed for Matt's lonely house.

But they were.

Some fifteen minutes later Matt turned off a winding B road on to the narrow track that led to his home.

'This is it,' said Alex, bringing his car to a halt and switching off his lights.

They watched as Matt's car pulled up outside the isolated house about a third of a mile ahead of them. Dimly they saw the two occupants emerge and head for the front door.

'Right,' said Russell, grabbing the door handle.

Alex nodded. No further words were needed. They were well rehearsed in their plan and knew exactly what they had to do.

Swiftly and silently, they retrieved their balaclavas and the shotguns from the boot of the car and began making their way down the road to the house. It stood there like a spooky haunted house from some ghost story, dimly silhouetted against the moonless sky.

## NINETEEN

'Another drinky poo," said Matt Wilkinson, his arm making a grand sweeping gesture towards the drinks trolley.

Laurence was well aware that he had to keep a cool head now – he hadn't drunk half as much as he had pretended to at the club – but he was also sure that it would be a capital mistake to refuse a drink now. Nothing, absolutely nothing must rouse Matt Wilkinson's curiosity or, indeed, animosity. Laurence knew that there was a savage brute quivering beneath that large, cool and apparently friendly exterior.

'A wee G and T would go down a treat.'

'We don't do small drinks here, pal. You'll get a big one and like it.' His tone was a strange mixture of the aggressive and the jokey. It unnerved Laurence. It reminded him, not that he needed reminding, how very vulnerable he was. If the Fifth Cavalry in the shape of Alex and Russell didn't arrive at the crucial moment, he was about to be dealt with in a very unpleasant fashion.

Matt handed him a giant gin and tonic. 'Come on, Sunshine, let me show you upstairs.' He held out his hand and Laurence felt obliged to take hold of it. They moved up the narrow staircase on to the upper floor and Matt led Laurence into the gym. It was as Alex had described it. To Laurence it was like a smooth and polished high-tech torture chamber. There was a running machine, a rowing device, dumbbells and an exercise contraption which looked like something out of a science fiction film. Any moment now Peter Cushing would appear and strap him into it while attaching electrodes to his forehead.

'You like to keep yourself fit, I see,' said Laurence lamely.

'You don't get a body like mine without working for it,' said Matt and stepped back, pulled off his black T-shirt to reveal an impressive, fairly sculptured waxed chest, although the tummy was

145

getting a bit podgy, thought Laurence. *Better not mention that though.*

'Very nice,' he observed, while his mind was groaning, 'Jesus, he's got bigger tits than Raquel Welch.'

Matt jumped on an exercise bike and began pedalling like fury. 'It keeps you toned and focused. Fit and active. Fit and eager, if you catch my drift.'

'Oh, I do,' said Laurence quietly – so quietly that Matt slowed down his manic pace of pedalling and cast a curious glance at him.

'You seem nervous,' he said.

Laurence shrugged. 'Nah, it's just not my scene. I'm too lazy for all this. I'm content to be the slob I am.'

'I could soon train you up, build up your muscles. As they say, the body is a temple. It should be treated with respect.'

It was with that comment that Laurence knew it would give him great pleasure to kill this arrogant self-centred bastard. And he wanted to do it now.

'My body is less of a temple, more of a Methodist mission hut.'

Matt grinned and clambered off the bike.

'I think we've done enough of the small talk now, don't you think? Let's move on to pillow talk, eh?'

So soon? thought Laurence, his body tensing. This fellow doesn't waste time. Very well, then, I can't wait any longer. I'll have to start without my back up. It's time for action stations.

'What's that?' asked Laurence suddenly, his

146

features contracting into a concerned frown as he pointed in the vague direction of the far corner of the room.

Matt, suitably distracted, turned his back and followed Laurence's gaze.

As he did so, Laurence snatched up one of the silver dumbbells lying on the floor and brought it down on the back of Matt's head with great force. There was the gentle sound of cracking bone, a brief spurt of blood which mingled with Matt's gelled hair, before he fell to the floor face down with the faintest of moans. Laurence bent over him and repeated the action with the now bloodied dumbbell. After the second blow, Matt lay still, apart from a strange twitching movement of his right hand which lay outstretched on the polished wood. For a few moments, his fingers danced erratically as though they were using an invisible typewriter and then they froze into the shape of a claw as death finally took dominion.

Slowly Laurence rose to his feet and stepped back, his heart racing, his mouth suddenly sandpaper dry. It wasn't supposed to happen like this. This is not how it was planned. Something had taken him over. Controlled his actions. What was it? Fear? Hatred? Impatience? Whatever. Some erratic and unreliable emotion had stormed the citadel of his cool and calculated nature. And he was horrified at the result. Not the fact that he had killed the bastard – just that he had fallen prey to undisciplined feelings. He should have waited until Alex was there, allowed his friend to witness the fear in the bully's eyes, to have given him the pleasure of being in at the kill.

He heard movement on the stairs and hushed voices in conversation. It was Matt's cronies. They had arrived for the fun. He slipped back and stood behind the door just as they entered. On seeing the body before them and the pool of blood which was now collecting around the damaged head they froze in their tracks.

'Christ all fucking mighty,' said one eventually. This exclamation broke the spell, reanimated them, and they both rushed forward and knelt by the body.

Bald-headed Dave, thickset with piggy eyes and a pock-marked skin, sensing another presence in the room, instinctively glanced behind him and saw Laurence. It did not take him long to size up the situation and with a roar of anger he launched himself forward, but Laurence was ready for him and kicked him with great force in the crotch. With a loud two note staccato cry, Dave fell back and dropped to the floor only a few feet away from the dead body of his friend.

Ronnie rose from his crouching position and began advancing slowly on Laurence, who backed away wondering what the hell he was going to do now. Dave also showed signs of recovery and with some effort began to clamber to his feet.

More noise on the stairs and Alex and Russell burst into the room. They were balaclava-ed up and each was carrying a shot gun.

The two assailants froze in their tracks

'Waste no time,' barked Laurence, with great relief, stepping back behind them.

They obeyed him without hesitation.

Almost simultaneously the shot guns fired, each barrel aimed at the stomachs of the two startled men.

It was over in seconds.

The three bodies lay side by side on the polished floor wood like some gory battlefield tableau.

Laurence, Russell and Alex stood for some time in silence gazing at the dead men, each experiencing a strong mixture of conflicting emotions.

For Russell, it had been a step too far. This wasn't killing as it had been in the old days. Randomly and for fun. There was something dirty about this project. Targeted victims. A vendetta. A motive. Dirty ... and dangerous.

Alex shared similar feelings but yet he was also disappointed that he had not been the one to kill Matt as had been arranged. Maybe it had got too dangerous for Laurence. He was taking the biggest risk after all. But the whole purpose of this project had been for him to try and bring a kind of closure to his pain and the deep-seated humiliation that he still felt through the cathartic action of killing Matt. Circumstances – whatever they were – had denied him that. He knew, too, that this particular set of killings had changed the dynamic of their operations. Probably it had brought them to an end. In many ways that would be a relief. Now perhaps was the time to bring the Brotherhood to a close.

If that were possible.

Laurence was simply relieved that it was all over. He was disappointed that it had not run as smoothly as he had hoped but the outcome at least was as satisfactory as it could have been. He too still had great reservations about killing with a motive. It was not part of the game – the game that he'd invented. Somehow, weirdly, it seemed immoral. But what the hell, they had done it and his plan had worked with remarkable efficiency. He should be pleased about that. Suddenly, he found himself grinning.

'Right,' he said briskly, turning to the other two, 'mission accomplished. Let's go.'

As they sped away with Russell at the wheel, the three men remained silent for some time. There was not the usual cheesy, cheery bonhomie that usually ensued after the completion of one of their projects.

As they neared the lights of Huddersfield, Laurence, who had been sitting in the back of the car, leaned forward. 'Right, gentlemen, a successful evening but one not without its dangers and possible repercussions. We split tonight and we do not – I repeat – do not contact each other for twelve months. We must not provide the police with any possible links. Is that understood?'

The other two men murmured their assent. They knew he was right.

'*I* will instigate the next meeting. Wait for me to get in touch. OK, now drop me here. I'll walk back to the hotel.'

Russell pulled in on the lower side of the town centre and Laurence clambered out.

'Well done, gentlemen,' he grinned and gave a sharp salute before disappearing into the night.

Back at Matt Wilkinson's house, the three bodies still lay prone on the shiny gym floor, the bright lights glistening on the fresh blood. Imperceptibly, to begin with, one of the men's eyelids fluttered. It was Ronnie Fraser, the blond-haired one. After a while, his eyes opened in a lazy drugged fashion. There was a lack of comprehension mirrored there. He groaned and grimaced, not understanding just how lucky he was.

## TWENTY

It was Alex who first learned the terrible truth. It was on the Tuesday lunch time following the killings at Matt Wilkinson's house. As usual he had taken lunch at the little café around the corner from the design studio where he worked. He liked to get away from the place and its stultifying environment for an hour and from the narrow-minded bores he shared an office with. He picked up the local paper which someone had left behind expecting to read of the multiple murders in an isolated house at Ravensfield. It wasn't a story he was going to relish. Indeed, he had already successfully blotted the memory of the event from his mind. It was something that he found relatively easy to do – even from the early days. In fact he knew he had to or he would be haunted by guilt. He knew he didn't possess what he perceived as Laurence's armour plated conscience.

151

Alex glanced at the headlines and his blood ran cold. What he read made him gag on his sandwich.

## HORRIFIC MURDERS
## IN ISOLATED HOUSE. TWO DEAD.
## ONE MAN SURVIVES
## <u>VICIOUS ATTACK.</u>

One word bore into his brain and knotted his stomach.

Survives.

*Survives!*

Christ Almighty!

Alex dropped the paper, the room already swimming before him, the other diners, chatting in a casual fashion, were slowly drifting out of focus.

Survives.

One of them was still alive. Miraculously. How on earth...?

Alex clasped his hand over his mouth, desperately trying to bring his emotions and his stomach under control, but the terrible implication of the news he'd just read, kept rocking his equilibrium. He had to pull himself together or people would start to notice. Become suspicious. God, they might begin to suspect the truth, his fevered mind suggested. The truth ... that he was one of the murderers. For one terrible moment he thought he was going to be sick then and there. He gulped loudly forcing the food back down his gullet.

With some effort, he rose from his seat, snatched up the paper and headed for the lava-

152

tory. Sitting himself down in the cubicle and locking the door, he held the newspaper in his trembling hands and read the article in full. He skimmed the details about the cleaner finding the bodies first thing on Monday morning and realising that one of the men was still alive. This was a Mr Ronald Fraser, *'a thirty-year-old accountant, who is now in a very serious condition in Intensive Care in Huddersfield Infirmary. Police are waiting by his bedside in the hope that he regains consciousness and will be able help them with their enquiries into these* – there was that phrase again – *horrific crimes.'*

Alex crumpled the paper and stared unseeingly at the cubicle door before him and the motto scrawled there with some sharp instrument: 'I LIKE TO FUK WOMEN'.

*'...in the hope that he regains consciousness.'* Those words pounded in his brain. The bastard was still in some sort of coma. So all was not lost. The devil still might die, taking any incriminating evidence with him to the grave.

He might die.

And then ... he might not.

It was clear to Alex that if this Ronald Fraser recovered he may well identify individuals who wanted revenge on Matt and his mates for their brutal sexual exploits. He'd have to confess to their little peccadilloes of course. Their luring innocent gays to the house and raping them, but what's a little buggery compared with murder, to *'horrific crimes'*. Then these individuals – these suspects – would be rounded up, interrogated, investigated and thrust under the microscope.

No stone would be left unturned; every dark corner of their lives would be scrutinised, analysed and dissected. Nothing would deter the police until they nailed the culprit.

Until they arrested *him*.

Alex Marshall.

For a brief moment, he wanted to scream. He needed some release or his heart would burst. Instead, he screwed up his eyes, clenched his fists leaned forward until his head rested on the door and moaned.

Time passed and slowly he began to relax and see things in a more practical, less dramatic light.

He realised that he would have to tell the others. No doubt they would find out quite soon anyway. This was not just a nasty local crime. It was juicy enough for the nationals and the television ghouls to deal with it in detail. He knew that contact should only be made in an emergency – but this was an emergency. He would have to write to Laurence – he never had a permanent telephone number – just a private P.O. Box number – but he would ring Russell that evening. As he rose to leave, his trembling legs gave way and he flopped down again. It was then he realised just how frightened he was.

Very frightened.

# PART THREE

# TWENTY-ONE

At police headquarters in Huddersfield, Detective Inspector Paul Snow was perusing a series of black and white photographs taken at the scene of the crime. They did not make pleasant viewing. Somehow the blood, registering as black on the photographs, seemed to Snow to be more disturbing than if it had been red. The images held a grim fascination for him and although he wanted to slip the glossy pics back into the brown envelope in which they had been delivered, he remained gazing at them with a growing sense of unease. This was not going to be an easy case for him to tackle. For the first time he rather wished that an important investigation hadn't landed on his desk.

His thoughts were interrupted by the lightest of taps on his door and Sergeant Bob Fellows entered carrying a couple of small boxes. He was a stout fair-haired man about thirty with a ruddy complexion and deceptively innocent eyes.

'Got some really interesting stuff here. A nice evening's entertainment,' he said wryly, plonking the video boxes on Snow's desk. The inspector raised an eyebrow in query.

'We found then under the floorboards at Wilkinson's gaff. In the gym. Seems he and his mates were into a bit of torture – bumboy style – and they liked to capture it for posterity.'

'Really.' Snow lifted up one of the video boxes and slipped the tape out. 'Souvenirs, eh?'

'Yup. We located the recording equipment hidden in the roof space. Basic stuff. Domestic but practical enough.'

'Nothing on the night of the murder, I suppose.'

'Nah. That would have been too jammy. They wouldn't have been prepared for what took place.'

'I suppose we'd better watch these then.'

Fellows nodded. 'I gave one a quick ten minute gander. To be honest that was much as my stomach could take. I'm not into gay porn, especially when there's violence involved as well.'

'You are a sensitive flower, Bob,' Snow observed in a monotone. 'Get a telly and video in here and we'll have a little film show. See if it'll toughen you up.'

Fellows gave the inspector a mirthless grin and nodded.

Sometime later, the two men sat uncomfortably mesmerised by the grim scenes played out before them on the screen. Neither spoke as they watched Matt Wilkinson and his cronies forcibly manhandling, abusing and raping their victims. There were six men – six victims – in total. It was gruesome and as a tough experienced copper, Snow knew that he should be able to watch this stuff without feeling as he did now, very uncomfortable and repelled by the grainy images that shimmered before his eyes. What made it worse were the cries: the men begging, screaming for mercy and the ghoulish laughter and increased brutality that these pleas invoked.

Snow found himself digging his nails into the palms of his hands in a kind of angered distress. These three vile men deserved to die, he thought. After what they had done, he had no sympathy for their fate. As for the bastard up at the hospital ... Snow would happily go up there now and pull the plug on the machine that was keeping him alive. But there was another reason, more haunting and much more disturbing that caused his unease. A reason that he could not reveal to any of his colleagues.

To anyone, in fact.

When the second tape ended, the picture having turned to a blurry hissing grey, the two men stared at the screen for some time as though hypnotised by it. Eventually, Sergeant Fellows leaned forward and switched off the television and extracted the video from the machine. He had been making notes as they had watched and he now referred to these.

'Six men over a period of nine months. All, it would seem, lured to Wilkinson's house on a promise and then surprised.'

'Until last Saturday when it was Wilkinson's turn to be surprised. It looks like revenge, Bob. A rather spectacular revenge.'

Fellows nodded in agreement.

'See if the technical chaps can grab reasonable images of the victims,' said Snow. 'If we can track these poor devils down, that should give us a lead.'

'A pretty sound one. Will do. And we could also get the artist to draw a likeness if the tape picture is too indistinct for a decent still.'

'Yes. Fine,' Snow said wearily, his mind reluctantly wandering back to those rough, violent and degrading images. And to the faces of the victims. Their expressions which initially showed shock, soon transmuted into horror, and then agony and disbelief. It seemed to Snow that a couple of them were already more than a little drunk before the proceedings began but were sober enough to experience the brutality of their physical invasion with crystal clarity. Each whelp and cry produced guffaws and animal grunts from the attackers. It was like some medieval torture chamber. It was strange but predictable that none of the victims had come forward to the police about these attacks. Obviously the shame and the fear of exposure were greater than their desire to convict their attackers. Snow empathised with their feelings. No doubt they thought it best to limp away, lick their wounds and try to wipe the whole ghastly business from their minds. All except... All except for those who returned for the ultimate revenge. Forensics had suggested that were probably three individuals there on the night of the murders. The three musketeers come to settle a score. Whether any or all had been victims was debatable.

One of the faces on the tapes, a young man with blond hair, had seemed the most overwhelmed and indeed the one treated most cruelly. He screamed to be let free, but his agonised cries only spurred on the assailants to more frenzied actions. Left on his own, Snow turned the television on again and began playing the first tape. He saw Wilkinson enter the bedroom with his victim, a chubby young man with dyed blond hair wearing a black T-shirt and cream chinos. As he moved forward to kiss the boy, Wilkinson turned and gave a knowing smile at the hidden camera.

Snow clicked the recorder on to freeze frame and gazed at the fuzzy image of that self satisfied face for some time. He gazed and remembered.

He had only been a young copper in his early twenties when he first encountered Matt Wilkinson about ten years before. He was off duty in one of the arty pubs in town when two men at the bar started an argument. Voices were raised and Snow could see things were going to get rough any time soon. His heart sank. He'd only come in for a quiet pint and a scan of the evening paper, but he knew that if a fracas developed he would have to step in to try and sort it out. He was an officer of the law after all.

The two men started pushing each other like kids in the playground. Under different circumstances it might have been funny. One of the men was Wilkinson, a man about his own age, smartly dressed with a good physique. The other, an older stouter man threw the first punch but it missed its target. Wilkinson pulled back, his face registering dismay that the situation had developed into such a violent one. He held up his hands in a defensive almost placatory manner, but his companion was having none of it. He picked up one of the barstools with the intent of bringing it crashing down on Wilkinson's head. It was then that Snow intervened. He stepped forward and grabbed the man's arm, freezing it in

161

mid-air.

'Don't be a pillock. Put the stool down,' he said quietly.

'Who the hell are you?' snarled the man as he tried to wrench his arm free from Snow's iron grip.

'I'm the law, matey and if you don't do what I say, I'll arrest you for causing an affray.'

Again the man tried to free himself and again he failed. He turned and stared into the face of this tall young man and saw something in his cold ice blue eyes that scared him and quelled his anger. Slowly he placed the stool on the floor.

'He's not worth the hassle,' he said with a sneer, attempting to regain some of his dignity.

'There's a good chap,' said Snow, still maintaining his hold on the man's arm. 'Now I suggest you leave. Pop off home to cool down.'

For a moment the man's eyes flickered with hot resentment again. He seemed about to retaliate but instead he turned towards Wilkinson. 'You can get lost, you pathetic bastard,' he jeered and jerking his arm free from Snow's loosened grip he headed for the door.

While all this had been happening, the other customers in the bar had been held motionless in frozen fascination and silence had fallen. As soon as the man had disappeared through the door, the place sprang back into life once more: drinks were ordered, conversation renewed, normality was restored.

'I think I owe you a pint,' said Wilkinson.

Paul Snow was about to refuse, but his copper's curiosity got the better of him. He'd quite like to

162

know what had been the cause of the kerfuffle and besides this fellow had rather a charming way with him.

'Just a half then,' he said with a gentle smile.

'Grab a seat and I'll bring it over to you.'

Paul did as he was told and when Wilkinson appeared he was carrying two pints and a couple of packets of crisps.

'Can't let you off with a half,' he grinned. 'A pint at least for the hero who saved me from a bloody nose. I'm Matt Wilkinson.'

'Paul Snow.'

'And you're really a copper.'

'Indeed I am. So ... what was that all about?'

Wilkinson took a gulp of his pint and then glanced shyly at Snow over the rim of the glass. 'Oh, something and nothing.'

Snow raised his brow. 'A little more, I suspect.'

'Personal stuff really. Nothing that would interest you, I'm sure.'

Snow was definitely interested but he decided not to push it and let the matter drop. He wasn't in the interrogation room now.

'So ... do you come here often?' said Wilkinson with a giggle.

Snow laughed too. The ice was broken. Both men relaxed.

What they talked about that night Snow could not remember now, but it was easy, engaging and somehow pleasurable. As they downed their third pint together, he had no doubts about Matt Wilkinson's sexuality. Previously when he had met men like Wilkinson, charming and attractive, but batting for the other side as his colleagues at the

163

station might have put it, he had walked away. It wasn't that he was in a state of denial but he wasn't yet prepared to cross the bridge from self acceptance to participation. That way madness lies, he told himself. Well, if not madness, various dangers. As a police officer with 'a promising future' as he had been told on more than one occasion by various superior officers, he knew he had to be careful – more particularly, he had to be straight or perceived to be straight. So, as a result, Snow preferred to remain isolated, intact for as long as he could manage it. He had been tempted in the past but his reserve and what he regarded as his own sense of self-preservation had always been greater than his physical desires. Tonight, however, he felt his defensive shield slipping a little.

Wilkinson was a physically attractive bloke, but it was more than his appearance that captivated Snow. There was something glamorous about his personality and dangerous, too. There was an edge to him that both threatened and appealed. Even in a casual conversation he could turn from the frivolous to the covertly threatening in an instant. There was no doubt about it, Mr Matt Wilkinson had a dark side – but that was part of the attraction.

They stayed until closing time and stools were being placed on the tables. Snow wasn't drunk but he had consumed more alcohol than usual, more than he should. Already, he thought, I'm breaking my own rules under the influence of this man.

'Pity to call it a night so early, Paul. How about

a coffee at my place, maybe a wee nightcap as well? I live not too far away. I have a flat in Orchard Row.'

Snow nodded.

On entering Wilkinson's flat, he was conscious that he had taken several steps forward on to the bridge. Both men knew that beneath their apparently innocent conversation, there were undercurrents, electrical impulses. Snow wondered how long it would be before they became overt.

He refused a whisky nightcap and stuck with coffee. Wilkinson put on a Miles Davis LP and disappeared into the galley kitchen of his smart but decidedly tiny flat. In his absence, Snow surveyed the sitting room, his policeman's antennae fully extended. The fittings were classy and stylish, with odd touches of extravagance like the real onyx ashtray and the top of the range hi-fi unit. It was meticulously tidy and organised.

He perched on the edge of a leather armchair and lit a cigarette and pondered the question: what was he doing here?

Wilkinson returned shortly with a tray bearing coffee in two smart black mugs and two crystal tumblers holding a generous measure of what Snow assumed was whisky. The smell told him it that it was single malt.

'Just in case you changed your mind,' he said impishly placing the tray down on a coffee table within Snow's reach. He stretched out on the sofa.

'Lovely music. Do you like Davis?'

'I'm not too familiar with him. Sounds fine though.'

'Cool is the word, man. Cool.' He took a sip of whisky and gazed directly at Snow. 'So ... where do we go from here?'

Paul did not know how to answer that question and after an awkward pause he responded with a slight shrug.

'You do know what I mean?' Wilkinson said casually placing his fingers to his lips and blowing a kiss in Snow's direction.

Paul felt his whole body tense. 'Yes,' he said quietly and then shook his head. 'I suppose I do. It's just ... I'm ... sorry. But I'm ... not ready...'

Wilkinson's face darkened. 'But I am. Ready and gagging, my dear.'

Snow stood awkwardly. This was going too fast for him. 'I think I'd better go.'

'Oh, my God, we're not a virgin are we?' There was an edge of frustrated disgust in Wilkinson's voice.

Snow made his way to the door. 'Thanks for the coffee,' he said, fully aware what an idiotic remark that was particularly as he had not touched it.

'And thanks for nothing, Mr Tease.'

'I'm sorry if... Well, I'm sorry.'

He hurried out of the flat and into the cool air of the street. For some moments Snow leaned against the wall and tried to bring his emotions into check. He hoped that he had done the right thing by leaving, despite the temptation to stay and all that it would have entailed. Sense had ruled over emotional inclination. As it should, he told himself.

As it should.

Only...

Fumbling in his jacket, he extracted another cigarette and lit up before moving on his way. Home to his tiny, empty terrace house. He had hardly reached the end of the street before he was experiencing pangs of regret. Suddenly he stopped, gazed at the night sky for a moment and then took a deep breath before turning round and retracing his steps.

## TWENTY-TWO

Paul Snow took a trip out to Matt Wilkinson's house at Ravensfield. He'd been there once before with Bob Fellows when the place had been crawling with the scenes of crime officers and grumpy old Dr Strong, the pathologist, was pontificating in terms very few could understand. Seeing the body of Matt Wilkinson, the back of his skull resembling a crimson sponge, had shaken Snow to the core. For a time, he felt nauseous and his vision blurred. Very little had sunk in and he quickly made his excuses to slip outside for a cigarette and gulp of air. This did not arouse anyone's suspicions. It was well known on the force that Snow was a bit queasy in the presence of a dead body, particularly one that had been disfigured.

Snow had leaned against the wall of the house and taken in several deep breaths before lighting up. It was so strange to see the man he had been

167

quite fond of all that time ago lying dead before him, his head almost beaten to pulp, his sightless eyes staring out at the living world in horror.

Snow had not seen or indeed heard of Wilkinson for about ten years. Not since their brief affair had come to a bitter close. What had started tentatively and gently ended acrimoniously. But before it did, there had been moments of an unusual kind of sweetness in their relationship. Wilkinson had in some strange way helped Snow admit and then accept what he was. For a few weeks he felt properly himself for the first time since he had reached manhood. However, Snow came to learn that Wilkinson was also controlling, devious, and cruel. He was a strange mixture of the possessive and the promiscuous. There was no way the relationship could survive and besides Snow knew that if it continued inevitably his private life would be discovered by his colleagues, whose job was curiosity after all. For a short time he walked a dangerous tightrope and although he was relieved when it was all over, Snow knew that he would be grateful to Matt Wilkinson for allowing him to be himself, even if it was for a brief butterfly moment.

And now he was engaged to solve his murder.

So here he was back at the scene of the killings on his own. He wandered around the ghost house, observing but not touching. Anything of real relevance would have been bagged up and taken for forensic examination anyway. The bloodstains remained on the gym floor, creating a weird dark crimson pattern on the polished woodwork, reminding Snow of a piece of Jackson Pollock artwork. The smell of death lingered in the room and he felt uneasy in its presence. He retreated and returned downstairs. While passing through the sitting room towards the outer door his eyes lit upon the onyx ashtray he had used that first night in Wilkinson's flat, that ocean of time ago. It brought a wry smile to his mouth. 'Come on, boy,' he whispered to himself. 'Put the past behind you and start dealing with the bloody present.'

Bobby Rawlins was a cockney skeleton in an Hawaiian shirt. Well, that's how Paul Snow thought of him. His pale face was crisscrossed with a thousand wrinkles, the result of a thousand late nights and thousand fags from a chain-smoking habit which began some forty years ago when Bobby was twelve.

Rawlins was the owner of the Starlight Club. Snow had never been into the club as a punter, although he had been tempted in his early days, but he had visited the 'cockney skeleton' a few times in recent years regarding various drug offences in the club. Nothing had been proved. 'Would I sell that stuff on my own turf, Mr Snow, I ask you?' He was right out of central casting as a dodgy small time East End villain. How he'd found his way up the M1 to Yorkshire was anyone's guess.

'Mr Snow, how nice.' He rose from his cluttered desk in his cluttered office and extended a bony arm and smiled, revealing a set of uneven yellow teeth. 'What can I do for you?'

'You've heard about the murders out at Ravensfield.'

169

'Oh, yeah. Terrible. You're not safe in your own home these days are yer?'

Snow slipped a set of photographs on to Rawlins' desk. One was of Matt Wilkinson which the SOCOs had found at his house. It showed him in some café raising a glass of wine in a toast to the photographer. The other was a mortuary shot of Dave Johnson.

'These are two of the victims. Do you recognise them?'

Rawlins averted his gaze. 'Recognise them. Why the hell should I recognise them? What are you suggestin'?'

'We have reason to believe they were regular customers of your club. In fact they used it as a pick up station.'

Rawlins grinned, the yellow teeth making another appearance. 'Now there's a surprise. Come on, get real, Inspector. I reckon that every club in this fair land is used as a pick up station, especially on a Saturday night. That's part of their function. In fact I met my missus in a dancing club.'

'Not in a gay club.'

'Now don't start slapping labels on my place. This is a disco, mate. I have no control over the clientele. I run a respectable business. As I've told you before, nothing goes on in my place that is against the law. I can't vouch for what happens outside.'

Snow sighed. 'I'm not here to discuss the nature of your club or what goes on here. I just want to know about these two men.'

He pushed the photographs along the desk nearer to Rawlins and placed a finger on the one showing Wilkinson.

'This fellow for instance. His name's Matt Wilkinson. You must have seen him before. He's been around on the gay scene for years.'

*I should know.*

With some reluctance, Rawlins glanced down at the photograph.

'Yeah,' he said at length. 'I reckon I've clocked him at the club a few times. A Saturday nighter. On the prowl. Usually with a couple of mates.'

'This one of them?' Snow indicated the other photograph.

'Could be. Not a studio portrait is it? And it's not exactly bright lights in the club y'know. Sometimes it's difficult to see people's faces.' He gave the photograph a second look. 'Yeah, I reckon he could have been one of them.'

'On the prowl?'

'As I said, that's the function of these places. A chance to meet new people. Chat 'em up. Find the love of your life.'

'Seems that didn't happen to these two.'

Rawlins shrugged. 'There's such a thing as a one night stand. You must have had one of those, Inspector. Red-blooded chap like you.'

Snow ignored the remark and slipped the photographs back in the envelope.

'Are you sure there's nothing more you can tell me about Wilkinson and his friend? Both men were brutally murdered hours after leaving your club.'

'Them's the key words ain't they: "after leavin'"? It had nothing to do with my place. If they'd been to the paper shop a couple of hours before they got the chop, would you be round the news-agent now giving him some hassle? I think not. Look Inspector, I'm sorry about these blokes, but to me they were just punters. Sure I saw them around in the club but I didn't know them personally and I can't answer for what they got up to or what happened to them after they left my place.'

'Who was serving behind the bar last Saturday night?'

Rawlins frowned. 'Oh, you're not going to bother him are you? He's just a young kid.'

'This is murder enquiry, Mr Rawlins. I'd question a babe in arms if I thought it would lead me to the truth. What's his name?'

'It's Sandy. Sandy McAndrew.'

'And where will I find him?'

Snow found Sandy McAndrew early that evening in his dingy bedsit in dingy bedsitland near to the railway station. He was a small, slightly built youth who looked younger than his twenty two years.

'This won't take long will it? I'm due at work in half an hour.'

'At the Starlight?' asked Snow perching precariously on the edge of the unmade bed.

McAndrew shook his head as he pulled a shiny red jacket from the clothes rail. It bore the logo 'Frankie's' on the breast pocket. He pointed to it. 'No, at Frankie's,' he said, 'the burger place on Firth Street. You know it? I work there three nights a week. I have four jobs in all. I need them in order to keep me in this lap of luxury.' He threw an arm out to indicate his shabby quarters.

'I work most days at the Crematorium, ashes to ashes, a stint at Starlight on Friday and Saturday night and help a friend out on his fruit stall at the Monday market. I aim to be a millionaire by the time I'm thirty. Either that or I'll be dead from exhaustion.'

Snow smiled. He warmed to the lad. At least he was trying with life. 'I shan't keep you long,' he said.

'Good, because Mr Frankie, Frank Armitage to you and me, is a stickler for timekeeping and I've already had a finger wagging off him in the last few days. Don't want another.'

'It's about last Saturday night. You were behind the bar at the Starlight.'

'Yeah,' McAndrew said, moving to the mirror over the tiny sink to comb his hair. 'It's hell on earth there on Saturdays. The boss really should get a second barman. It gets so busy I hardly have time to wipe my nose or any other part of my anatomy, if you get my drift.'

'Have you read about the murders that happened at Ravensfield this week? Two men battered to death.'

'Yeah, well sort of. I didn't actually read about it but heard a bit on the radio and one of the guys at the crem was talking about "them nasty murders on our doorstep". Sounds horrendous.'

'Well, I suspect you served the victims on Saturday night.'

McAndrew froze, his comb poised over his quiff. 'You're kidding!'

Snow shook his head and produced the two photographs of Wilkinson and Johnson. 'These

173

are the two men. Recognise them?'

Gingerly McAndrew took hold of the photographs and scrutinised them. 'He doesn't look well, does he,' he said pointed at the photograph of Johnson. 'Was it taken on the slab?'

Snow nodded. 'Do you know them?'

'Well, yes, I reckon I do recognise them. Especially this chap.' He held up Wilkinson's picture.

'What can you tell me about him? His name is Matt Wilkinson.'

Sandy McAndrew screwed up his face in thought for a few moments. 'Well, not a lot really. You don't get much time to chat with the punters, business is so brisk. He was a ginger ale man, I seem to recall. He was pretty regular on a Saturday night. Had a charming way with him, I suppose. He seemed a nice bloke to me. He appeared to score pretty regularly. You know it is a gay club I suppose.'

Snow nodded again.

'Not that I'm gay. But ... well I reckon that's why Mr Rawlins gave me the job. He didn't want me flirting with customers from behind the bar, if you know what I mean. Be brisk and use a deep voice.' He smiled at his own observation.

'Did you see him score on Saturday night?' He held up the photograph of Wilkinson.

McAndrew revived the face screwing routine again. 'There was one chap with him for most of the night, I seem to remember. They did a lot of chatting and buying each other drinks.'

'What did he look like, this other chap?'

'Heck, I don't know. I can't remember really.'

'Think. Give it a go.'

McAndrew stared at the ceiling for a few seconds. 'Tallish. Thinnish. Long nose. Almost aristocratic,' he said at length. 'Looked a bit like Peter Sellers without the glasses.'

'Would you recognise him again?'

'I think so. Maybe. I'm really not sure. My God, you don't think he...'

'It's a possibility. Anything else you remember about this man or Saturday night in particular.'

'Not really. Ah ... wait a minute ... I did see him, this Peter Sellers bloke, talking to another man whenever the Wilkinson bloke went to the bog.'

'And what did he look like?'

'That I can't say. It was beyond the lights of the bar. All I can say was it was a white man of a normal build ... with glasses. I thought he looked a bit out of place.'

'In what way?'

'I never saw him dancing or talking to anyone – apart from the Peter Sellers guy. It was probably his first time. You get to recognise the behaviour.'

There was nothing more that young Sandy McAndrew could tell Snow. It was just crumbs. But, thought the policeman, gather enough crumbs and you make a loaf.

Snow left the young lad to finish his preparations for his stint at Frankie's burger bar and drove home. He lived in an Edwardian terraced house situated in a quiet street near Greenhead Park. It was furnished in a very Spartan style, not in any way to be fashionable or chic, but simply because Snow did not acquire possessions. They

175

weren't important to him. In all manner of ways he travelled light. He had no really close friends, no hobbies or passions to fill up his time away from the job and because of the dangers, no romantic involvements. Sometimes, wryly, he thought of himself as a kind of modern urban monk.

He sipped a can of lager while he waited for the microwave to ping telling him his meal for one was red hot and ready to burn his mouth.

As he ate, he thought about the case and prayed for a swift straightforward conclusion.


## TWENTY-THREE

'I know I shouldn't be talking to you. I know what we agreed. But these are bloody exceptional circumstances. I've been putting this call off all day. It's been doing my head in. I mean we can't just do nothing. We can't sit tight and hope the bastard dies.' Alex's voice on the phone was almost hysterical.

Russell didn't know what to say. He didn't know what to think. Like Alex his mind had been transformed into mincemeat since he had heard the news about Ronnie Fraser.

It was close to midnight and he was sitting at his desk in the downstairs room which he had converted into an office, a single desk lamp throwing a narrow beam down on to the telephone. Upstairs his wife and unborn child were

176

sleeping soundly. He had been in a quandary all day as to whether he should break the rule and contact the others, but now Alex had beaten him to it.

'If he wakes up, comes round, he could land us right in the shit.' Alex's voice rose an octave.

'And what do you suggest we do?' asked Russell softly, lobbing the ball back.

There was a pause. Both men knew what the other was thinking – the options were few – but neither had the courage to voice their thoughts. After a while it was Alex who spoke. 'Well,' he said hesitantly, 'I suppose we'd better get in touch with Laurence. He'll know what to do.'

As usual it was Russell who contacted Laurence, their bond being the stronger and more intimate than Alex's.

Initially Laurence was irritated that Russell had broken their rule. He had told them clearly that they should remain incommunicado for twelve months. Of course, he had not reckoned on the way things had turned out. How could he have been so stupid not to check that all three of them were dead? Really dead. However, his initial response to the unpleasant news that one of the men had survived their attack was just to lie low. It would all pass. Surely even if this fellow was able to talk to the police about the event, there was nothing definite that he could say that would link the killings to the Brotherhood. But now Russell's call had begun to sow seeds of doubt in his mind. Maybe he was fooling himself. The coppers would be looking for a motive and as robbery was not involved it would be suggested to them that the attacks on Wilkinson and cronies had been carried out as some form of revenge. The crime was too vicious and calculated to be random. This line of thinking surely would lead them to seek out Wilkinson's victims, one of whom was Alex. Once that had been established, the coppers had their link, *the* link to all of them. And although Alex and Russell had been balaclava-ed up on the night, he had not. OK, he had been in disguise but this was simply a camp persona and a long-haired wig. Window-dressing. Certainly not an iron clad protection against identification. Slowly, uncomfortably Laurence also began to get pangs of concern. It was a feeling alien to him and he didn't like it.

'Look, allow me a little time to give this some thought and I'll ring you in the morning. Early before you set off for school. Say around 7.30. And for God's sake tell Alex to remain cool.'

Russell said he would, knowing that it would be a futile gesture, and replaced the receiver. As he did so, he sensed another presence in the room. He turned sharply and saw Sandra standing in the open doorway.

'What was that all about?' she said softly. There was no edge or tone to her voice to indicate to Russell whether this was a vague enquiry or that she had heard most of the conversation.

'Are you OK, my love? The baby...?'

She shook her head sleepily. 'Yes, I'm OK. Baby's fine. Who were you talking to?'

Suddenly Russell felt very weary. It was all going wrong. Things were spiralling out of control. He was starting to build lie upon lie. What had been his pleasant dark secret now seemed a ridiculous and dangerous burden. It should never have brought them this close to discovery. For a fleeting moment he wished it were all over. Everything. He just wanted to rest in the dark and never be troubled again.

His brain worked sluggishly as Sandra stood waiting for his response. 'It's ... it's an old school friend. He's got some health issues. Cancer.' He paused, gathering up further strands of the lie. 'He's not got much time left and he's been getting touch with people he knew. A final chat ... you know.'

Lame as a three-legged dog, thought Russell, bringing to mind one of Laurence's pithy expressions.

'At this time of night?'

'He can't sleep, poor devil. He's not thinking straight.'

In the dim light he couldn't tell whether Sandra believed him or not.

He rose swiftly, crossed to her and placed his arm around her shoulder. 'Come on love, let's go back to bed. We've work in the morning.' After a moment she responded and moulded herself into him. 'Thank God *we've* got our health and sanity,' he murmured, leading her back to their bedroom. A tag line he hoped would add a touch of credibility to his lie.

Sandra did not reply.

Laurence, his sleep interrupted by Russell's phone call, sat up in bed smoking and thinking. His

179

bedroom was illuminated solely by a tiny bedside lamp and as though in a trance he watched the tendrils of smoke spiral away beyond the spill of light up into the darkness above. He felt that he was caught in a mental maze. Each time he tried to think his way out of the dilemma, he ended up in the same spot. The same conclusion, the same resolution. It would not go away. It would not go away because it was the only practical and sensible thing to do. He knew that he was trying to avoid the obvious for the obvious meant more planning, more effort, more danger and enhanced the possibility of exposure and capture.

He swore gently under his breath. It was a gesture of defeat.

'Oh, ma wee boy, it looks like you'll have tae grasp the nettle,' he murmured in a comic Scottish accent and allowed himself a faint smile at his enforced whimsy. Fate, it seemed, was now leading him by the hand, taking him off any planned route and down a doubtful side road. He had no choice in the matter. He just couldn't resist it.

With a sigh of resignation, he stubbed out the cigarette, clicked off the bedside lamp and slid beneath the covers and lay on his back, fully aware that sleep would not visit him that night.

Alex was also having a sleepless night. His mind was a riot of thoughts, but at the heart of his cerebral turmoil was one idea which, like Laurence's, would not be shifted. It was logical, inevitable. It was, he believed, necessary. He would have to kill Ronnie Fraser. The bastard had to die before he regained consciousness and blabbed. Of course,

180

he may well have regained consciousness already. If so the three of them were going to hell in a handcart.

Whatever, he had to find out and act accordingly. It was, he reasoned, his fault that his friends were in this mess and so it was up to him, and him alone, to try and get them out of it. If he failed, he would be the only one to suffer.

What a pillock he had been to get involved with Matt Wilkinson in the first place. He had allowed his dick to rule his brain and his common sense. And then he was a pathetic twat running to his mates with his sob story, wanting them to punish the naughty man for hurting him. If he'd kept his bloody mouth shut and suffered in silence they wouldn't be in this precarious position now. So, quite rightly, he had to resolve it.

First thing in the morning, he'd be up to the hospital...

He prayed he wouldn't be too late.

It was just after seven o'clock in the morning when the telephone rang in Russell's house.

'Not your sick friend again,' observed Sandra with too much irony for Russell's comfort.

He shrugged. 'I'm not telepathic.' It came out nastily and not as light-hearted banter as he'd intended.

Sandra frowned.

'I'll take it in my office.' Russell left the kitchen in a hurry, desperate to silence incessant ringing.

He shut the door of the little room and lifted the receiver and recited the appropriate mantra. 'Hello, this is Russell Blake. Can I help you?'

That told Laurence that indeed it was Russell answering the telephone and that he was free to speak openly.

'Good morning, squire,' said Laurence.

'Bloody hell, man, I thought you said you'd ring me at seven thirty. It's only just after seven. I wasn't ready for you. Now the bloody wife is getting suspicious.' It came out in torrent of anger, the voice a harsh whisper, the face strained with mixture of frustration and annoyance.

'Sorry, my friend, but I have to leave shortly to catch a train. A train up to Huddersfield.'

'What?'

'Huddersfield. I'm coming up to complete this job. I'm going to silence our surviving friend. On my own, I hasten to add.'

'What the hell are you talking about?'

'Oh, Russell, you know what I'm talking about. You know as well as I do the only way to knock this matter on the head is to silence this Ronnie character for good.'

'Well, yes.'

'Good. Glad we're agreed on that. And I'm the fellow to do it. With all due respect, I reckon you two guys might cock it up. Alex is too emotionally involved and therefore unstable. As for you ... well, my old mate, you can't suddenly set off to Huddersfield without explanation to the wife, the headmaster and those snotty, spotty morons you teach just to pull the plug on some toe rag in the Huddersfield Infirmary. The last thing you want to do is draw attention to yourself. Act out of character. The situation is so delicate, any suspicious move on your part or Alex's might make things a whole lot worse. So let Uncle Laurence sort it out. A white coat, a false moustache, glasses and one on my nice wigs and I'll be in and out of that intensive ward before you can say Christiaan Barnard. A quick click of the switch of the magic contraption that's keeping the bugger alive or whatever else is appropriate to stop him breathing and all our troubles will be over.'

Russell couldn't help but smile and not for the first time he felt a hot wave of love for Laurence crash over him. 'You're like bloody Superman coming to the rescue.'

'That's me, that's what I'm here for. I'll just nip into the nearest phone, change my underpants and zoom off to Yorkshire. It's in all our interests. We're brothers after all.'

'Sure. But you take care, Laurence.'

'I always do, *mon ami*,' he answered in the comic French accent he used to adopt when they were at college and for a brief moment Russell was transported back to Alf's pub, the dusty light filtering in through the tall windows, the grumpy old men in the corner staring into space and his eighteen-year-old self was sitting holding a pint and laughing at something Laurence had just said. The memory brought an ache to his heart. It welled with sadness. He had been so happy then, so content. If only he could go back. But life isn't like that.

'One thing I'd like you to do,' Laurence was saying. 'Let Alex know what I'm up to. Put his mind at ease and tell him to carry on as normal. I worry about him sometimes. He comes very close to flipping his lid these days. Since the little incident with Wilkinson, he's not the same steady fellow he used to be with a reliable firm hand on the tiller.'

'Sure, I'll ring him now.'

'Good man. Don't contact me again until the appointed time. You'll read the results of my actions in the paper or on the telly. Ciao.'

The line went dead.

Russell stood for some time just holding the receiver, staring into space, the ache was still there. With a sigh he replaced it and dialled Alex's number.

There was no reply.

## TWENTY-FOUR

He had not expected to find a policeman sitting in the corridor outside Ronnie Fraser's room by the Intensive Care Ward at the Huddersfield Infirmary. On guard no doubt to prevent any unauthorised person entering the room and on hand to take down any information that Ronnie might provide should he regain consciousness. Of course Alex should have known if he had been thinking clearly, but his thoughts had been mangled ever since he'd learned that the Fraser creep was still in the land of the living.

Alex had arrived at the hospital just before five in the morning. Unable to sleep or to wait until daylight, he had made his way there at this early hour reckoning that the place would be quiet and that he would find it relatively easy to gain access to Fraser. He was existing in a strange dream world where his actions were somehow not a part of him. Perhaps at any moment he would wake up and find that it was some kind of night-time hallucination.

And then, perhaps not.

He parked a few streets away and jogged to his destination. The sky was still grey with only the faintest promise of dawn as he pushed through the swing doors and entered the hospital. The building was eerily quiet, like a ghost hospital with an empty foyer and deserted corridors. Illness, it seemed, had been put on hold until the dawn chorus. He felt vulnerable, the solitary stranger wandering along the empty corridors. It would have been so much easier if he could have blended in with a throng of patients, nurses and visitors, but he did not have the luxury of time to wait until the place became busy. What he had to do, he had to do as soon as possible.

He did encounter the odd nurse who wandered by him in a preoccupied manner, but no one questioned his presence or took any interest in him at all. He had dressed smartly but wore a flat cap which he'd pulled as far down as he could without looking ridiculous in order to shade his face.

Following the copious signs on the walls, he had found his way via the lift up to the third floor where the Intensive Care Ward was situated. The enquiry desk was dark. No one was on duty. That was a real bonus. He scurried past but then he hit the buffers in the shape of a bulky policeman.

Although, far from looking alert, the constable, slumped in a chair outside Fraser's room engrossed in a paperback novel, was a real problem. Casually, Alex strolled past the copper who did not raise his eyes from the printed page as he did so.

To Alex it was clear that the presence of PC Plod meant that Fraser was still clinging on to the wreckage of his life and had not yet spilt any beans. That was good but the burly rozzer was not. Decisions had to be made and made fast. Alex glanced around him. Apart from the policeman the corridor was deserted. He knew what he had to do and it had to be done quickly while the coast was clear. He caught sight of a stone bottle on a trolley by the wall. It was a medieval device to pee into used by bedridden patients. Alex could see that it was suitably heavy and would work well as a weapon.

Snatching it up, he approached the policeman from the side. Just as the copper sensed a movement near him, Alex brought the stone bottle crashing down on the side of his head. There was a sharp crack and, with a muffled groan, the constable slid smoothly from his chair onto the polished floor.

Quickly, Alex knelt down and felt his pulse. He was still alive. Alex was relieved. He hadn't intended to kill the man – just knock him out. Opening the door to Ronnie Fraser's room, he dragged the unconscious policeman inside. He didn't want a passing nurse to spot the fellow lying on the floor with blood seeping from a wound in his head and raise the alarm. It was not an easy task: he was quite a weight and took some shifting. And then his size twelve boots caught on the corner of the door frame. Alex cursed silently and reached forward to pull them free. He was sweating now and his clothes were beginning to stick to his body. Eventually Alex got the lumpen copper into the room and dumped him by the wall. Catching his breath, he turned his attention to the man in the bed. Ronnie Fraser was lying on his back with only his head and arms visible above the sheets. Various tubes and wires were attached to him and what Alex assumed was a heart monitor bleeped eerily in the corner like a sonar in one of those films set on a submarine. The patient appeared to be breathing regularly.

Like a man possessed, Alex pulled as many of the tubes and wires from Fraser's body as he could. He unplugged the various devices placed near the bed, including the heart monitor, yanking the plugs from their sockets with great force. At first there seemed no obvious change in the patient. His chest continued to rise and fall in a regular fashion but then slowly the face began to contort and the mouth to open and close like a manic ventriloquist's doll. Spittle foamed at the lips and a strange, hoarse gasping sound emerged from the snapping aperture. Alex watched mesmerised as Fraser's body began to writhe slowly beneath the covers as though possessed by some alien force not his own. For a brief moment the eyes flickered open and glared at Alex. They seemed to bore into his brain. Alex stumbled backwards with a gasp of terror; and then as swiftly as they had opened, Ronnie Fraser's eyes closed again.

Snatching one of the pillows from beneath his head, Alex thrust it down on Fraser's face and pressed hard. There was a little resistance: the hands fluttered slightly and the body shook but this lasted for only a few seconds until the damaged creature lay still, the life squeezed out of him. Alex continued to hold the pillow firmly in place for almost a minute.

There must be no mistake this time.

Eventually he pulled the pillow away and looked down at the gaunt, contorted face of Ronnie Fraser whose eyes were now open once again and staring back at him with the fixed gaze of a dead man. For some moments Alex was held mesmerised by this sight but then suddenly he heard a slight noise behind him. On turning around sharply he saw a nurse entering the room. When she caught sight of Alex and the body of the inert policeman lying on the floor by the wall, she let out a scream and dropped the metal tray she was carrying. It fell to the floor with a resounding crash, the noise seeming to fill the room like a cacophony of clanging cymbals.

Alex leapt forward and grabbed the distressed nurse before she could reach the door. As he gripped her by the shoulders and shook her, her screams died away and she fought against him, desperately trying to pull herself free of her assailant's grasp. With a savage thrust Alex hurled her to the ground. As she hit the floor, she banged her head on the side of a cabinet and lay still.

Alex rushed from the room, slamming the door

behind him and raced down the corridor, his heart pounding. As he rounded the corner, he collided with a white coated porter who was pushing an empty wheel chair.

'Sorry mate,' he grunted and ran on. Behind him he could hear the porter's cries of protest.

Alex knew that it was too dangerous to use the lift and so he made for the stairs. He raced down them, missing his footing on one occasion and tumbling to the bottom of the flight. Undaunted, he jumped to his feet and carried on. Panic, for the moment, dulled the pain of the fall. By the time he reached the ground floor, there were signs that the hospital was gradually coming to life. There were nurses, porters, doctors, cleaners and other assorted souls meandering gently in the foyer. As casually as he could, Alex made his way to the exit. He was within a few feet of the doorway when someone tapped him on the shoulder. He froze.

'Just a minute,' said a voice and he felt a hand on his arm.

He knew he had to respond. He couldn't ignore this and rush away. To make a bolt for it now would only draw attention to himself. There were loads of witnesses to pass on his description to the police.

Slowly he turned round to face the voice. It belonged to an old man, dishevelled in appearance, unshaven and wild eyed. 'Can you tell me where gents' bogs are? I'm bursting.'

Alex shook his head, 'No, mate. I've no idea,' he muttered, shaking off the man's hand which was still resting on his arm, and with as much relaxed aplomb as he could muster he resumed his flight.

Once out into the early morning light, he breathed in the cool fresh air in large gulps. He could hardly believe what he'd done. In his mind's eye he saw Ronnie Fraser's pale, gaunt face with the frothy spittle oozing from his mouth. He visualised the pillow slowly descend on his face with his own hands, fingers spread wide, pressing down.

Pressing down.

Squeezing the life out of him.

And there were his eyes, those wide staring eyes.

Staring at him.

Accusing him.

Suddenly Alex retched and he felt the foul taste of bile as it rose up into his mouth. With an effort, he swallowed it down again. His footsteps faltered for a moment, but he carried on. With a grimace, he wiped his mouth with his hand-kerchief and moved briskly towards the labyrinth of streets behind the hospital where he'd parked his car.

Well, he thought, as he hurried along, I've killed the devil, but it's been a bit of botched job. In my cack-handed eagerness, I've been seen by various people who may well be able to identify me and I've attacked a nurse who, no doubt, has my phizzog well and truly imprinted on her mind. I could hardly have made things worse. What have I gone and done?

# TWENTY-FIVE

On reaching police headquarters, Paul Snow made himself a strong coffee before wandering into his office. On this occasion, the morning after he had interviewed Sandy McAndrew, he found a manila file waiting for him on his desk. It contained two plastic wallets. In one was a set of six dark grainy photographs, each showing the face of one of Matt Wilkinson's victims. Paul could see that although they had been technically enhanced the features still remained indistinct. The images were harsh and blurred and lacking sufficient definition to ensure accurate identification. Even the mothers of these individuals would have difficulty recognising them, Snow thought, and gave a grimace of disappointment. Studying them he noticed that there was one thing that each of the vague faces had in common: their eyes. Wide and staring, they were. Wide with ... what? Fear? Disgust? Pain? Guilt? Even perhaps a hint of pleasure? Maybe a mixture of all those emotions. It was difficult to determine.

The second wallet held individual pencil sketches of the same men. Snow examined them carefully. These were more promising. The artist had done a very competent job considering the original material he had to work with. While it was clear that the faces were only an approximation of the originals, the features were at least distinctive enough that they might possibly jog someone's memory. He'd certainly seen worse images of Elvis. In policing terms it was better than nothing. And it was still those wide haunted staring eyes which were a prominent feature. They had obviously fascinated the artist also.

Snow spaced the drawings out across his desk and scrutinised them while he finished his coffee. Where are they now? he thought. These poor buggers. These poor buggers who had been buggered, he added as a gloomy afterthought.

Suddenly the door of his office burst open and Bob Fellows leaned into the room. His face was red and agitated.

'A rather dramatic development, sir. Ronnie Fraser has been murdered up at the hospital.'

'What do we know?' asked Snow as he and Fellows set off for the hospital in Snow's Cavalier.

'Not a lot. Apparently a chap got access to Fraser in the early hours of the morning, pulled out all his tubes and stuff and suffocated the life out of the poor devil.'

'What about the officer on duty?'

'Cracked on the head from behind. He's all right though, apart from a stonking headache. Apparently the murderer was interrupted by a nurse. He just belted her to the floor and scarpered.'

'Let's hope she got a good look at him.'

'There was a porter, too, I believe. He saw him.'

Snow chewed his lip. He didn't want to admit it openly but he had no sympathy for Fraser and his death did not upset him unduly. To him he wasn't 'a poor devil', just a nasty piece of work who had got what was due to him. A politically incorrect view, of course, but as far as he was concerned one that was morally just. However, the rash action of the killer who was desperate enough to risk exposure and indeed capture to silence Fraser could be a very useful breakthrough. He had to hope so.

There were several police cars parked around the entrance of the hospital, each with a vibrant flashing light. A stout uniformed sergeant led Snow and Fellows up to the intensive care ward where the Scenes of Crime Officers were busy at work in the tiny room where the body of Ronnie Fraser still lay in the bed.

'Got a nice set of prints off this,' said one of the officers, holding up the stone bottle. 'It was used to bash Carmichael on the head.'

'The constable on watch?'

The officer nodded and rolled his eyes. 'I reckon he'd not been keeping his eye on the ball. He's not the brightest bauble on the tree.'

'Where is he now?'

'They've got him bandaged up and lying down in one of the rooms further down the corridor. But he'll be no use to you, sir. The only thing he saw were stars.' He grinned at his own little joke but Snow did not respond.

'And the nurse?'

'Susan Watkins. She's in the nurse's rest room. She suffered a minor concussion, but she's OK. WPC Sparrow is taking down a statement.'

Without a word, Snow turned and went to the bed to look at the victim. Grey faced, wide eyed, open mouthed with the veins like rope running down his neck, Ronnie Fraser looked like an old man rather than someone around thirty.

'Not a pretty sight, eh, sir,' said Fellows over his shoulder.

Snow was about to say something about getting his just desserts but thought better of it. He simply nodded instead. He couldn't explain the revulsion he felt about what this man along with his evil companions had done time after time to their unsuspecting victims. Well, certainly not without revealing more about his own feelings and sensibilities.

'Come on, let's have a word with this nurse,' he said turning away from the bed and its grim occupant.

Nurse Watkins, a plump and pretty woman somewhere in her mid-thirties was sitting in the nurse's rest room, cradling a cup of tea in her hands and chatting to a young police woman. Obviously the statement had already been taken for WPC Sparrow was also sitting casually drinking a cup of tea. On seeing Snow she stood up awkwardly.

'Morning, Sir.'

'Morning, Sparrow. I'll take over from here. Make sure I get a typed version of this lady's statement on my desk by lunchtime.'

The policewoman nodded vigorously. She knew it would not do to let DI Snow down. He had exacting standards which he upheld himself and woe betide anyone who failed to meet them. WPC Sparrow gave a brisk nod at Snow and Fellows and with some relief she left the room.

Snow sat beside Susan Watkins in the same seat

that Sparrow had just vacated. Her face was puffy from crying and her eyes were still moist. There were faint spidery traces of mascara advancing down her cheeks.

'Hello,' he said softly. 'I'm Detective Inspector Snow. How are you feeling?'

Susan tried a smile but the lips just twitched for a few seconds. 'I'm all right really,' she said with little conviction. She had a strong Yorkshire accent which made her seem older than she was. 'Physically, there's no real damage. It was just a bit of a shock, like.' She tried to smile again; this time it was a minor success. 'Well ... more than a bit of a shock. I mean ... he could have killed me.'

Snow nodded sympathetically. 'I'm sorry but I'm going to ask you to tell me what happened again.'

'But I've made a statement to that lass.'

'I know but as officer in charge I need to know myself ... from you. There are some questions I need to ask.'

Susan Watkins gave a sigh. 'What do you want to know?'

'Just tell me what happened this morning. Go through it slowly. Tell me everything you saw and felt. Leave nothing out no matter how small or insignificant it seems to you. Run it like a film in your head and give me the commentary. OK?'

'Yeah. I think so. Well, I started my shift at two and I knew I had to check on Mr Fraser before six but I had other duties to carry out before then. Do you want to hear about them?'

'Not now, I think. Just tell me what happened when you got to Mr Fraser's room.'

'For a start, the copper that was usually sitting outside wasn't there. I thought it a bit strange but I supposed he'd just gone for a pee or something.'

'Your suspicions weren't aroused in any way?'

'Not really.'

'Go on.'

'So I opened the door to Mr Fraser's room and the first thing I see is the copper lying on the floor by the wall. I think I was so surprised, well shocked at this, that I just opened my mouth and sort of gave a little gasp. I didn't make much of a sound. It just seemed so unreal. Then I saw him, the man.'

'What did he do?'

She shook her head in some distress as she relived the moment. 'It all happened so quickly. He rushed towards me and before I knew what was happening, he grabbed me by the shoulders and threw me on the floor. Well, I banged my head and lost consciousness. Can't have been for more than a few moments, like. When I came to, he'd done a bunk. That was it. It was all over in a matter of seconds.'

'What was he like? Can you describe him?'

'Well as I told the police lady it were dim lighting and so everything was shadowy-like.'

Snow realised that he'd have to lead her by the hand through the various categories. Often the sub-conscious registered more details than one was aware and it was only by gentle probing and prompting these could be released and brought to the surface.

'Was he a tall man?'

'Not especially. Not much more than my

height. I'm five foot six.'

Snow glanced at Fellows to check that the sergeant was making notes. He was.

'What kind of build. Was he slim? Fat?'

'He was slim. Wiry, you might say. He moved quickly. Light on his feet.'

'A young man, then.'

'Oh, yes. I reckon he'd be in his late twenties or early thirties.'

'How could you tell that?'

'Well, he had a boyish face...'

'So you saw his face?'

Susan seemed surprised at her own revelation. 'Well, yes I must have.'

'Describe it. Think carefully.'

Nurse Watkins sat forward in her chair and screwed up her face, attempting to drag images to the forefront of her mind. 'Well he had a thin face,' she said slowly. 'Taut. Longish. To be honest he looked more frightened than I was.'

'What about his hair?'

'He had a cap on. It covered most of his head, but his hair was quite long – it went over his ears.'

'The colour?'

'Lightish, I think. Not quite blond ... but close.'

'How was he dressed?'

'He had on an anorak kind of thing on. Blue and jeans, I think. And trainers.'

Snow smiled and patted her hand. 'That's brilliant.'

She sighed again. 'Is that it now?' she asked unable to keep the anxious tone out of her voice.

'Nearly,' said Snow. From the manila file which had been resting on his lap he withdrew the set of sketches of Wilkinson's victims.

'Would you have a look at these?' he said, holding out the sketches to Susan. 'Take your time. Was any one of these the man you saw, the man who attacked you?'

Susan gave an involuntary shudder as she took the drawings and began to examine them. She went through each of the six sketches carefully and then returned to one again. 'I think ... I think this is the one.'

Snow felt a tingle of pleasure but his features remained neutral. 'Are you sure?'

'Well, as sure as I can be. As I said it was dark and it all happened so quickly. But this fellow's hair, his nose ... yes, I reckon that's him.'


## TWENTY-SIX

By the time Laurence reached Huddersfield, he was a changed man. Physically, that is. Shortly after the train had left Doncaster Station, he had made his way to the cramped lavatory and assumed his new identity. He had stripped off his white shirt, jeans and blazer, packing them in his canvas holdall, after extracting his new apparel: a pair of baggy corduroy trousers, a tweedy jacket, along with a checked shirt which he adorned with a moss coloured tie. This was his countryman model, based on a part he'd played the previous year in rep in Worthing. After donning his 'costume', as he regarded it, he set about

198

altering his features: a little rouge on the cheeks, some grey powder to the hair at the temples and on the eyebrows followed by the application of a false but realistic salt and pepper moustache. The whole appearance was topped off by a jaunty checked cloth cap. He now looked like a fifty-year-old codger, a small landowner up from the country to the town to see his bank manager. He grinned at himself in the pitted mirror, pleased with his appearance.

When Laurence arrived at the hospital, having taken a taxi from Huddersfield Station, the first things he observed were the two police cars with flashing lights parked right by the entrance. Two uniformed officers were leaning against the side of one vehicle, each with their arms folded engaged in a casual conversation.

With assumed casualness, Laurence sauntered past the policemen as though they didn't exist and made his way into the foyer; they in return took no notice of him.

Once inside the hospital, he approached the information desk. 'I've seen the cops outside. Been a bit of trouble?' he said cheerily, with a strong trace of a Yorkshire accent.

The buxom grey-haired lady behind the counter looked puzzled.

'The police. Two cars, flashing lights. Something up?' Laurence prompted her again.

'Oh, that. Yes...' She leaned forward conspiratorially. 'There's been a bit of funny business up in Intensive Care. They're not saying much but I heard there'd been an intruder.'

Laurence felt his mouth go dry. 'Oh, I see,' he

found himself saying as his mind whirled, trying to digest this surprising piece of information: 'A bit of funny business up in Intensive Care ... there'd been an intruder. What kind of 'funny business'? Surely it must have something to do with Mr Ronnie Fraser. An intruder? Who the hell was that? An answer struck him immediately. He hoped to God...? What the hell should he do now?

'I said, how may I help you?' the woman was saying. Laurence hadn't heard her the first time. He had been caught up in his own desperate thoughts. He smiled apologetically and desperately trying to bring his mind on track said the first thing that came in his head. 'Blood tests. Where do I go for blood tests?'

'Down Corridor B and take the stairs to the basement.' She leaned forward and pointed. 'You'll see it signposted on the wall down there.'

He thanked her and, moving away, followed the directions he'd been given until he was out of the woman's line of vision. Then he made his way to the little cafeteria and bought himself a coffee, wishing it were a whisky, and sat at a table by the fish tank to ponder what he was going to do next.

'A bit of funny business in Intensive Care'. What the hell had happened up there? Who was this intruder? What had he done? Had they caught him? He prayed that it wasn't Russell. Stupid Russell, trying to take the law into his own hands. He closed his eyes to squeeze this terrible thought from his mind, for he knew that if this were the case, the whole world could soon come tumbling about his head. His mission now had taken on a completely different and somewhat more dangerous dimension. He knew that he'd have to try and get up to the Intensive Care Unit and see if he could find out more details.

He took a sip of the brown water that professed to be coffee and grimaced. God, he thought, no wonder there are ill people in here if they have to drink this stuff. Pushing the offending plastic cup away he rose from his chair. Time for action he told himself and after consulting the map of the hospital on the wall by the café entrance, he rode up to the third floor in the lift. On exiting, he followed the signs for the Intensive Care Unit. It was strangely quiet, no bustling nurses, tired doctors or ambling porters and no patients abandoned on the corridor on a trolley or in a wheelchair. And apparently no police presence. Thank heaven. The whole area had an air of desolation about it. Turning a corner, he approached a pair of double doors above which bore the legend painted in black: Intensive Care. Ah, thought Laurence, here they are: plods on the port bow. There were two policemen standing on guard outside. As he approached, one of them held up his hand.

'I'm sorry, sir, you can't go in here. The ward is closed for the moment. Only medical staff are allowed entry. I suggest you come back this evening.'

'Oh dear. That's a beggar,' Laurence said, shaking his head. 'What's going on, officer?'

'There's been a bit of trouble. Nothing to worry about. It's all under control.'

Laurence knew that he had to tread carefully,

but that he still had to tread.

'It's not to do with that Fraser chappie is it?'

The policeman's eyes narrowed. 'What do you know about Mr Fraser? Are you a friend of his?'

Laurence shook his head vigorously. 'Not I,' he said. 'It's just what I read in the paper. Has something happened to him?'

'Nothing that need concern you, sir.'

'I'm just concerned about my mother in there.' He pointed at the double doors.

Laurence knew that this was taking a big risk. He had no knowledge that there was an old woman in the ward and if there was he certainly had no name for her.

'All the patients are being treated as normal, sir. They are receiving the appropriate care. I'm sure your mother is in safe hands and as I say you should be able to visit her this evening.' With lifeless eyes, he spoke in strong measured tones, like an automaton that had been programmed to spout this message. If I press his stomach, thought Laurence, I'm sure he'd repeat his spiel, word for word in exactly the same way. Laurence knew that there was no way that he was going to find out what had actually happened behind those cream doors in the Intensive Care Unit and if he pushed any further, he would begin to raise suspicions. In a sense he believed that he had sussed out what the situation was, he just needed confirmation.

'Thank you,' he said quietly and was about to turn and go when the door swung open and two men emerged. The leading figure was tall and lean with very short cropped hair and eyes that glittered fiercely even when his handsome face was in repose. He was accompanied by a sandy-haired man, chubbier and from his expression and gait a much more relaxed fellow. The uniformed officers stiffened almost to attention on their appearance.

The tall man gazed at Laurence keenly. 'A problem here?' he asked one of the constables.

'Not really, sir. This gentleman was wanting to visit his mother inside. I told him to come back this evening.'

'Sir' looked more intently at Laurence. This is the last thing he wanted. His disguise was fine for casual observations, but not for the close eyed scrutiny of these two blokes, whom he assumed were police detectives.

He turned slightly so that his face was away from the detective's gaze. 'Yes, sorry to be a nuisance. I'll come back this evening.'

He was about to walk away when the leading detective touched him on the arm.

'What name was it, sir?'

'Sorry?'

'The name of your mother.'

'It ... it was Crowther. It's Doris Crowther.' He snatched the name from God knows where. 'But I can come back this evening.' Laurence made to take another step away but the bastard detective's hand was still on his arm.

'Wait a minute, Mr Crowther. I'll see if we can help.' The detective smiled. It was probably his normal smile but was without much warmth.

Laurence could feel the perspiration building up under his collar and on his forehead. Tendrils of panic started to form around his heart. This isn't how it was meant to be.

The detective turned to one of the uniformed officers. 'See if you can find a doctor or a nurse through there who can give this gentleman an update on his mother's condition. Mrs Doris Crowther.'

With a sharp nod the constable disappeared through the swing doors.

'You're very kind,' said Laurence, apparently addressing his shoes, desperately trying to control his breathing.

'That's all right, sir. Now if you'll excuse me...' With that he walked off in the direction of the lift, followed by his partner.

Laurence waited until they had disappeared from sight before he turned to the remaining constable.

'I need a quick pee. Is there a loo nearby?'

'Down the corridor on your left near the end.'

'Thanks. I won't be a tick.'

He hurried off in the direction he had been given but carried on past the lavatory and through another set of double doors. Here he encountered a porter carrying a pile of blankets.

'Which way out, mate?' he said rather more abruptly than he meant to.

'The lift is back the way you came.'

'Can't stand lifts. I get a bit panicky. Prefer stairs.'

'Just on here at the end. Through that green door.'

'Ta, mate.'

Some minutes later to his great relief, Laurence

found himself in the hospital foyer once more. Keeping an eye out for the two detectives he made his way to the gent's lavatory and, locking himself in a cubicle, he discarded most of his disguise. Now having been seen in close up by four coppers and several other hospital staff he thought it best to return to his anonymous self. He slipped the cap into his coat pocket, wiped the rouge from his cheeks and washed his face. Then he whipped off the tie and clapped on a pair of spectacles to alter his appearance further. He could do nothing about the clothes, but with floppy hair, an open necked shirt and a more assured gait, he was sure he looked like a different person from the one he'd been impersonating. Checking his appearance in the mirror, he was not surprised to see that the face which looked back at him was somewhat pale and disturbed.

Meanwhile up at the Intensive Care Unit, the uniformed officer had returned from the ward to his colleague on duty at the door. He wore a puzzled expression. 'Where is that guy who wanted to see Mrs Crowther?'

'He's gone for a slash. Said he'd only be a few minutes.'

'Well, there isn't a Mrs Crowther in there. There's only two patients left in the ward now. An old bloke called Forsdyke and an Indian lady.'

'That's funny.'

'Yeah. Very funny. I've a sneaking feeling that we won't see Mr Crowther again. I reckon I'd better let Snow know about this.'

On leaving the hospital, Laurence walked for some

time in the direction of the town centre some two miles away. He moved slowly as though a figure caught in slow motion contrasting with the real world around him: the pedestrians who shouldered past in a hurry and the traffic that whizzed by him on the road. He was deep in thought, oblivious of his surroundings, trying to make some sense of the whole Matt Wilkinson/Ronnie Fraser farrago. He had dragged his mind back to the night of the killings and followed the scenario from there. In cold, sober broad daylight he saw that the whole thing was crazy. It was surreal, foolish and pointless. Like his whole life. Suddenly his entire existence seemed like a dream, a warped illusion, and he desperately wanted to wake up or, failing that, stop dreaming altogether. A deep rumble behind him temporarily attracted his attention and looking back he saw a large juggernaut rattling and juddering down the highway at speed – far faster than it should have been on such a road. There was an anonymous shadow up high up in the driving seat behind the shiny windscreen. For a fleeting second Laurence considered stepping out in front of it. That would solve his problems all right. Oblivion in an instant. He stared at the massive radiator grille and the giant throbbing tyres on the monster machine which was fast approaching. That would make light work of his body, his skull cracking like a bird's egg.

All he had to do was step out.

The thing rumbled nearer.

Just, step out.

He moved to the edge of the pavement and

took a deep breath.

And then the juggernaut thundered by with a mind-numbing roar, creating a spiral of dust and grit which enveloped him in a thin grey shroud. He coughed and spluttered for a moment and then with his handkerchief wiped the smuts from his face and eyes. With a tight grin he resumed his journey.

On reaching the outskirts of town, he discovered a small dingy pub which had just opened its doors for the lunchtime trade.

Sitting in the gloom, with a pint of bitter which he really did not want, Laurence tried hard to martial his thoughts into sensible and practical channels, casting all fanciful and melodramatic thoughts of suicide aside. From nowhere came some words from Shakespeare's *Macbeth,* a play he'd appeared in twice but only as minor characters. The lines were apposite and helped to point the way:

*'I am in blood*
*Stepped in so far that, should I wade no more,*
*Returning were as tedious as going o'er.'*

He took a sip of his beer and smiled. It looks like it is time, he told himself with a mixture of sadness and relief, it looks like it is time to make the last few moves in this grand game that I have been playing. This grand game of my own devising. I have been the puppet master all along and now I think it is the moment to start cutting the strings.

The landlord at the bar, lonely for customers, found his thoughts interrupted by the sound of laughter. He gazed over at the youngish chap in

207

glasses sitting in the shadows at the far corner of the room and saw that he was chuckling heartily to himself. Crikey, we get all sorts of nutters in here, he thought wryly as he absentmindedly wiped down the bar counter with a tea towel.

## TWENTY-SEVEN

'Right, get this picture out to the press and the TV companies pronto, please. Someone is bound to recognise him, surely. And we've got the finger-prints on the weapon he used to bash Constable Carmichael on the head. That should act as a clincher. With a bit of luck, we could have an arrest on our hands within the next twenty four hours.' Snow slumped back in his desk chair and smiled. It was a rare expression and it didn't last long.

Sergeant Fellows could see that his boss was in an unusually buoyant mood and this puzzled him slightly. He knew that it had been a productive morning with Nurse Watkins identifying one of the sketches, but this did come on the top of another killing. Three men had died now and this fact did not seem to affect Snow at all. He was a strange fellow. As one of his colleagues Sergeant Bradley had observed once, Snow was an appro-priate name for him. He was like the snow in the carol: 'deep and crisp and even'. You could never tell what was really going on beneath the surface. Smooth, cold and unfathomable was DI Snow. That, thought Fellows, is probably what made him a good copper.

'I'll see to it right away,' the sergeant said, snatching up a copy of the sketch and heading for the door.

'Oh, Bob. Get me a spare photocopy too, would you? I'd like to have the blighter to hand.'

'Will do,' came the reply as the door closed, leaving Snow alone.

He stroked his chin thoughtfully. He was aware that he shouldn't get his hopes up high, but he desperately wanted to bring this case to a swift conclusion and if they could track down the fellow in the sketch it was very likely that this could happen. There were his accomplices to track down, of course, but it often followed that once you had one rat caught in the trap, the others were usually easier to nab.

However, it was the nature of the crime and the motive behind it that disturbed Snow more than he liked to admit. It brought to the surface the secret of his own sexuality, a sexuality which he hoped he had managed to subdue and imprison deep within his consciousness. He knew he lived a lie and it was one he accepted. It was part of him now. He was determined not to let old memories and feelings rise up and contaminate his well-ordered life. The little worrying niggle at the back of his mind was the thought that someone digging deep into Matt Wilkinson's history might well discover his connection with the dead man. Although it was years ago since he'd had any contact with him, the fact still remained. And now it was like an albatross around his neck ... until the case was closed at least.

He hoped.

Exposure would be disastrous.

Snow shut down this idea instantly. It was time to channel his thoughts into other directions. But first a brew. He was just about to move when the phone rang on his desk.

With practised ease he snatched up the receiver. 'Snow,' he said sharply.

'It's PC Yeats here, sir. I was on duty this morning at the hospital outside Intensive Care when you came to the crime scene.'

'What is it, Yeats?'

'It's that bloke, sir. The one who turned up to see his mother.'

'Crowther – sports jacket and cords. Yes, I remember.'

'Well, sir, there weren't no Mrs Crowther in Intensive Care and there hasn't been anyone of that name in there for ages – eighteen months at least. And after you went, the bloke disappeared.'

'In a puff of smoke?'

'When I went into the ward to see if I could find out about this Mrs Crowther, he went off for a pee and never came back. It all seemed a bit funny, bit suspicious to me, sir. I just thought you ought to know'

'Yes, you were right. It may be something and nothing ... and then again... Thank you Constable. If you find out any more information, let me know.'

'Yes, sir.'

Snow replaced the receiver and stroked his chin again. Curious, he thought, and tried to bring to his mind's eye an image of this mysterious Mr

Crowther. He remembered a Harris Tweed-type sports coat and a flat cap. The face ... yes the face was constantly being turned away from him: but Snow had an automatic filing system in place for such encounters. Without thinking, he stored details away. That face. Yes. Moustache, ruddy cheeks. A countryman – or someone pretending to be a countryman. But it was a good performance. Well, it had convinced him at the time. Facts had shown that the man obviously wasn't who he said he was and that certainly made him a suspicious character. Where is he now? Snow sighed. Needle in a haystack time again. He needed a coffee.

If Laurence had known that his alter ego, Mr Countryman Crowther, was in the thoughts of Detective Inspector Paul Snow, he would have had second thoughts about booking in at the Huddersfield Centre Hotel in that name the same afternoon. Laurence realised that the way events had turned out, he could hardly return to London until this ugly matter was resolved one way or the other.

And he reckoned it would have to be the other.

Fate it seemed was lubricating the passage towards the Great Game finale. The realisation of this brought a strange melancholic mingling of sadness and relief. The performance had dragged on too long perhaps and it was probably time to ring down the curtain and bring up the house-lights. He who lived by the greasepaint must die by the greasepaint. Laurence smiled at his own conceit.

But he had to be certain of the facts. That's why he was staying around, registering at the Huddersfield Centre Hotel as Walter Crowther, sans moustache, baggy pants and the other parts of his disguise ensemble.

With a sigh, he dumped his bag on the floor, flung himself on the bed and fell asleep almost immediately. It had been a long day and a disappointing one. The only remedies for such outcomes were sleep and alcohol. For now sleep would suffice. Alcohol would come later.

On waking, he freshened up by washing his face and brushing his teeth. Feeling more alert, he returned to the bed and switched on the television just in time to catch the local early evening news. The hospital murder was the first item. It was as he suspected, someone had gone into the Intensive Care unit at Huddersfield hospital in the early hours of the morning and murdered one of the patients, a Mr Ronnie Fraser. The newscaster explained that Mr Fraser had been recovering from a violent attack he had suffered on the previous Saturday night. What happened next almost brought Laurence's heart to a halt. A pencil drawing appeared on the screen. The newscaster explained that this was an artist's impression of the man the police were anxious to interview in connection with the murder. The face that flickered before him was Alex's. Or a close approximation of it. Close enough for anyone who knew him at all to recognise him.

Laurence stared open-mouthed in shock at the drawing on the screen. He found himself shaking his head in some form of pointless denial. My

God, he thought. Now we're for it. The applecart has been well and truly overturned.

Alex has been a prize pillock.

A very dangerous prize pillock.

A telephone number was flashed up on the screen while a voice advised viewers to contact this number if they recognised the face in the drawing.

Laurence let out roar of anger at Alex's stupidity and incompetence, but he knew that he did not have the time for futile emotions. He imagined the phone lines already hot with callers all identifying Alex. He had to act fast in order and get to his wayward colleague before the police did.

## TWENTY-EIGHT

Paul Snow was also watching *Calendar*, the local news programme, which paraded the sketch of the man they were looking for. He was sitting alone in his office, gazing at the screen with cool detachment. He knew that somewhere out there were a number of people looking at the same picture and being amazed because they thought they knew this man. They were shocked, too, because he was involved in a murder investigation. Very soon someone would ring the telephone number provided and give them the information they wanted and bingo! they would have their man. That was the hoped for scenario at any rate.

When the newscaster went on to another story, Snow switched off the set but kept staring at the screen deep in thought. How much of Matt Wilkinson's history would emerge when this case was solved? Or more particularly, how safe was his own history? He had no doubts that this was a dangerous time for him and somehow Fate had thrust him on to the front line.

His reverie was interrupted by a gentle knock on the door. A large face appeared around the edge.

'Might I have a word, sir?'

It was Sergeant Michael Armitage. Snow had only a passing acquaintance with him. He'd worked with him before on a couple of minor investigations and he had been drafted in to help out on the Wilkinson case. There was something about the man that Snow did not like. His demeanour and deportment suggested arrogance and a lack of sensitivity. Armitage had a blokish swagger and a ready sneer that Snow found off-putting. He was a man's man in the worst sense of the phrase.

'Sure,' said Snow as Armitage came into the room and shut the door. He was a big man, over six feet tall and bulky – overweight with a beer belly, broad features topped with thinning blonde hair and the possessor of two large gobstopper eyes.

'It's this Wilkinson case. It's thrown up some interesting evidence.'

Snow's face expressed interest but he said nothing.

Suddenly Armitage's lips formed themselves into an unpleasant grin, more of a leer to Snow's thinking, and then with an attempt at a melodramatic gesture he pulled an envelope from the inside pocket of his jacket and waved it airily before Snow.

'It seems we have a poofter on board. A brown noser on the force.' The leer broadened and eyes sparkled with malice.

Snow felt his stomach muscles tighten. Suddenly things began to seem a little unreal and yet, strangely, he knew what was about to happen.

'I have evidence,' continued Armitage as he placed the envelope down, his spatula fingers spread widely, pressing it flat on the desk. 'Evidence. Shirtlifters in our sights, Captain.' With the theatricality of a second rate magician, he extracted the photograph contained inside the envelope. It was an ordinary black and white snap and showed two men grinning at the camera with their arms over each other's shoulder, their faces touching.

The two men were Paul Snow and Matt Wilkinson.

Snow remembered the photograph. He used to have a copy of it himself. He also remembered the occasion when it was taken. Someone's birthday party. He was a little drunk. So was Matt. The snap was over ten years old.

Snow pursed his lips and looked up into Armitage's face with its gargoyle grin, but continued to say nothing 'Cosy. They make a lovely couple don't they? I found this at Wilkinson's place along with a lot of other ... what shall we say ...

215

less sedate pics? Bum boys on show and at it. I reckon you'd be familiar with the sort of stuff I mean. Funny I should find this little gem slipped in amongst them. I should say that this is fairly compromising. Wouldn't you say so...? Sir?'

Just at that moment Snow wanted to lash out with his fist, and hit Armitage squarely in the face. He wanted to hear the satisfying crack of bone as his knuckles demolished that thick mound of flesh that Armitage used as a nose. He wanted to see blood spout from his cavernous nostrils; hear the surprised grunt of pain as he fell backwards to the floor.

No. He wanted more than that. Just at that moment he wanted to kill the bastard.

'I knew Wilkinson many years ago,' Snow said at length, his voice steady and unemotional.

'Knew him ... in what sense do you mean... Sir?' It was quite a feat, Snow thought, for Armitage to inject so much sarcasm and derision in one short word.

'We were friends for a while.'

'Boy friends?' His eyes shone with vicious humour.

'What are you after, Armitage? What little game are you playing?'

'Oh, I think it's you ... you're the one who's playing games. Little fairy games.'

Snow's hands, which had slipped down below the top of the desk out of sight, formed themselves into tight fists, the nails digging hard into his palms. He was determined not to lose his temper with this low life bastard, but he needed to do something to help contain his anger, to

216

subjugate it. Inflicting pain on himself did the trick – for the present at least.

'I wonder what they'd say out there,' Armitage gestured to the door, 'if they knew that their DI was a queer, a member of the Queen's own.'

'It isn't true,' Snow said softly. He tried to make light of the accusation, to smile but it never made it to his lips. His response sounded defensive and weak.

'Oh, I reckon this picture and the circumstances under which it was found say otherwise.'

'Only to those with a nasty mind.'

Armitage laughed. What was particularly chilling to Snow was that the strange sound he produced was a genuine laugh; it wasn't an artificial gesture. He really was amused by what Snow accepted was his rather lame and naïve response to the foul taunts.

'So, this is a threat.'

'You didn't get to be DI for nothing, did you Mr Snow?' Armitage tapped his brow with his forefinger. 'Smart, that's what you are. Smart and ... queer.'

Snow knew it was pointless to protest, deny or bluster. In essence this Neanderthal in a policeman's uniform was right. Yes, he was 'queer'; but not in *his* interpretation of the word. He wasn't a promiscuous, sibilant camp floozy who was after anything hunky in trousers, the creature so effectively portrayed in films, comedy shows and in the press. He was far from that. In truth he was a sad bugger, repressing his natural sexuality, slipping on the mask of dull normality in order to maintain his career and retain his image of respectability.

217

He played a part and was good at it. Certainly that was more comfortable to deal with than the alternative. Admitting his sexuality, or being found out, would be suicide in the force where, even now in the nineteen eighties, you were required to wear your butchness on your sleeve.

Armitage perched on the edge of Snow's desk, still grinning in his ghoulish fashion. 'I don't think your superiors would be happy to know that you are in charge of an investigation dealing with the murder of one of your old flames, would they? Or that their star detective is a limp-wristed faggot? Not good for the old career, eh?'

With a Herculean effort, Snow kept his hands below the desk, the nails sinking deeper into his flesh, desperately controlling his fury.

'That photograph proves nothing,' said Snow, wishing he could sound more convincing.

'I'll grant you that. It doesn't prove you're a gay boy – but it as hell as likes suggests it. And that is all that is needed. You know that.'

Snow did know that. The 'no smoke without fire' principle. Armitage was right. That photo-graph would soon set things going all right. In a close-knit community like police headquarters there were no secrets. The rumours would soon spread like a rampant disease. Then there would be the scrutiny, the whispered jokes behind his back and then to his face. Gradually a total lack of respect. Questions asked upstairs. And toe rags like Armitage would dig around for more evidence.

If they dug deep enough...

'What are you after? What exactly do you want?'

Snow still sounded cool and in control, only allowing a trace of irritation to show in his voice.

Armitage grinned again and raised his right hand, thrusting it towards Snow's face, rubbing the first finger and thumb together in a vigorous fashion.

'Moolah,' he said breathily.

So that was it. Blackmail. As simple and as sordid as that.

'You open your wallet and I'll keep my trap shut.'

Snow did not know what to say or how to react. He had been taken off his guard. This bizarre and threatening scenario had presented itself to him suddenly without any warning. It seemed so unreal. Here he was being threatened by a fellow policeman with exposure as a homosexual unless he coughed up with some cash. And if he did pay this pariah, how long would he be safe before another instalment was requested? He allowed his gaze to wander down to the photograph on his desk. It was slender evidence of his sexuality. Two tipsy men hugging each other. For God's sake footballers hug and kiss each other in front of thousands of spectators every Saturday. No one suggested they were queer. He knew this was a weak argument. There he was in close intimacy with a gay man who it turned out had gang-raped other men on a regular basis. Any connection Snow had with him, even though it was over ten years ago, would be damning in the extreme. He knew that Armitage would be able to stoke the rumour bonfire with ease until the flames destroyed his reputation and his career.

He could reach over and snatch up the photograph with ease and rip it to pieces but what good would that do? No doubt Armitage had several copies stashed away. He wouldn't be so foolish as to bring along the only one.

Snow knew that he was trapped. In a corner. He had to protect himself. What alternative did he have?

'How much do you want?' he said.


## TWENTY-NINE

Laurence had never been to Alex's house before. None of the Brothers had trespassed on each other's domestic scenes. That would have been a kind of contamination. Isolation had been a key feature of their arrangement. Contact was kept to a minimum. Of course, all that had been swept aside now by Alex's desperate and ill-conceived actions.

Once more attired in his middle-aged countryman costume, complete with greying temples, moustache and flat cap, Laurence had travelled by cab to the district where Alex lived, only a few miles from Huddersfield town centre. He remembered a pub called The Albion which Alex had mentioned as his local and that was the destination he gave the cabbie. He'd find his own way from the pub. Circumspection was the name of the game. He stood on the threshold of The Albion, pretending to sort out his change after paying his fare, while the taxi reversed and disappeared. He had no intention of actually going inside the pub. Strangers in suburban hostelries were eyeballed to a great degree. It was as though you were an alien from the planet Zog, thought Laurence, and enough people had seen him today already.

He waited a while on the pavement and then caught sight of a young woman with a push chair. He enquired of her the whereabouts of Oak Tree Grove. With flailing arms and an almost impenetrable accent she sent him in the right direction.

On reaching Oak Tree Grove, a quiet street of newly built townhouses, he was relieved to see that there were no police cars and vans with flashing lights pulled up outside number eleven.

He was still in time.

After ringing the bell and receiving no response, he tried the door. To his surprise and delight it was unlocked. He entered. The hall, like Alex, was smart and tidy. There was no clutter. Few signs of habitation, in fact. He found Alex in the sitting room, or lounge, as he was sure the estate agent's brochure would deem it. His friend was sprawled unconscious on the sofa like a dead body in a western movie, an empty whisky bottle by his side. But Laurence could see that he wasn't a dead body. He was just drunk. Alex's chest rose and fell in a gentle regular motion, the alcohol having taken the poor sod away from the real world and its trauma for a short time, but eventually he would wake up. The pain would be still there, along with a throbbing headache.

That's if he did wake up. Was allowed to wake up.

Laurence sat in the chair opposite him and gazed for quite a while at his old friend. That word 'friend' flittered into his mind but it seemed odd. It was a strange way to consider Alex really. Was he a friend? They certainly went back some years and had shared a number of exhilarating moments together. They were Brothers in Blood, but was he really a friend? And more to the point – if so, could he kill a friend?

Suddenly Laurence felt an overwhelming sense of sadness seep into him. He shivered with the sensation. It was the brutal realisation that this was the end. Or at least, to be more precise, the start of the end: an irrevocable step that heralded the grand finale. He had known it would be, had accepted that fact, had come to terms with it – or so he thought. But now ... now the moment had come to take the first step he felt close to tears. Not for the death of this 'friend' but for the death of a dream – a dream that had been conceived long ago and nurtured by him like a child. In the end, it was all as he had expected, allowed for, planned for even, but, of course, theory and strategy make no allowances for emotions.

He rose slowly and wandered into the kitchen – neat again, sparkling, Spartan, smelling of lemons – and found the cutlery drawer. From this he extracted a large carving knife. Its stainless steel blade shone and flashed as it caught the light.

This will do, thought Laurence. This will do.

Russell had gone to the lavatory to be sick. After

catching the early evening news and seeing Alex's face on the screen – albeit as a vague sketch – he had begun to retch. Leaning over the bowl, he felt as if the whole of his insides were pouring out of him.

When he had finished, he sat back on the edge of the bath and wiped his mouth on a towel. 'My God,' he said to himself and then repeated the phrase several times like a mantra, as though it would make things better. Of course it didn't.

His stomach lurched again and he moved to the bowl once more where he deposited the rest of his lunch.

'Are you all right?' Sandra said when he came downstairs some time later. Patently he wasn't. He had caught his reflection in the bathroom mirror and thought he looked dreadful. His face was suddenly haggard, dark circles ringed his watery eyes and his skin was pasty white with a fine sheen of perspiration.

'I've been sick. Something I ate, I reckon.'

'Nasty. Well I was aiming to make a chili for tea but...'

Russell shuddered at the thought. 'I think I'll skip on tea. Give my stomach a rest.'

'Probably wise. In that case I'll just rustle up an omelette for myself.'

'Yeah. OK. Listen, love, I think I'll go out for a walk. Get some fresh air.'

Sandra moved over to him and stroked his damp face. 'You do look washed out. Perhaps you ought to go to bed.'

'I just ... I just need to get some air.' The close proximity of his pregnant wife and her concern for his health brought the panic welling up inside him again. He was desperate to be on his own. He had to have time to think, focus on the disaster that was about to overwhelm him. He hadn't the strength to play normal just now. With undignified haste, he grabbed his jacket and bolted from the house.

He walked aimlessly, not noticing where he was going, the world a soft blur before him while his mind tumbled with awful thoughts. He knew that if he had managed to recognise Alex from the drawing on the television, dozens of others would. Perhaps Alex had made a run for it. If he had, that was only delaying the inevitable. It was possible he was already in the hands of the police. At this thought, his stomach reverberated violently again, but it was too empty for him to be sick this time. Instead he felt a strong, salty bile surge upwards into his mouth.

How long had he got? How long would it be before the police came knocking on his door? How long before they discovered his dark history? He suddenly remembered the journal, the one in which he'd recorded those early days in Huddersfield with Laurence. He needed to destroy that, without a doubt. It was in the garage.

*The early days in Huddersfield with Laurence.*

His own phrase came back to him. If only Laurence were here now, he thought, to comfort him or joke him out of his dark malaise. He would have ideas of how they could get out of this mess.

If only he could talk to Laurence, but he knew that was impossible.

224

Suddenly he realised that he was crying. This awareness of the tears trickling down his face seemed to upset him even further and he gave a gasp of agony and his shoulders shook with emotion. He turned down a quiet side street to avoid attracting attention and while not really wanting to master his feelings, he did try to pull himself together.

He stepped into a telephone box and dragged his handkerchief from his trouser pocket and mopped his face. A bleary-eyed, blotchy featured face that stared back at him from the small rectangular cracked mirror in front of him.

It was, he thought, the face of a sad and doomed killer.

## THIRTY

Paul Snow sat quietly staring into space. His mind was a blank. He had deliberately made it a blank. He didn't want any thoughts to bother him in any way. He was seated at his desk in the growing gloom, like a thin Buddha, the only sign of movement was the revolving of his fountain pen between the fingers of both hands. It was a signature nervous tic developed from those early days when he had tried to give up smoking and he had needed something to occupy his hands.

Armitage had been gone for nearly an hour and yet Snow was not ready to let the real world and hurtful thoughts seep back into to his consciousness and so he remained still and silent, turning the pen over and over between his fingers, contemplating nothing.

Raised voices in the room beyond his office broke his trance. Reluctantly, he dragged himself back into the present. With a deep sigh, he hauled his slim frame from his chair and wandered into the incident room. There were four officers there, including Bob Fellows who gave him a friendly wave.

'I think we may have struck oil, guv,' he said cheerily.

'Yes, sir. We've had quite a few responses to the TV appeal,' chirped in WPC Sally Morgan, a tall, plump but sexy woman heading towards her forties. 'Some weirdos as usual, but one name keeps cropping up. An Alex Marshall. And I've just got an address for him. It's local.'

Snow took the printed sheet from Sally and studied it. 'Good,' he said at length, but his voice registered no emotion 'Let's you and I take a ride out there, Bob, and take a shufty before we send the posse in.'

'Could be dangerous on your own, sir,' said Sally.

'What d'you think, Bob?'

Bob Fellows allowed himself a grin. 'You know me sir: I'm always in favour of the softly, softly approach.'

'Me too. Right, let's go.'

They found Alex Marshall in the front room of his tidy townhouse. He was lying on the sofa with his throat cut. Blood had seeped from the wound on to the cushion and down on to the cream carpet where it looked like a rather nasty red wine stain. An empty whisky bottle lay a few feet away from the body. There was no sign of the weapon.

'Well, this is a turn up for the book,' said Bob Fellows, bending over the body and peering at the savage wound.

Snow peered closely at the dead face. 'Well, it looks like this is our man all right. He matches the drawing perfectly.'

Fellows nodded. 'No sign of a struggle.'

'Looks like he was slashed while under the influence.' Snow indicated the empty bottle and the packet of pills on the coffee table. 'Some kind of ritual killing perhaps? Victim puts himself in a dopey state and then his mate cuts his throat.'

Fellows grimaced. 'That's a bit far fetched isn't it, sir?'

'Yeah, maybe you're right. But there's a great deal that is far fetched about this affair. It seems to me that we're following an unpleasant chain of murders, each one linked to the next. I believe that Ronnie Fraser was killed in order to keep him quiet. He shouldn't have survived the attack at Matt Wilkinson's house and when he did he posed a threat...'

'...the threat of identification.'

'That's how I see it, yes.'

'And this guy?'

'Well there were two others involved in the Wilkinson killings. It could be that one of them is snuffing out anyone who could provide a link with him. He's just protecting his own back,

227

eliminating traces.'

'If that is the case, then there's going to be at least one other murder.'

Snow nodded grimly. The phrase 'watch this space' came to mind, but he kept it to himself.

'We'd better get the SOCOs in here and get this turned into a proper crime scene.'

'Not just yet, Bob. I'd like to do a little poking around myself first. I have some idea what I want to find.'

'Sir, you can't mess about in here before the forensic boys have had their turn.'

Snow took out a pair of plastic gloves from his jacket pocket and started pulling them on. 'Don't worry, I'll be neat and tidy, Sergeant. No one will know a thing. Besides, I don't intend to do anything in here. This isn't the room where this fellow's secrets are. They'll be upstairs. Come on and join me. You have your own gloves I know.'

Despite himself, Fellows grinned.

'You look in the spare bedroom. I'll tackle the master suite. There is so little space in these modern rabbit hutches, if there is anything of significance we'll soon root it out.'

Alex Marshall's bedroom was, like the rest of the house, tidy, pristine and minimalist. Snow rifled through the chest of drawers, all neatly set out with underwear, socks. T-shirts, jumpers, carefully folded shirts in separate compartments. The wardrobe was similarly organised. Mr Marshall was quite a precise person, thought Snow, as he dragged over a chair and clambered up on to it in order to examine the contents of the top shelf. Towards the back, covered up by a couple of wool scarves he found a rectangular tin box. He pulled it out and examined it. It was the sort used as a cash box. It was locked. He shook it. The contents rattled dully but Snow was certain it contained no coins. He tried without success to prise it open.

Dumping the box on the bed, he continued his search but failed to discover anything else which he considered significant. There were no diaries, letters or photograph albums. Maybe Fellows was having better luck.

But he wasn't. 'All I can tell you is that Marshall has a penchant for Monty Python – he has some of their records along with The Jam in there. In general the house is holding its secrets,' he said, as he wandered into the bedroom.

'Well, there's this.' Snow picked up the tin box. 'But it's locked. We need to find the key.'

'Keyring?'

Snow nodded. 'Let's check downstairs.'

A further search produced nothing.

'Where do you put your keys when you come home?' Snow asked Fellows as they stood in the tiny kitchen area.

Fellows crumpled his face. 'I just sling 'em on the hall table or put them in a jar on the kitchen window sill.'

'Well, we've looked in all those places.'

'I suppose sometimes I just slip them in my trouser pocket.'

Snow's eyes brightened. 'Right you are.'

Moving into the sitting room they stared at the bloodied corpse which lay frozen like an exhibit in a gruesome waxworks show, the glassy eyes wide

229

with surprise and the rubicund mouth agape. The poor sod probably knew little about his murder until the last few moments when he realised all was not well. He would be puzzled rather than anxious as darkness descended. He was probably too far gone to feel the pain, thought Snow. He supposed that was some kind of consolation. And then he reprimanded himself for thinking of this man as a 'poor sod'. He was a killer after all.

Snow knelt down by the corpse.

'You're not intending to ... er, well to interfere with the dead man, are you, sir?'

Snow was aware of the rather bizarre farcical element of the situation and also amused at Fellows' failure to find a word other than 'interfere'.

'I'm just going to get the man's keys out of his trouser pocket, Sergeant. Look away if you wish,' he said handing Fellows the metal box.

Snow studied the two pockets of his trousers. One seemed bulkier than the other. He felt waves of Fellows' disapproval as his hand reached inside the pocket. He knew that he should not be tampering with a murder victim in this fashion. He should wait for the SOCOS to complete their investigation and take the crumbs from their table but he'd never been one for the rules when his instinct told him that his way was better – that his way would lead to a result.

Within seconds he had the key ring in his hand. A little skull with a circle of wire through its nose containing several keys. A house key, a car key and several others, including a miniature key that Snow knew instinctively would fit the lock of the metal cash box.

He slipped the key from the ring and held it up in triumph for Fellows to see. His sergeant gave a wan smile.

'Now let's open the treasure chest and see what goodies are inside.' Snow took the box from Fellows and led him into the kitchen. Placing the box on the work surface, he slipped the small key into the lock. Snow felt a tingle of pleasure as it turned easily releasing the lid.

The box contained very little. There a few sheets of paper, a faded old letter, a brown manila envelope and one photograph. The photograph was of a bulky individual sitting astride a motorbike looking arrogant in a kind of moorland setting. The letter was on hotel headed notepaper – a place called The Sea Royal in Brighton – and dated eight years ago. The letter just had a date, time and location 'August 6th 1976, 1.00 p.m.', and a signature, simply 'L'.

He passed it to Fellows. 'A few things to check up on here and there's the handwriting, too.'

The other sheet was a series of dates going back to the beginning of the seventies, each one followed by a red tick. The most recent date was less than a week ago. The tingle came again. It was the date of the murders at Matt Wilkinson's house.

'This is all very interesting,' he murmured, more to himself than his companion. Then he turned his attention to the manila envelope. Gently, he tipped the contents out on to the work surface. There were a series of cuttings from various newspapers, some of them brown with age. He sorted them out into a neat pile and scrutinised a few for some moments.

'What are they?' asked Fellows.

'They are all reports of murders. Some of them going back ten years.' He read a few more of the cuttings before continuing. 'The murders took place all over the country. And they all seem to be without motive – or at least that's what the press are saying. Fascinating stuff. This gives us quite a lot of material to sort out and follow up. We should be able to find about these killings and whether the culprits were caught.' He shook his head in disbelief and held up the tin box as though it was exhibit A. 'What have we stumbled on here, Bob? It's a bit of a Pandora's Box. Either Mr Marshall had a fascination with murder or ... he was a keen participant.'

'What, for ten years?'

Snow raised his eyebrows. 'The idea is fantastic, gruesome, I agree, but you know as well as I do in our job we encounter this sort of thing – and worse – on a regular basis. This affair is far more complex than it first seemed and there is something sinister and uniquely nasty about it.'

He began scooping up the newspaper clippings and slipping them back into the envelope. 'Right, you'd better ring HQ and tell them we have a body here – another homicide.'

Fellows looked relieved. He wasn't a maverick like his boss and was not happy with them tampering with the murder scene before the appropriate officers had dealt with things in the approved manner.

'Right, sir.'

'But at the moment, not a word about this little

232

treasure chest.'

Sergeant Fellows opened his mouth but Snow silenced him with a glance.

'I need to give it my close attention. I don't want it leaving my sight to be dusted, tested and photographed etc., etc. It's timewasting. There's likely to be another murder and I'd like to prevent it. I am sure I can extract all the relevant juice out of this particular lemon overnight.' He held up the box and shook it. 'This could provide us with all the answers we need.'

## THIRTY-ONE

Laurence sat in the Boy and Barrel pub staring into space. He had returned to the hotel and once again ditched his disguise. He had been in two minds whether to try and make it back to London straight away but he was tired and he didn't want to raise suspicions at the hotel by leaving without spending the night there having paid for the accommodation. Besides, he was emotionally and physically drained. To avoid thought and pain, he shut down various systems in his own mechanism to reduce himself to an automaton. He almost succeeded – but not quite.

However, he couldn't bear sitting in his bedroom alone and so he wandered up the road from the hotel and landed in this shabby but busy pub filled with rowdy teenagers and a pulsating juke box. The noise, the crowd and the atmosphere thick with cigarette smoke were a comfort to him as he sat in the corner, a silent, immobile character amidst the whirl and cacophony. He was still coming to terms with what he had just done. It had been necessary, he reasoned, and inevitable but that didn't make it palatable. He was surprised how upset he felt. It wasn't as though he hadn't killed in cold blood before and, indeed, enjoyed the experience – but they had been strangers and losers. Not someone he knew. Not a 'friend'. More importantly – not a Brother. Although he had known from the beginning that he would do it one day, he had not been prepared for the emotional turmoil it would unleash. He had thought it would bring an extra frisson of delight to the killing. That had been the whole point. He thought of all those years of climbing up the mountain to achieve the greatest thrill on reaching the peak, but this had not been the case. Perhaps he wasn't as strong, as detached, as nihilistic as he imagined. Or was this just a blip, an irritating nervous reaction that would vanish with the morning light. It had to be – because it wasn't over yet.

And yet he could not shrug off this strange depressive mood which enveloped him. The weariness and futility of life, *his* life weighed him down with such heaviness that he could hardly move. Lifting the glass to his lips was a major effort. Perhaps he should top himself and have done with it all, the whole weary business of living.

He growled in anger at his own weakness and with an effort, he finished the pint of beer in three gulps, the liquid dribbling down either side of his mouth in the process. He knew that alcohol was not the answer, not the permanent answer anyway, but it was a very effective anaesthetic: it softened pain, remorse, guilt and thoughts of the future. Just what he needed. With leaden limbs he made his way to the bar and ordered another pint.

Oblivion tonight could not come quick enough.

It was hot black coffee that Paul Snow was consuming with relish as he sat at his dining room table, studying the papers from the tin box he'd found in Alex Marshall's house. He was able to correlate the press cuttings about a series of apparently unrelated unsolved murders with the dates and locations recorded on the separate sheet of paper. The last one on the list, before the Wilkinson killings, was less than two years ago, in Norwich. A small time drug dealer had been knifed to death and then his clothes set alight in the Tombland district of the city. Tombland. How ghoulishly appropriate, thought Snow wryly, taking another sip of coffee.

It seemed that all the victims were some kind of ne'er do well. There was a prostitute, a mugger, a couple of drug addicts, a few tramps and other similar low life characters. In many ways – easy targets.

Snow placed his hands around the mug, receiving a pleasurable warming sensation as his mind wandered. Was it some kind of game? A bizarre game? The murders were apparently motiveless and took place with such regularity. What had a prostitute in Glasgow got to do with a drug peddler in Doncaster? It would need a super Sherlock Holmes type genius to provide some kind of credible link between these victims. No, they had to be random killings which took place in different locations approximately a year apart. *Like an annual game.*

What kind of person would do something like that? Treat murder as a sport. Had Alex Marshall carried out these crimes himself or were others involved, sharing the game? His pals at Matt Wilkinson's house.

Ah, but that was the fly in the ointment: the Matt Wilkinson murders. Alex Marshall had been a victim of Wilkinson and his cronies and this crime had all the hallmarks of revenge. Here there *was* a definite motive. That spoilt the pattern – but nevertheless there was a pattern. If forensics were correct, there were three men at Matt Wilkinson's house the night of the killings: three murderers. One for each victim. One of these murderers was Mr Alex Marshall who had made sure that Ronnie Fraser, the surviving victim, did not recover sufficiently to talk to the police and help them to identify the perpetrators. Now Marshall had been eliminated also. No doubt for the same reason Ronnie Fraser was silenced. Presumably he was killed by the other two murderers, or one of them, in a desperate bid to protect their anonymity. Things had got messy and they had grown desperate. That was good. People make mistakes when they are desperate.

Snow rubbed his forehead in a vain attempt to banish the headache, which was developing rapidly. He believed that his ideas held water and

236

fitted the facts but they were built on a great deal of surmise and naked guesswork. While the scenario was neat and feasible, he could be wrong. His theory implied that he was dealing with madmen. Unhinged bastards at least. Murder, however unacceptable, was to some extent understandable if the crime brought about some tangible benefit to the killer, but to end someone's life for no reason was madness. What prompted them to go out and kill without any apparent motive? Just for kicks? For a laugh? Just to prove that they could? Only madmen would maintain such a grisly routine over a long period of time. Oh yes, if this were the case, these chaps are candidates for Broadmoor, pals for Hindley and Brady, thought Snow.

However, even if he was right in his assumption that there was a strange homicidal vigilante group on the loose – three men who kill someone they don't know every year in a different location – he still didn't have sufficient evidence or information to guide his future actions. He was no nearer identifying the remaining murderers.

Not yet anyway.

He looked again at the brief note which was signed by the single letter 'L'.

The date and location mentioned – The Sea Royal Hotel, Brighton, August 6th 1976 – coincided with the killing of some alkie derelict on the beach. The letter 'L' wasn't going to get him very far. But he could try. He knew from experience that successful policing often depended on the little things.

Then he remembered something else he

needed Fellows to check up on in the morning and made a mental note of it.

He sat back, sighed and rubbed his temples again. He realised how tired and stressed he was. This case was a devil and... For a split second Michael Armitage's face flashed into his mind and a wave of depression crashed over him. What on earth was he going to do about him? The bastard was not going to be satisfied with one payment was he? He would have to drip feed him on a regular basis. Snow knew he couldn't allow that to happen. But what was the alternative?

That night as Laurence crept between the nylon sheets in his hotel bed, he had decided what his next move was going to be. He accepted that he had reached the last act of the drama and there was no point in prolonging it. It was time to bring down the bloody curtain at last. With this thought, he slipped into a gentle untroubled sleep.

## THIRTY-TWO

Laurence sat in his rented Cortina parked across the street from the school gates. Once more he was in his countryman disguise. He was relaxed and patient, smoking a series of his favourite small cigars. Shortly after 3.45, the kids began pouring out of the building, shouting, laughing, pushing, pulling, and jumping, all celebrating the release from their scholastic confinement.

It was a mild October afternoon, although the sky had remained implacably grey, hinting at the gloom of the winter months to come. It suited Laurence's mood. He didn't like sunshine anyway.

With the aid of a map, he had spent the early part of the afternoon seeking the ideal location for his purposes. He had been successful.

He watched the flood of children reduce to a trickle and then members of staff began to emerge from the building heading in a weary fashion for the car park, clutching bulging bags and briefcases. There was no jollity or exuberance with them, just grey, tired faces and shoulders rounded by invisible burdens. Laurence waited a further ten minutes before leaving his vehicle and crossing the road towards the school.

Once inside the building, he put his head through the hatch of the reception desk. Beyond was a cramped and untidy office inhabited by two chunky middle-aged women with crisp perms, woollen cardigans and fancy glasses. They could have been twins. They were self-absorbed in their own tasks and took no notice of Laurence.

'I'm looking for Mr Blake's classroom,' he said cheerily, realising that he would have to make the first salvo if he wanted to elicit any response from these cardiganned worker ants.

One of the women looked up from the pile of papers she was sorting through. She appeared flustered and annoyed at being interrupted. She threw Laurence a suspicious glance.

'I'm here to see him about my son,' he said.

'Down the corridor to your left, go right to the bottom, turn left again. It's 13G,' the woman announced in peremptory and charmless fashion before returning to her chores.

'Much obliged,' returned Laurence with as much sarcasm as he could inject into the phrase.

The school was virtually deserted as Laurence made his way as directed. A couple of spindly youths in gym kit hurried by him and an ancient lady in a blue smock was sweeping up the day's debris, a cigarette dangling from her lower lip. She didn't give him a moment's glance as he strolled past.

He knew that it was Russell's habit to stay behind after school finished for a good hour in his class marking books so, as he'd told him many times, that he didn't have to 'take too many of the buggers home'. On reaching Room 13G, he peered through the glass panel in the door. To his dismay he saw that the room was empty.

Laurence swore softly under his breath. He felt that his old friend had let him down deliberately. His absence was some kind of treachery. Russell should be here involved in his allotted task. Indeed there was a pile of exercise books on the teacher's desk. One of them was open and a red biro was resting on the page. It was, thought Laurence, like an academic Marie Celeste. He opened the door and entered. It was then that he observed another door at the far end of the room. It was slightly ajar. In the area beyond the door he could see shelves of textbooks. Obviously, it was some kind of stockroom. As he approached it, he sensed movement inside. Then there was a gentle cough and a sigh and a distracted looking Russell appeared in the doorway. Laurence could see at once that he was tense and ill. His face was drawn and pale while dark shadows gave him the panda look of the serial insomniac.

Catching sight of someone in his classroom, Russell, dropped the pile of books he was carrying and his mouth opened in shock. 'Christ,' he said, staggering backwards. 'You gave me a surprise.'

It was clear to Laurence that as yet his friend had not recognised him.

'Are you wanting to see me? I'm Mr Blake, second in the English department.'

'Oh yes, I'm wanting to see you,' replied Laurence in his own voice.

Russell blinked and came closer, peering at his visitor. 'Laurence?' he said hesitantly.

Laurence grinned. 'The very same, my good fellow,' he intoned in the voice he used as his old countryman.

For a moment Russell forgot the worry and depression that had dogged him all day and just grinned. He was delighted to see his old friend. He felt a lightening of the spirit and, rather like a young child who had been terrified by a nightmare and was comforted by his father, he experienced the heady feeling that now everything would be all right. Laurence would know what to do. Laurence would make everything better. Instinctively, he moved forward and hugged his old friend.

'Am I glad to see you,' he murmured.

'Hail fellow, well met,' replied Laurence, pulling away from the embrace.

'We're in a bit of a mess, aren't we?' said Russell, the clouds of depression gathering once more. 'This Alex business. What on earth possessed him...?'

Laurence gave a casual shrug. 'I'm sure he thought he was doing what was for the best ... for all of us.'

'The stupid bastard. You saw that picture. The one they paraded on the telly. He's probably in police custody already.'

Laurence shook his head. 'Oh, no he isn't. I can guarantee you of that.'

'What do you mean?' Fear gripped Russell's heart. There was something in Laurence's tone that gave him the answer already. There could be only one answer. 'What... You don't...'

Laurence gave him a wan smile. 'He had to be silenced didn't he?'

'Silenced.'

Laurence nodded. 'The link had to be severed and quickly. There was no time for soul searching.'

'What do you mean?'

'I think you know what I mean.'

'You ... killed him?' Russell could hardly believe that he had uttered these words.

'Yes.'

Russell felt his body turn to ice. He shook his head vigorously as though to dislodge this terrible notion. 'But ... he was our friend. Our Brother.'

'Our dangerous brother. He'd become too much of a threat to our safety I'm afraid.'

242

'My God.' Russell slumped down onto one of the desk chairs, his face drained of all colour.

'You knew from the start that we had to protect our anonymity whatever happens. With Alex identified as the killer of Ronnie Fraser, our liaison and past deeds were open to exposure. Coppers are clever these days – they can do much more than just put two and two together. It wouldn't take long before they were knocking on our doors.'

'That still could happen.'

'Absolutely. Which is why I've come to see you. Certain things need to be set in place in order to protect ourselves. To secure our safety. But I'm afraid that in order for us to survive ... we shall have to sever our relationship forever. With Alex's death we have reached the end of the road: the end of the Brotherhood.'

Russell couldn't think straight. He felt as though he was in some dark Monty Python sketch. Here he was in a school room, a teacher sitting at a pupil's desk talking to a man wearing a false moustache about the murder of a friend and the end of a sixteen year friendship. It was bizarre and surreal.

'Look, we can't talk here, it's too public,' said Laurence in an attempt to rally his friend. 'I've a car outside. Let's go for a run to a private spot I've found where I can outline my plan and we can say our final goodbyes properly.' Laurence reached over and took hold of Russell's sleeve and gently hauled him to his feet. He was too dazed to resist.

The car pulled off the road and veered down a

rough wooded track for a few hundred yards before the foliage began scraping against the side of the car. And then Laurence brought it to a halt.

'Where are we?' asked Russell, still feeling somewhat disorientated. He hadn't really come terms with the fact that Laurence had murdered their friend. Things didn't seem real to him any more.

'Just a country spot. Let's go for a walk.' He was out of the car before Russell could respond. Slowly, he hauled himself from his seat and then made an effort to catch up with Laurence who was already several yards away.

'Why are we here?'

'I want to explain my plan to you in detail. It's a little complicated but I reckon it will leave us completely in the clear.' He paused and smiled. 'And it's rather a pleasant place to say goodbye and dissolve the Brotherhood forever,' murmured Laurence, snatching up a twig and beating a crop of nettles with it. 'You know how sentimental I am. Further down here we come across a large pond. Very gothic, fairy tale-like. Appropriate.'

'Appropriate?'

'Yes. We've been living an enchanted gothic fairy tale life haven't we? Ever since we clubbed old Mother Black's dog to death. All those years ago. Remember – when you and I were sweet seventeen. I say all those years ago but really it was only yesterday. It has all happened in a trice, the winking of a malevolent eye. During that time we entertained ourselves, we fought off the morphine of boredom by killing other creatures, other

244

pointless souls. We saved them from the slings and arrows that we still endure. We were doing them a favour. But now, sadly, it has to end.'

'I see that. And it makes me sad, too. Sad that I shall not see you again. I love you, you see. Not in queer way. That would be trivial. I love you as a kindred spirit. As a real brother. You've been a rock for me. I've never been strong. I needed someone like you in my life. You gave it shape and purpose.'

'Touching sentiments, old boy. I will miss you, too. My dear dependable Russ. But all good things must come to an end.' Laurence bent down and picked up a small stone. He threw it high into the air and watched it as it curved and fell with a gentle plop in into the scummed surface of the pond.

'You said that there were things we should do...' said Russell quietly, moving to the edge of the pond and staring at the dark waters as though they would provide an answer to his worries.

'Indeed. Even with Alex no longer with us there are still tentative links between us. Who knows what clues we've left over the years, casual careless overheard comments, appearances together that could eventually expose our relationship ... and the rest.'

For a moment Russell remembered the journal. Bugger, he'd forgotten about it. He must – *must* destroy it when he got home. Guilt pierced his heart. He had been stupid to keep the thing – to write it in the first place. He turned his back on Laurence so his friend wouldn't see his pained expression.

'I don't see how there is anything that we can do about that now,' he said awkwardly.

'*Nil desperandum, mon ami,*' said Laurence as bent down and picked up another stone. A much larger one this time. 'There's always a solution. A way out. Trust your Uncle Laurence,' he added and then as a thin smile touched his lips, he brought the stone down on the back of Russell's head with as much force as he could.

Russell gave out a sharp cry of pain and eyes wide with shock sank to his knees. Laurence struck him again. And again. And again.

And again.

Russell was now slumped down by the water's edge, his dead eyes staring balefully at the reeds rustling in the early evening breeze. Laurence knelt down by him and raising the stone brought it down once more on to what remained of Russell's skull. The back of his head was now the colour and consistency of raspberry jam.

Just like Old Mother Black's terrier. There was a fitting unity to the act. The Great Game had come full circle.

'Goodbye,' he crowed, throwing his head back to the shifting branches above him. 'Goodbye, my old friend.' There were tears in his eyes.

Laurence remained motionless for some moments before he dragged the body into the shallows and then launched it out into the pool. He watched as the corpse floated away from the shore for a few seconds and then sank slowly beneath the sooty surface.

'You see, Russell, old friend, this was how it was meant to be. This is how I planned it, all those years ago. This is why I took you under my wing. To nurture you as my final victim. I knew one day, my dear Russell, that I would end your life. That was part of the game. The cunning, ruthless game. My game. It was no fun otherwise. I created the Brotherhood and now I have destroyed it. Good night sweet prince, blah, blah fucking blah.'

With an angry gesture he scooped up a handful of pebbles and flung them into the pond.

## THIRTY-THREE

That same morning, Paul Snow overslept – a rare occurrence for him. It was, he thought, a sub-conscious response to the events of the previous day. He had no desire to wake up to the realis-ation that he was a victim of blackmail. As he downed an extra strong coffee while hurriedly getting dressed, he determined that he should shove this particular problem to the back of his mind. While he was sensible enough to accept that it wouldn't go away of its own accord, he knew that there was nothing practical he could do about it at present and there were other press-ing concerns he had to deal with.

Despite his desperate efforts to catch up the time by driving like a mad thing on his journey to police HQ, he arrived after most of his team were already at their posts. Somewhat sheepishly he made his way to his office, asking Bob Fellows to join him. As he did so, he caught sight of Michael Armitage grinning maliciously in his direction. The lips may have given the impression of joviality, but the eyes registered a sneering malevolence. It was a clear message that the mischief was far from over. It only confirmed what Snow already suspected: from now on Armitage would loom like a dark spider at the corner of his life. Something must be done.

'Bastard,' murmured Snow under his breath as he ushered in his sergeant and closed the door behind him.

'What was that, Sir?' said Fellows.

Snow shook his head distractedly. 'Nothing, nothing. Ignore me. I'm a little disorientated this morning.'

Fellows thought it best to say nothing in response.

'Right,' said Snow, sitting behind his desk, 'I've a few tasks for you to attend to. First of all pass this box on to forensics. I've got what I can out of it. Let's see if they can do any better.' He handed over the tin box that he'd brought with him from home, carefully wrapped in anonymous brown paper.

'And then I want you to follow up a couple of frail leads.'

'Frail leads are my speciality,' said Fellows, with irony.

Snow ignored the levity. 'Get on to the Brighton police. I'd like them to check if there was a guest staying at the Brighton Sea Hotel on 6 August 1976 with a name, probably a first name that begins with L. See if they can come up with the info.'

Fellows groaned. 'That is a mighty frail one, if

you don't mind me saying so, sir. That was eight years ago.'

'I know, I know. But when you have little to play with, you play with the little you've got.'

'Where d'you get that piece of crap wisdom from, sir?'

'Out of a cracker, I shouldn't wonder. Just do it, eh?'

'Anything else?'

'Get on to BT. See if they can give us the details of any incoming or outgoing calls that Alex Marshall received on the day he died.'

'Phone numbers?'

'If possible.'

'That's a big stretch, sir. You know that could take for ever unless it's a London exchange. The technology's a bit basic up in this neck of the woods.'

'I know it is but that doesn't mean we don't try.'

'OK.' His response was without much enthusiasm, but Fellows was used to Snow's wild goose chases and he had to admit that on rare occasions they did actually manage to corner a wild goose.

'In the meantime, I think I'll take myself out to Marshall's house again. Another visit might very well reveal a little more.'

'You going on your own, sir?'

'I think it would be best.'

There is something about a house in which a murder has taken place that announces itself to the sensitive. Or at least that's what Snow thought. As he let himself inside Alex Marshall's neat little townhouse, he could still smell the blood and the faint aroma of dead body. There was a special kind of silence, too, which was strange and unique. He was tempted to make a noise to break that suffocating blanket of quiet, but something prevented him. It would be like shouting in church, he thought.

Slowly he moved into the sitting room. Alex Marshall's corpse was gone now, of course, but his dried blood remained spattered in a grotesque pattern on the sofa and light coloured carpet. He stood by the spot where the body had been and let his eyes scan the room. Could there be anything here that would provide some clue, some illumination on the case? The SOCOs had already scrutinised the whole house so there would be nothing obvious and indeed, probably nothing at all. Still he had to try.

Room by room he explored and examined. Snow was convinced that Marshall's murderer was known to him. It may be that he had visited the house before. They certainly had been in touch with each other. Somewhere there must be an address or telephone number... Unless, of course, they had just been memorised for safety reasons. If the only repository was a dead man's brain then there was no way of retrieving them.

Snow spent an hour in the house. A fruitless hour. While he was in the bedroom, he glanced out of the window and saw a young man gazing up in fascination at the house. One of the local rubber neckers, he thought at first, come to take a gander at the 'murder house'. Even properties gain a kind of ghoulish celebrity when a horrible crime had taken place there. Snow didn't give him another thought until he returned to the living room some five minutes later and observed that the man was still there, sitting on the garden wall, staring at the house. He went to the door and as he appeared on the threshold, the young man stood up, turned abruptly on his heel and began to move away.

'Just a minute, please,' Snow called out to him. 'Just wait a minute.'

The man hesitated, half turning to look at Snow who was advancing on him quite quickly.

'I'm a police officer,' he said, extracting his warrant card and flashing before the youth. 'I'd just like to have a word.'

The man's face paled. He looked nervous and tense, his eyes twitching as though he was about to do a runner.

'I just wanted to know why you were so interested in this house,' Snow said gently.

There was a pause, fear and uncertainty registering on the young man's face. He coughed awkwardly and then he spoke. 'I ... I used to live here.'

'Before the present owner?'

The man hesitated again for a moment before replying. 'No... No, I used to share with Alex.'

'I see.' Bonus time, thought Snow. 'When was this?'

'Up until to a few months ago.'

'Why did you leave?'

He shifted awkwardly, unsure how to phrase his answer. 'We had a falling out. It just wasn't working.'

'What wasn't working? The relationship?'

The man's eyes narrowed. 'You could say that.'

'Look, I need to talk to you. I'm investigating Alex's murder and I'm sure you can help me.'

'How? I haven't seen him for a couple of months.'

'You can tell me about him. It'll be an informal chat. Nothing to get worried about. Nothing official.'

It was a lie. Snow knew that if this fellow came up with the slightest fragment of information that could help the case he would have to log it and the man would be called in to make a formal statement. 'How about coming inside and having a brief chat?'

The man shook his head vigorously. 'No. No. You'll not get me in there. It's filled with too many memories for me. There's a café a couple of streets away. We could go there.'

'Right you are.'

By the time they had driven to Sue's Café, Snow had established that the man's name was John and had deduced that he and Alex had been lovers. In the car he had begun to ask Snow how his friend had died, but the question had hardly left his lips before he added, 'No, don't tell me, I really don't want to know. It's bad enough that poor Alex is dead without being told the gory details. I will have nightmares enough. We didn't part on the best of terms but he was a special person in my life and I have good memories of him. I don't want them blighted more than they are.'

Sue's Café was a modest little affair with affectations above its calling for a small establishment in the suburbs. There were a group of round tables with white cloths and a little vase of flowers on each one. When Snow and John entered there were just two other customers, an elderly couple having tea and cakes.

'Well, the most obvious question,' said Snow once they were seated and had acquired a pot of Earl Grey for two, 'is can you think why anyone should want to kill Alex?'

John shook his head. 'No. It's all a mystery to me.' He turned away and gave a little cough. Snow could tell that he was upset. He would have to treat this fellow very gently if he were to elicit anything from him that would be of use.

'Tell me why you left.'

'It was rather strange in a way. We always bickered a bit but it got much worse after that night.'

'That night?'

John took a deep breath before responding. 'We used to go to the Starlight Club most Saturdays and one night we had a bit of a tiff and I left early. Alex didn't get back until the next morning. It was daylight when he walked in. He was in a right state. I think he had been beaten up or something. His clothes were a mess and he looked like he'd been crying. He was quite strange and emotional but he wouldn't talk about what had happened. He just clammed up. From then on he changed. His personality, I mean. He behaved oddly with me and he ... he didn't like to be touched or anything. It was as though whatever happened that night had taken part of him away.

Whatever went on it seemed to haunt him. I tried to prise it out of him several times ... but nothing. Suddenly it was like living with a stranger. As a result we just drifted apart. I realised it was time for me to move on – and so I did. It was a pity because he was a nice bloke and I was very fond of him. And now he's dead.'

'Does the name Matt Wilkinson mean anything to you?'

John didn't need to think about this one. He shook his head. The response was so immediate and easy that Snow knew that he was telling the truth.

'What about Alex's other friends? I believe there were two other men that he was friendly with.'

'To be honest, Alex was a bit of a loner. He had no family and apart from me, I don't think there was anyone else close in his life ... except perhaps the midnight caller.'

Snow leaned forward with interest. 'And who was he?'

'I don't know. I used to refer to him as the midnight caller – I assume it was a him – because he would ring late at night. The calls would be brief and Alex made sure they were taken in private. At first I used to joke about them, saying that he'd found another boyfriend. He denied it, but he wouldn't tell me who was on the other end of the line. I accepted this. We all have private parts of our lives that we want to keep to ourselves. Anyway, I eventually lost interest, especially towards the end. But there was a time when I was determined to ring the chap up and ask him who he was.'

'And how could you do that?' said Snow, hardly containing his excitement.

For the first time since they'd met, John smiled. ''Cause I managed to get the number, didn't I?'

'Tell me more.'

'Alex always used to doodle on a note pad when he was on the phone. Very late one night – well, it was more like early morning – he had one of these calls. When he'd finished he put the phone down and went to the small bedroom for a few minutes before coming back to the phone and I could hear him dialling back.'

'Did you hear what he was saying?'

'No. He always spoke in whispers. Anyway, later on that night, I got up for a pee and then I went downstairs to get a glass of water because my throat was very dry. Too much red wine at dinner no doubt. Out of curiosity, I looked at the note pad and I saw that as well as a few abstract squiggles, there was a phone number there. My friend had been very careless. He'd been on the red wine, too. So I made a note of the number but left the original in place. And sure enough by the time I came down in the morning that page of the notebook had gone.'

'What did you do about the number?'

John shrugged. 'Nothing.'

'Weren't you tempted to ring it?'

'I suppose I was to begin with but then I reckoned if Alex was so desperate to keep this a secret, then let him. By this time his behaviour in general was beginning to exasperate me. I knew that a parting of the ways was on the cards and ringing up a mysterious person was not going to change things.'

'Did you think it was another lover?'

'Not really, I think there would have been other signs if that was the case. It's funny I suppose that once I'd got hold the number all my curiosity ceased. I knew that I could ring if I wanted to – but I didn't want to.' He gave a gentle shrug.

'Do you still have the number?'

John paused for a moment and gazed at Snow directly in the eyes. 'Actually, I do. Initially I put it in my wallet inside my driving licence and I never bothered to take it out again.'

'I think you'd better let me have that number now. It could be vital to our enquiries.'

## THIRTY-FOUR

Laurence felt that his journey back to London was spent in some strange state of suspended emotion. He functioned fairly efficiently on a practical level – buying his train ticket, finding a seat, ordering food from the buffet bar – but he felt nothing. It was as though his mind had gone into hibernation.

Immediately following the death of Russell, he had undergone a ferocious rush of conflicting feelings from regret to elation. Regret that after all this time the Great Game was finally over; and elation for the same reason. There was little room for sadness; it was an emotion that he never fully comprehended. All his life he hadn't got as close to anyone as he had done with Russell, but this had been a deliberate decision, practical, planned and engineered. There had been nothing sentimental about it. It was, to his intents and purposes, an artificial pairing. He didn't do intimate. He knew how that could very easily fuck you up. Even at the relaxed moments in his friendship with Russell there had been a controlling Machiavellian edge that always took precedence in his dealings with him. He never lost sight of the grand plan. However, Laurence did accept that in being closely associated with someone over a period of years, however calculated the reason, one couldn't help developing a liking and a fondness for that individual. He'd read of how kidnap victims had grown to care for their captors. He supposed that it was a little bit like that with him and Russell.

However, he had slept soundly that night in a cheap B & B in Durham and by the time he had boarded the train for his journey south, he had contained any disturbing thoughts and feelings and was self-immunised against deep contemplations and emotion. He knew that in time and certainly in drink he would return to the events of the last few days when he had killed his two comrades of many years in cold blood, but for now, enough was enough.

When he arrived in London and strode out of Kings Cross Station into the autumn sunshine, he felt happy and content. All shadows had been banished. There were important things to consider: the future. How was he going to proceed with his life from now on and when would the next killing take place?

On reaching his little flat in Chiswick, he could hear his phone trilling as he made his way up the stairs. Flinging open the door, he dropped his bags and snatched up the receiver as it was making its dying call,

'Hello,' he said abruptly and rather breathlessly.

'My God, at last,' said an urbane, affected voice at the other end. 'The wanderer returns. Where the hell have you been?'

Laurence recognised the caller immediately. It was his agent, Gavin Swan.

'Hello Gavin. And how are you?' replied Laurence smoothly with a smile. It was good to hear a friendly voice from the real world again.

'I've been calling you for two bloody days, you terrible man.'

'Well, I'm here now. What can I do for you?'

'It's more a case of what I've done for you.'

'Ah, work. What shitty part in what crumbling theatre have you got for me now?'

'The gratitude of the fellow! Oh, ye of little faith. I've got you a telly, darling.'

Now Laurence was really interested. 'Tell me more.'

'It's in a soap, but it's a decent part. Not a regular character but guaranteed five episodes – maybe more. You play a dodgy estate agent who shows this girl around a house and tries to have it off with her.'

'Typecasting then?'

Gavin chuckled.

'What's the soap?'

'It's *Emmerdale Farm*. They shoot it up in York-shire. It'll mean popping up to Leeds for a week or two...'

Laurence's heart sank. Bloody Yorkshire. He'd just come from bloody Yorkshire and he didn't want to see the place again in a long while.

'I'm not sure...'

'I beg your pardon?'

'I don't really want to traipse all the way up to the land of pork pies, mushy peas and whippets for a cough and a spit.'

'You ungrateful bastard! I can't believe what I'm hearing. It's not a cough and a spit. It's a nicely written part with potential and decent money. This is your big chance, Larry my boy. Make a good impression and who knows where it may lead. I warn you – to turn it down at your peril. I'm certainly not going work my arse off for you in future if you are going to be so fucking fickle...'

Gavin was really angry now and his hot words had their desired effect. Reluctantly Laurence squashed his reservations. Gavin was right. Accepting this part could take him down new and exciting roads. If only it wasn't up in Yorkshire.

'Sorry. I'm a little tired. Of course, I'll do the part.'

'I should bloody well hope so.' Gavin's anger had not yet fully subsided. 'There are some actors who'd give their eye teeth to get a part in a soap.'

'Yes, of course. Me, too. Thank you.'

'I'm glad to hear it. Read throughs begin at Yorkshire TV next Tuesday. Filming should start on Friday.'

'That's great,' said Laurence with as much

enthusiasm as he could muster.

'Good. I'll put the contract and other details in the post. OK.'

'Yeah. Thanks Gavin. This is good news. Really good news.'

'You'd better believe it. Telly is where the money is, darling. You don't want to end up playing in revivals of old Agatha Christie stinkers as the murderer do you?'

'No,' said Laurence with a grim smile.

'You look the bee's knees in that.' The shop assistant fluttered around him like a mother hen.

Michael Armitage had to agree. He did look like the bee's knees – whatever that really meant – in the leather jacket he had tried on. It was light tan, the colour of caramel, and had the fine, smooth, shiny texture of a baby's bottom, not like the tough low grade stuff you got on the coats in the market. This was *proper* leather. He gazed admiringly at himself in the shop mirror and beamed. The jacket, blouson in style, made him look even bulkier than he was already, but this pleased him. His kind of women liked a bloke with a bit of meat on them.

'It is expensive,' the assistant was saying, 'but one has to pay for quality. It is striking but sophisticated at the same time. It really suits you.'

My God, thought Armitage, he was working overtime on making a sale. It wasn't necessary. He was determined to have the jacket.

'How much is it?'

'Three hundred and fifty pounds,' came the answer. It was swift and casual to underline the insignificance of such an amount to the customers of this exclusive emporium.

Armitage smiled sweetly at the little man. 'I'll take it.'

'A wise choice, sir. How will you be paying?'

'Cash,' said Armitage, his smile broadening.


## THIRTY-FIVE

Jack Turner called to the dog in vain. It took no notice of him as it lolloped off into the undergrowth. It was all very well Margaret, his wife, doting on the black Labrador puppy, but he was the poor sod who had to take it out for walks and try to make the thing obey him. He pushed his way down the narrow woodland path in pursuit of the hound until he came out into a clearing, and there before him was a large pond, murky and muddy. The dog was on the water's edge gazing at it with great curiosity.

'You're not to go in there,' cried Turner racing towards the dog. Seeing his master advancing on him at speed and thinking this was part of the walkies game, the dog splashed into the water with enthusiasm and swam out towards the middle of the pond.

Turner groaned out loud in despair. How was he going to get the mutt to come back? He threw his head to the heavens in frustration but when he looked again he saw that the dog had found something in the water and was growling and snapping at it. Eventually, the dog grabbed something from just below the surface and dragged it up into the air. Jack Turner couldn't believe his eyes. It was the sleeve of a jacket but what chilled him to the bone was the sight of the livid white human hand dangling from the end.

Snow knew that there came a time in every investigation when things seem to fall into a torpor. After the initial flurry of activity and responses from the public, there was a dead period where everything hangs fire waiting for the big breakthrough. If it ever came.

They were just about to enter this period now with the Matt Wilkinson/Alex Marshall murder case. There had been a big response to Marshall's picture shown on the television, most of it genuine. Inevitably there had been the usual loonies who came up with wild stories and accusations ranging from the victim being an alien to him having set fire to their Ford Fiesta in a pub car park last Bank Holiday. However, they all needed checking out, wasting valuable police time and resources in the process. In this case, apart from identifying Marshall and his place of work, there was no new information received. His work colleagues had been interviewed but all they could say was that he was a quiet chap, possibly gay and kept himself to himself.

There had been no progress with tracing the calls to Alex's house and it was unlikely there would be. The technology was simply not in place. Meanwhile Sergeant Fellows was still waiting for the Brighton police to get back to him about the guest with the initial 'L' staying at the Sea Hotel in 1976. The only bright light in the gloom was the telephone number that the young chap John had passed on to Snow. Although he had been tempted to ring the number out of the blue, he knew that this would have been far too reckless. Such an action could easily tip off whoever was on the other end of the line that the police were interested in them and a speedy disappearing act would result. No, he needed an address. And so once more he had put in a request to BT for help. He handled the matter personally rather than delegating it to Bob Fellows or others. On this occasion BT had managed to come up with an address for the number.

'Would you mind telling me where we are going?' enquired Bob Fellows with a certain amount of irritation. He was used to his boss keeping his cards close to his chest but he usually gave him some sort of clue as to what he was about. Here they were haring up the A1 to God knows where – or precisely only Snow knew where.

Snow allowed himself a terse grin. 'We're headed for 12 Willows Walk, Gillesgate Moor, near Durham.'

'Oh, that's OK then,' he said drily. 'And why exactly are we going there and what do you hope to find?'

'Not quite sure. I think I'd better explain.'

'That would be useful, sir.'

Briefly, Snow told of his encounter with John and how he had secured the mysterious telephone number. 'It could be something and nothing. That's why for now I've not logged it.'

'I see, sir.' Fellows rolled his eyes. This was typical of Snow. Even if it turned out to be the phone number of the local Samaritans, he should have logged it. That was the procedure. That was the rule. Now here we were off on police business without an official reason. Snow loved to play things this way – his way. If only he didn't include me in his little intrigues, Fellows thought.

'But fingers crossed, sergeant, it could turn out to be the break we need.'

'Yes, sir.'

Snow laughed. 'I love your enthusiasm, Bob. Now if you'll drag that map book off the back seat and work out a route for us from the motorway to Gillesgate Moor.'

Willows Walk turned out to be one of a series of similarly named streets on a modern housing estate some five miles north of Durham itself. There was Oak Avenue, Larch Crescent, Chestnut Way etc. It was a fairly smart complex, most of the houses being detached, albeit situated very close to one another. However there wasn't a willow in sight or indeed a tree of any kind.

After a few wrong turns in the labyrinthine estate, Snow eventually pulled up outside number twelve. 'Right, Bob, let's see where this leads us.'

The door was opened by a pretty woman, aged around thirty with short blonde hair, intelligent blue eyes and haggard features. It was clear that she was pregnant. Snow held his identification card for her to see but before he could say a word, the woman grabbed his arm.

264

'Has there been some news. Have you found him?'

'No,' said Snow instinctively.

The spark of hope died in the woman's eyes and her shoulders slumped as though she had just been presented with a giant invisible burden. For a moment Snow thought she was going to faint, but then she rallied.

'May we come in?'

Without a word, the woman stood back and allowed the two men to pass by her into the hall.

'What is it, Sandra?' asked a woman who emerged from the sitting room, holding a mug of tea. She was around forty with a homely face and dressed in jeans and a woollen top.

Sandra shook her head. 'The police. They still haven't found Russell.'

Snow was not sure how to play this, but before he had time to think any further, Sandra introduced the other woman as 'my neighbour Joan'.

Snow smiled at Joan. 'If you don't mind, we'd like a word alone with Sandra. Perhaps you could make us both a cup of tea, eh? Milk, no sugar.'

Joan nodded and scuttled off to the kitchen without a word.

Sandra led them into a comfortable, well-ordered lounge. Snow surveyed the room professionally, building up ideas and evidence to try and understand what had been going on here. The furniture was modern, stylish and of a reasonable quality. The house belonged to a professional couple he guessed and there they were framed on the mantelpiece, caught in gaudy colour on their wedding day. The man – Russell he assumed – had

265

unfashionably long hair and peaky features. The grin that he wore was not his own, it was borrowed for the occasion. He certainly didn't look comfortable having his picture taken. The woman was a slightly younger looking Sandra.

'When did your husband disappear?' Snow asked.

Sandra frowned heavily in response. 'What on earth do you mean? You know all this. I've made a statement.'

'You've made a statement to the Northumberland police no doubt. We're from West Yorkshire.' Snow held up his ID again.

Sandra shook her head. 'I don't understand.'

'We're here for a different reason, a different investigation. Not the one about your missing husband – but it is possible that the two cases are linked.'

Sandra shook her head in some confusion and sank into an armchair.

'When did your husband disappear?'

'Two days ago. He didn't come home from school. He's ... he's a teacher.'

'Is this unusual?'

'Of course it's bloody unusual!'

'And you have no notion where he may have gone or what has happened to him?'

'Of course I don't.' Sandra was shouting now and her eyes had begun to moisten.

'I'm sorry to upset you, but I need to get the situation clear. Does your husband know someone called Alex Marshall?'

Sandra thought for a moment. 'Alex,' she said softly to herself and her mind went back to a few

266

days earlier, to that strange midnight phone call Russell made. Did she catch the name Alex? Was it her imagination? What on earth did it mean? Why was everything suddenly such a mess? Instinctively she stroked her bulging tummy and allowed her tears to fall.

Snow threw a glance at Fellows but said nothing. He knew that it was best to wait, to allow the woman to control her own emotions. Anything he said would not help matters.

At length, Sandra Blake pulled a handkerchief from the sleeve of her cardigan and staunched the tears. 'I'm not sure if he knew anyone called Alex or not. But if he did, I didn't know anything about him.'

'Did your husband have any friends in Huddersfield?'

Sandra seemed puzzled at this question. 'He might have,' she said slowly. 'Old friends, I suppose. From the past. He was from Huddersfield originally. He came up to Durham to the University and stayed. Look, what is this case you're investigating? How does it involve Russell?'

'A man was murdered in Huddersfield and he had your husband's telephone number. We know that on one occasion at least the victim rang this number here in the early hours of the morning.'

'You ... you think that my Russell is involved in this murder?'

'We'd just like to find out more about his relationship...'

'With this Alex?

Snow nodded. 'He could provide us with a vital clue.'

'Well, he can't can he, because he's missing and no one knows where the hell he is.' Her face flushed and the tears began again.

'What have the police done so far about finding him?'

Sandra shrugged and her features stiffened. 'Not much as far as I can see. They took a statement and a photograph which they were going to circulate. They said that as it's only just been over forty-eight hours, there's still time for him to walk in through the door. They said it wasn't unusual for men who are just on the brink of fatherhood to disappear for a few days without warning.'

Snow nodded. It did happen but it wasn't exactly a common occurrence.

'Did your husband have a desk, a workspace, somewhere he kept his correspondence?

Sandra hesitated. She didn't like the sound of this. 'Yes,' she said at length, 'he used a small office at the back of the house – where he did his school work – lesson preparation and stuff.'

'May we see it?'

Snow could tell that she was going to refuse. 'I know this may seem an imposition,' he added swiftly, his voice soft and reasonable, 'but it really may help in finding out what's happened to your husband. Clearly there is a mystery here and mysteries can only be solved by investigation.'

For some moments Sandra stared ahead of Snow, her eyes focused on nothing in particular. 'Very well,' she said after a few moments. 'It can't make things worse, can it?' She rose and led them into the hall just as Joan the neighbour came from the kitchen carrying two mugs.

'Your tea,' she said brightly.

'Thank you. Later perhaps,' said Snow as he and Fellows followed Sandra down the hall.

For a little cramped office, the room was reasonably tidy. It contained a desk, a filing cabinet, a book case and a small wardrobe. Papers were scattered across the desk and there was a pile of play copies – *Romeo and Juliet* – on the floor.

'Thank you, Mrs Blake. If you wouldn't mind leaving us alone for a while, we'll be quick and tidy. There will be no mess, I promise. Just give us fifteen minutes.'

Reluctantly she withdrew without a word.

Snapping on his latex gloves, Snow began examining the contents of the desk drawers while Fellows investigated the wardrobe.

'Here, sir, look at this,' he said after only a few moments. He held up a train ticket. 'A return to Huddersfield dated the day before the Wilkinson murders. It was in one of his jacket pockets.'

'Then we're on the right track. Good man. Keep looking.'

The filing cabinet was locked but Snow soon found the key in an empty vase on the window sill. Pulling out the drawers in turn they all seemed to be filled with school related material: test papers, lesson plans, exam schedules. One folder near the back contained Blake's own academic certificates: his O levels, A Levels, his BA degree and his Cert Ed. Slipped in with these were a few other items. There were a couple of play bills: one for the York Theatre Royal for an Alan Ayckbourn comedy and one for the Library Theatre in Manchester for a drama Snow had

269

never heard of before. He scrutinised these for a few moments, coming to the conclusion that the only connection between the two was an actor who appeared in both productions – an actor by the name of Laurence Dane. Laurence. Could he be the 'L' on the letter from Brighton? There was a kind of desperation in such a thought, but nevertheless it was possible. Snow made a mental note of the details before returning the flyers to the folder. There was one other loose item that claimed his attention: a faded photograph. It was of a burly youth astride a motorbike.

Snow had seen the snap before. There had been an identical one in the tin box he had found at Alex Marshall's house. The connection was sealed – surely? He allowed himself a brief grin of satisfaction before showing the photograph to Fellows. Without a word the two men exchanged knowing glances. Now, thought Snow, all they had to do was find this Russell Blake.

'Bloody hell!' Inspector Ray 'Dinosaur' Daniels gave a cry of dismay as his size elevens slipped in the mud and he ended up plonking one foot into the water. (He was known as 'Dinosaur' partly because he had the size and clumsiness of a prehistoric beast and partly because he seemed to have been in the force since the beginning of time.) 'Why can't they murder 'em somewhere where it's dry?' he moaned. None of the other officers offered a response.

Stepping back on to firmer ground and wiping his shoe on the grass, Daniels watched as the two officers in wet suits pulled the body onto the

270

banks of the murky pool. The bulk of it was covered with the slime and silt, but the head and face were comparatively clean.

'My God,' said Daniels, gazing at the back of the victim's skull. 'He certainly had his brains bashed in and not half. His killer was taking no chances for him to survive. I think we've got a nasty one here, Sergeant.'

His pale-faced companion nodded.

'No worries about the fellow's identity, sir,' cried one of the wet-suited officers. He held up a small black object. 'It's his wallet. Got all his info inside: credit card, NUT membership card. It seems he's a teacher. Lives at Willows Walk.'

'Name?'

'Russell Blake.'

## THIRTY-SIX

That evening as Paul Snow was attempting to unwind with a can of lager and some pap television, the doorbell rang. It had a soft tone, but whoever had his finger on the bell was holding it down, creating a long-winded irritating, muted cacophony.

With a frown of annoyance etched deep in his forehead and a grunted sigh, Snow dragged himself from his armchair and answered the front door. Michael Armitage was standing on the threshold. His stance was macho: legs apart, arms folded across his chest, a cocky smile nailed

271

to his lips, eyes glittering with malice. A parochial Rambo.

'Evenin', sir,' he said, the cocky smile spreading. 'Sorry to bother you at home, but I've got some business to discuss and I reckoned it were better done on your own patch, rather than at work. Can I come in?'

For the moment Snow was lost for words. He had a good idea what the 'business' was that Armitage wished to discuss but he had no notion how to respond. He had not expected this. Well, not yet anyway. Not so soon. Armitage it seemed was already moving matters into the fast lane.

Snow pulled the door back and stood aside to let his visitor inside and guided him into the sitting room.

Armitage saw Snow's can of lager by his chair and nodded. 'Wouldn't mind one of them myself. Got a spare?'

Still without speaking, Snow retrieved a cold can from the fridge in the kitchen and handed it to Armitage.

'Ta. The perfect host. Still you lot are good at the niceties, aren't you?' He softened his voice to an effeminate sibilance on the word 'niceties'.

'What can I do for you, Sergeant?' Snow said.

Armitage pulled the ring on the lager can as though it was a hand grenade and took a large gulp.

'Do you like the leather jacket? Pretty cool, eh? Cost a packet. Normally I wouldn't be able to afford such things ... but now...'

Snow found himself clenching his fists again with suppressed anger. He wanted to kill the man. To beat the sneering, arrogant corrupt bastard to death and then stamp on his face. That's what he wanted to do. It was as simple as that. It took all his self-control not to launch himself at Armitage and strangle the life out of him, to watch the light fade from those mocking eyes and that grin to twist into a grimace of pain. But instead, he just raised an eyebrow and waited for Armitage to continue.

'I reckon it's time that we came to a regular arrangement. The one off cash payment was good but now the money's spent, I find I'm in need of more.'

Snow continued to remain silent.

'I think you know what I'm saying.'

Armitage still received no response. His face darkened with annoyance. 'If you want me to keep stum about you being a pansy boy, you're gonna have to cough up on regular basis. Like an insurance policy.'

Snow was about to say, 'And if I refuse...?' but he was well aware that this would be a redundant query. He already knew the answer. Armitage would take great and malicious pleasure in demolishing his career.

The same feeling of despair that Snow had experienced the first time Armitage had issued his blackmail threats swept him once more. He was cornered, snared like a rat in a trap. There was nowhere for him to run, to hide, to escape. He had to meet his miserable fate head on.

'I think you know what I mean,' sneered Armitage.

'And I think that you'd better get to the point,'

Snow said.

After a sleepless night, Snow drove into the office early. He felt a leaden weight upon his soul and in truth he didn't know how he was going to get through the next few days, let alone the rest of his life. It wasn't just the financial damage that Armitage was imposing on him, but the fact that in a sense he was now the prisoner, the plaything and puppet of this foul and evil man. Apart from money, what else could this swine demand of him?

Once in his office and cradling a cup of the blackest coffee, he tried to shun thoughts of Armitage for the moment and force himself to concentrate on the case in hand. As it turned out, events aided him in this pursuit.

There was a tap at the door and Sally Morgan came in. 'A bit of news, sir. We've had a response from the Sea Hotel in Brighton at last.' She smiled and it was a warm, almost affectionate smile. In Snow's rather delicate and tortured state, it touched him, almost bringing a lump to his throat.

'Good,' he said and attempted to return the smile.

'Apparently there were three people staying at the hotel on that day with a letter L in either their first or last name.' She consulted a sheet of paper she held in her hand. 'A Lorna Hirst, a Laurence Dane and a Gladys Lightfoot.'

Snow made a note of the names. Of course, one leapt out at him: Laurence Dane. That was the name of the actor on the two play bills in Russell Blake's office.

'See if you can find out anything about Mr

Dane, Sally. See if he's got form. He's an actor and probably registered with Equity.'

'I'll get on to it.' She gave a mock salute.

'Thanks.'

'And there's more,' added Sally brightly. 'I've been able to identify that fellow in the photograph, the big chap on the motorbike. *He* certainly had form.'

'Go on,' said Snow.

'Darren Rhodes. Huddersfield chap from Sheepton. He did time for aggravated robbery. The old biddy he robbed died of a heart attack. And then he won the pools. He was a bit of a local celebrity at the time. This was back in the late sixties. He was involved in a mysterious motorbike accident in 1970. He lost a leg.'

'Why was it mysterious?'

'Well, he lost his memory for a while and when some of it came back he claimed he had been tricked into speeding and that his bike had been tampered with. I doubt if anyone believed him ... but you never know.'

'Where is he now?'

'Sorry, sir, he died of a drug overdose in 1978.'

'Dead, eh? Well, he's not going to be much help to us at the moment.'

'I know sir, but it's another piece of the jigsaw. The more pieces we get...'

Suddenly Snow found himself grinning. His emotions were off the radar this morning.

'Are you always this positive, Sally?'

'Well, in this job, you've got to be, otherwise you'll go under. Crikey, you know that better than me.'

Snow nodded. He certainly did.

'Are you all right, sir? You look a bit...' She struggled for the word, conscious she was speaking to a senior officer. She didn't want to use the word 'depressed' although that fitted her observations exactly, but the word had all sorts of clinical implications.

'...a bit down,' she said at last.

Snow gazed up at Sally's soft, sensitive features and smiled. He was not only touched by her concern but a little devil within him tempted him to tell her all his problems, to spill the beans about Armitage and wait to be comforted by her like a mother hen.

'I'm just my usual early morning grumpy self.'

'It's living alone that does it. No one to confide in. No one to share your problems with, things that are troubling you. It's good to get things off your chest now and then.'

Snow knew that Sally was not only referring to him; she too lived alone after a messy divorce some two years before. Nevertheless, he didn't want to travel any further down this road. Not because he did not like Sally or appreciate her unspoken offer, it was that his baggage was too sensitive to unpack with her – or anyone.

'We make life choices,' he said and immediately regretted it. Sally hadn't made her life choice. Her cheating husband had. He'd dumped her and run off with his fancy bit on the side leaving Sally to face life as a single woman once again. She'd had no choice in the matter.

For a moment Sally's smile faded but very quickly it came back. She nodded as though in agreement. 'Well, sir, any time you need to bend someone's ear...'

Before he could respond, she left the room.

'Handled that well,' he murmured to himself and sighed heavily.

The telephone on his desk rang shrilly, preventing any further negative thoughts from invading his mind. He snatched up the receiver, but before he was able to speak, a breathy voice at the other end said, 'Am I speaking to Detective Inspector Paul Snow?'

'Yes.'

'Good. This is Inspector Ray Daniels, Northumberland Police. I gather you've been doing a bit of plodding on my patch.'

'Just making some enquiries.'

The voice at the other end laughed. It was a deep-seated wheezy laugh. A heavy smoker, Snow thought.

'Don't get your knickers in a twist, Inspector. I'm not one of those fellows who gets upset if an officer from another force comes snooping around his manor. We're all in the same boat after all. We're all trawling for wrong 'uns.'

Colourful imagery.

'Yes.' Snow wondered where all this was going.

'I gather you were interested in a certain Russell Blake.'

'I still am.'

'Well, we've got him.'

The nape of Snow's neck tingled. 'Have you?'

'Well, to be more precise, we've got him on a slab. He's not up to answering questions, unfortunately.'

'Can you give me details?'

'Certainly. I can do more than that. If you'd like to pop back up here I can show you the body and fill you in on all that we've got.'

'That's very generous of you,' Snow said and he meant it.

'As I say ... same boat.'

'How did he die?'

'Head smashed in ... to a pulp actually and dumped in a pool.'

Snow grimaced. Another corpse to add to the growing list.

'I can be with you around lunchtime.'

'Good. We can down a pint or two together after viewing the exhibit,' said Daniels with another wheezy laugh.

Ray (Dinosaur) Daniels plonked down a glass of sparkling mineral water on the table in front of Paul Snow with a scowl of disdain. 'I thought you Yorkshire lads like to sup ale,' he said, lowering his considerable weight onto a bar stool.

'I have to drive back to Huddersfield. Don't want to be breathalysed on the way.'

'Hey lad, just show 'em your badge and they'll let you off.'

Paul had already sussed that Daniels was that kind of policeman, one who ignored the rules except for those he made up himself. He certainly was of the old school and should they ever bring 1956 back again, Detective Inspector Ray Daniels would feel at home. They had visited the morgue where the body of Russell Blake was still lodged after his autopsy which, as Daniels commented, 'had told us bugger all that we didn't know already'.

He had been beaten about the head with a stone – particles of which had been found in his hair – and had been dead when he hit the water. He was a teacher at a local secondary school – taught English – was married to Sandra and she was expecting their first child. He seemed, on the surface at least, a decent respectable sort of bloke. His wife had no idea who would want to kill him. That, as Ray Daniels explained, was about it.

It was interesting information but, like so much that Snow was learning in recent days, it did not really throw much light on the dark events he was trying to investigate. What exactly connected a school teacher from Durham with the murders in Huddersfield still eluded him. But he was certain there was a connection.

'So now, lad,' the large inspector intoned, leaning forward, after taking a large gulp of bitter, the froth leaving a faint creamy moustache on his upper lip, 'I want to hear your story. Why are you so interested in our dead school master?' He sat back and lit a cigarette.

'It's complicated and somewhat tenuous at the moment, but...'

'I can do tenuous and complicated,' grinned Daniels.

In simple and concise terms, Snow recounted the details of the killings at Matt Wilkinson's house and grim events that followed. By the time he had finished, Daniels had consumed his pint and was ready for another.

'Crikey,' he said, 'it'll take me a while to get my head around all that. I'm off for a Jimmy Riddle and to get another pint. D'you want another drink?'

Snow had hardly touched his water and shook his head. 'I'd better be making tracks soon. Get back to base.'

While Daniels was away, Snow went over the facts again in his mind, trying to edit out the insignificant details and concentrate on those elements that forged connections. Three men had been brutally murdered – three men who were in the habit of raping homosexuals. They were killed by three murderers, one of whom, Alex Marshall, had been brutalised by Wilkinson and his cohorts in the past. Therefore it was reasonable to assume that this was a revenge scenario. Well, Snow hoped it was reasonable. It appeared that two of the killers – and he was taking a leap in assuming that the school teacher Russell Blake was one of the trio – had been murdered themselves. And so the question was, who by? Was the culprit killer number three to protect his own identity or some unknown, a Mr X?

There was one interesting piece of information that Daniels had relayed to him: Blake had spent a great deal of his youth in Huddersfield, only moving away when he came to Durham University. It was during this period he could have got to know Alex Marshall. Perhaps the whole thing had its seeds back then – the time when Darren Rhodes had his nasty accident. They each had a photograph of the guy.

And then there was Laurence Dane, who had

stayed at the Sea Hotel, Brighton in 1976 and sent a message to Alex Marshall to meet up. Perhaps he was the one to track down.

'You look miles away,' said Daniels returning to his seat with a fresh pint of bitter.

'Just thinking.'

'Ah, thinking ... that gives you a headache.' Daniels gave a weary smile and lit another cigarette. 'It's a bit of a bugger, this case, but these bastards often have a way of sorting themselves out. We'll need to keep in touch, pass on any tidbits that can be of use.'

Snow nodded. 'Certainly.' He drained his glass. 'Now I think I'd better be on my way. Thanks for the help.'

Daniels raised his glass in reply. 'No problem.'


When Snow arrived back at his office, it was dark and most of the team had gone. There was just Sally and Bob Fellows in the incident room and he was shrugging on his coat ready to leave. Snow wandered to the little kitchen area to make himself a coffee.

'Where've you been, sir?' asked Fellows.

Snow told him. 'Thought I'd spare you the drive this time,' he added.

'Anything you want me to do tonight?'

Snow shook his head. 'No, you get off. I'll see you in the morning.'

Fellows didn't need telling twice. He was out of the office in a trice.

'You get off, too, Sally,' Snow said, putting the kettle on.

'Yes, I think I'm done for the day.'

'You and me both.' Suddenly he felt very weary and it wasn't simply a tiredness brought on by two long drives in one day; it was like a dark depressive languor that had suddenly settled on him.

'You all right, sir?'

Snow smiled. There she was mother-henning him again.

'Right as I'll ever be,' he replied with more gravitas than he had intended.

'You need a hot meal and a drink to perk you up, I reckon. What you having to eat tonight?'

Snow shrugged. He hadn't thought. Meals were not very high on his agenda at the moment. But the mention of food made him realise that he'd had nothing to eat since breakfast.

'Why not come back to my place. I've a home made steak and kidney pie in the fridge – enough for two. Washed down with a glass of red, it'll do you the world of good.'

The world of good. Oh, that's what he could do with.

He hesitated for a moment, sorely tempted and then slowly shook his head. 'Thanks, Sally but...' his voice trailed off.

'That's all right, sir,' she said quickly, somewhat embarrassed that she had made the offer to her boss in the first place. What was she thinking of? 'It was just a thought.'

'And it was a very nice thought, too. I appreciate it. Really. Thank you. Maybe another time.'

Grabbing her coat Sally headed for the door. 'Good night then, sir,' she said in a muted fashion before making a swift exit.

'Damn!' Snow slammed his fist against the wall. He felt both angry and guilty for turning down Sally's offer in such a dismissive fashion. Why the hell shouldn't he have gone to her place for a bite to eat? He could do with the company. Take his mind off things. Off Armitage. Of course he knew why. He was frightened that Sally might have motives behind the invitation. Might have some kind of romantic agenda. As soon as this thought slipped into his mind, he realised how ridiculous it was. She was a lonely woman, he was a lonely man and all she'd done was ask him to share a meal together. What an idiot. A clumsy idiot. And as if to prove his point he accidentally knocked over his coffee mug, the granules spilling over the work surface.

## THIRTY-SEVEN

'And this, of course, is the most important room in the property.'

'Oh, really.'

'Yes ... the bedroom.' The response was heavy with innuendo. He paused for a moment and then pushed the flimsy door open. 'I'm sure you'd like to take a look inside.'

The girl frowned slightly but entered nonetheless. He followed behind her, closing the door.

'You must test the bed,' he said, plonking himself down on it and pressing both hands on the mattress. 'Come and try it.'

'I'll take your word for it,' the girl said, a note of concern in her voice.

'I insist,' he said, reaching out and with a sudden movement, pulling her towards him.

She gave a little cry of surprise as she landed on the bed by his side. He just grinned. It was not a pleasant grin. He leaned over her and stroked her face. She gave a little whimper.

'OK. Cut. That's a take. Well done you two,' said Ted Torrance, the director. He gave a little chuckle. 'We can't get any steamier than that before the watershed. We don't want the old ladies gagging on their chocolate digestives.'

There was general muted laughter from the crew.

'We'll break for lunch now. Scene 14b at 2 p.m. please.'

'That's me done for the day then,' said Laurence who had wandered over to Torrance.

The director nodded. 'Good work, Laurence. You're a natural for television. You did very little in that scene but you were fully convincing as a sleazy bastard.'

Laurence smirked. 'Is that supposed to be a compliment?'

'Indeed. I reckon you're an asset to the show. I've already had a word with Piers, the producer, to suggest that they keep your character on a bit longer.'

'Well, cheers for that. I must admit I am rather enjoying myself.' He cast a glance at Sarah Cracknell, who was checking her make-up. 'Still, dragging darling Sarah under the covers has its plus points.'

284

'There'll be no under the covers on *Emmerdale,* I'm afraid. You'll just have to find your thrills elsewhere.'

'Not a problem,' said Laurence. 'Not a problem.'


'Call it a hunch, although it's not really a hunch because I've nothing to back it up. Call it "the need to do something when all other ideas have run out." Am I making sense?'

Sergeant Bob Fellows grinned. 'Not really. Perhaps you'd like to start from the beginning and simply.'

'It seems to me,' said Snow as though he was thinking aloud, which in a sense he was. 'It seems to me that all this stuff began in Huddersfield some time ago. Maybe around 1970 when Darren Rhodes had his accident – if it was an accident. Why Russell and Alex should have the guy's photo I do not know. I can't think they would be friends with such a low life but he does somehow link them together and probably to the other fellow in the frame.'

'This Laurence bloke.'

'Laurence Dane, yes. Sally's had no luck with him yet. Certainly he hasn't got a record, that's for sure. Apparently he's not with Equity. But we'll trace him in the end. But back to this morning's business ... in 1970 Russell Blake was attending Greenbank Sixth Form College doing his A levels...'

'And that's why we're on our way there now?' There was a note of incredulity in Fellows' voice.

'Yes. We're off to see one of the English

teachers, a fellow by the name of Colin Simpson.'

'Who's he?'

'He taught Russell Blake. I just wanted to get a snapshot of the young fellow circa 1970 and see if it leads us anywhere. I rang the Head yesterday and very obligingly he did a little digging and came up with Colin Simpson. He's the only member of staff still around from 1970 who had Blake in his group.

'Let's hope he's got a good memory and he's not senile.'

Colin Simpson did have a good memory and as a fellow in his mid-forties, he was far from senile. He looked tired though, haggard even, with a lumbering gait and bowed shoulders; the years of teaching were taking their toll. He was dressed in an ancient shiny suit which had obviously seen great service in the classroom. A knitted tie of indeterminate colour hung loosely knotted around his neck.

He saw Snow and Fellows in one of the smart 'study rooms' off the library and had even arranged coffee for them. It was, thought Snow, that for Simpson this was a pleasant interlude from the rigours of the classroom. Contact with the real outside world during school hours.

'So,' Simpson said, pulling on his chin 'you've come about Russell Blake.'

Snow nodded. 'You remember him?'

'Oh, indeed. Bright lad but ... somewhat self-contained.'

'What exactly do you mean by that?'

'He kept a kind of protective shell around him-self, as though he didn't want to get contaminated with human intercourse. You could only get so close to him. He was a difficult boy to understand. Intelligent though. That was his saving grace. But arrogant with it. Didn't mix. But he did have a close friend and they were joined at the hip. They both thought they were above it all. A memorable pair. I must admit they intrigued me.'

'Who was this friend?'

'A boy called Laurence.'

Snow threw a glance at Fellows. 'Not Laurence Dane?'

Simpson shook his head. 'No. Laurence Barker. Tall, snooty lad. He and Russell were inseparable. They were on their own idiosyncratic wavelength, in their own little world. It was rumoured they were queer but I never subscribed to that theory. There was something else other than sex which bonded them together.'

'What was that?'

Simpson shrugged. 'Don't really know. They had a kind of weird sense of humour and the same bleak view of the world – of life itself, I suppose. They viewed most things with sarcasm and disdain. Intellectually miserable you might say. But they were not in the least bit camp – if you know what I mean. To be honest, I didn't dislike them but at the same time I didn't understand them.'

'Did they get into trouble at all?'

'Nothing serious that I can recall. They skipped lessons from time to time but in many ways they were too mature to get involved in the usual teenage scrapes. I will say one thing however, they both seemed to have a very cruel streak, especially Barker. For example, they ragged one of my colleagues, Irene Black, something awful. She was a sensitive soul and not really suited to teaching, but that's not the point. You expect respect from your students – or at least you did in those days. The two lads sent her up rotten. She confessed to me that she used to dread going into the classroom when they were there. She's dead now, poor thing.'

'How did she die?'

'Heart attack I think.'

'Did you teach someone called Alex Marshall around the same time?'

Simpson thought for a moment and then shook his head. 'Not that I recall. Name doesn't ring a bell, but if he was a run of the mill student I wouldn't remember him. I get so many of those.' Simpson curled a weary lip.

'Russell Blake went to Durham University. Where did Laurence Barker go?'

'He went to York. I seem to remember he tried his hand at acting. He was quite good at that. Read Shakespeare very well in class. He had a natural bent for showing off, I suppose.'

'Do you think these two kept in touch after leaving college?'

'Well, I don't know for certain, but I would assume they did. Lifelong friendships are formed at school and these two were so close and so...' He searched momentarily for a suitable phrase. '...so *simpatico,* I can hardly believe they wouldn't have kept in touch.'

Simpson gave a brief self-indulgent smile,

shifted his position in his chair and placed his empty coffee cup on a bookcase beside him. 'So ... have these fellows been up to mischief?'

'Can't really say at the moment, Mr Simpson. Our investigations are ongoing. However, I can tell you that Russell Blake is dead. He was murdered.'

Simpson's hands flew to his face in shock, covering his mouth as he emitted a groan. 'Good gracious,' he said, looking even more tired than ever. 'He must have only been in his early thirties. How awful. Do you know who did it?'

Snow thought he had a good idea but he wasn't prepared to share his notion with Simpson, nor indeed with his sergeant. 'As I said our investigation is ongoing.' He rose to indicate the interview was at an end. 'Thanks for your time.'

'Well, that was interesting,' said Snow once he and Bob Fellows were outside the building.

'Interesting, maybe, but it doesn't get us much further down the road.'

Snow glanced at Fellows. He liked the man: he was easy to get on with, responsible and decent and in many ways a bright copper. But he lacked an essential ingredient that would propel him further up the career ladder: imagination. He couldn't take facts and information and play with them, and attempt to form some theory or possible scenario. Bob Fellows needed everything cut and dried before he was able take action.

'What now?' said Fellows as he hauled himself inside the car and began buckling his seatbelt.

'Back to HQ and a little more sifting. But

tomorrow, I fancy a trip to York. Not been there for ages. Nice city. I think I'll go on my own. Take a trip on the train.'

Fellows seemed a little puzzled at this but said nothing.

Laurence stared unseeingly at the muted television in his hotel room. He was bored. Really bored. He felt he was no longer connecting with life. He did enjoy working on the soap opera but it was hardly engrossing or demanding work. Performing a series of short two minute scenes was easypeasy and, because his character was a subsidiary one, his work seemed to be over in a flash, leaving him with oceans of time to kick his heels. As he took a swig of whisky from a half bottle he had by his bedside, he had to admit that he was not only bored but also lonely.

He missed his Brothers: Russell and Alex. He missed them and yet strangely he did not regret killing them. That had been part of his plan and he could not have veered from it one iota. But now there was a void; one that he had not been expecting. Although he only met up with them once a year for their annual project, in a strange way they had been with him all the time. He felt their presence and he thought of them often. Now ... there was nothing.

On an impulse he dragged himself off the bed, slipped on his overcoat and went out.

He headed for the city centre. It was dusk and pedestrians hurried by him, alien silhouettes against the lighted shop windows. He walked aimlessly, like a man in slow motion against the flurry of passers-by. After a while he went into a coffee shop off Briggate and sat there with a weak Americano eying up the customers. Like the old days, he analysed them individually, working out which of them would make a suitable victim. It was only hypothetical now, but he derived great pleasure from it.

Hypothetical?

Well, he supposed, it needn't be.

With a grin he cast a fresh eye upon his fellow coffee drinkers. There was certainly no one here that appeared to be a suitable candidate for his special attention. They all seemed clean-washed middle class dullards. Even the couple of teenagers over by the window appeared sedate and God-fearing.

Then he had an idea. Wouldn't it be fun to revisit the scene of his youth? He was sure there would be plenty of scruffy ne'er-do-wells ripe for plucking there. After all Huddersfield was only a thirty minute train ride from Leeds. He could visit his old alma mater. The nostalgia element appealed to him. It would be a return to the heart of the circle. Where it all began. He thought of Old Mother Black and her wretched dog and experienced a warm glow ignite within him. He felt happier than he had done for days.

It was settled. Tomorrow – another day free from filming – he would take himself off to Huddersfield.

# THIRTY-EIGHT

Laurence was humming gently to himself as he emerged from the gloom of the booking hall out on to the steps of Huddersfield station. He gazed at the spread of St George's Square before him bathed in a pale autumn sunshine with a mixture of unease and nostalgia. It amused him how fate and some other intangible force kept bringing him back to Huddersfield.

'Hello, the black sheep returns,' he murmured to himself with a grin.

As he looked around him he observed that while there were some changes visible from his old days, the heart of the old industrial town remained the same. 'Age cannot wither her, nor custom stale her infinite sameness,' he muttered to himself as he gazed around him at the sooty edifices surrounding the square. He gave a stiff salute to the statuesque lion that stood high atop the chambers that bore its name. The beast stared back with timeworn indifference.

Laurence sauntered slowly up the hill towards Greenbank College, about three quarters of a mile out of the city centre, remembering how he used to take the same route when he was a sixteen-year-old student. He reached the college and stood at the gates and allowed the memories to flow. Little had changed on the outside. One of the tennis courts had been converted into a car

292

park for the increasing number of staff cars, but apart from that the old building looked the same. In his imagination he saw the throng of students milling outside just before the eight-thirty bell. And there over by the laurel bush having a crafty fag was Russell, looking bored and disdainful as usual. He glanced towards Laurence, grinned and waved. Laurence almost waved back before the image faded.

To his surprise Laurence felt a powerful wave of sadness crash down on him. He shuddered from its effect.

'Can I help you?'

It was a man in a brown smock who had, it seemed to Laurence, materialised out of thin air. But this was no relic from the past. He was real flesh and blood.

'No, no.'

'I'm the caretaker,' the man said formally but not unkindly. 'Are you looking for a student?'

Laurence shook his head. 'Old Thompson's gone then?'

'Old Thompson? Oh, you mean Frank, my predecessor. Yes, he retired early about four or five years ago.'

'I was a student here. I was just passing.'

'Oh, I see. Well, if there's nothing I can do.'

Laurence shook his head. 'No. Nothing.' He turned slowly and walked away.

The next port of call was The Sportsman. It was nearly noon and Laurence thought it would be fun to sink a pint in the very corner that he and Russell used to occupy when they had bunked off afternoon lessons. But on arriving there he had a

293

great shock. The pub was closed and boarded up with a 'For Sale' sign projecting at right angles above the main door. From its tattered and grubby appearance, it was clear it had been there for some time. He stared at the premises for quite a while, disappointed at the demise of the old boozer. This was his real seat of learning rather than the college. He remembered those relaxed afternoons in the grey, dimly lighted interior indulgently plotting, moaning, back-biting and generally enjoying himself. It suddenly struck Laurence for the first time that these snatched hours in the Sportsman – Alf's place – were the best, the happiest time of his life.

His reverie was interrupted by a husky voice. 'Can you spare the price of a cup of tea, sir?'

He turned and looked into the face of the devil: a countenance seared with a thousand wrinkles, each one deeply ingrained with sooty grime, thin lips which barely concealed two rows of small rotten teeth and two blank raisin eyes, sunken in puffy flesh, set so far back in the head that they were barely visible. The creature stank of urine and alcohol.

This derelict scrap of humanity, wrapped in a greasy, ragged raincoat, repeated his request, his body swaying unsteadily. Whether this was the result of lack of nourishment or cheap alcohol, Laurence wasn't sure.

'A cup of tea, eh?' Laurence said with a sneer.

The tramp, unable to detect the venom in his voice, nodded. 'Yes sir. A cup... I'm dying for a cup of tea.'

'Are you? Sure you wouldn't prefer a large

294

bottle of whisky, eh? In preference a single malt. I can recommend Laphroaig.'

The tramp blinked his tiny eyes uncomprehendingly.

'Certainly, my good fellow, I can give you some cash in order that you can quench your thirst. The problem is I've left my wallet in my car. However, I'm parked not far from here. Come along.'

Laurence moved away, but the tramp remained where he was, swaying slightly, confused by events.

'Come along. Follow me. I'll give you cash. Mon-ey.' He addressed the man as though he was an errant puppy.

After a few moments, the man stumbled forward in Laurence's direction.

'That's right. Follow me.'

He led the man around the corner on to St John's Road and then left up a very narrow cobbled street which ran parallel up past the rear of The Sportsman. Laurence remembered it as one of the red light thoroughfares where at night prostitutes waited to be picked up. For all he knew this was still the case. It certainly remained a dank and dirty – but, more importantly, it was deserted.

He pointed to an ancient Cortina parked towards the top of the lane. 'My car,' he lied. 'Where my wallet is.' He spoke in a slow staccato, childlike rhythm so that the befuddled tramp could grasp the purpose of their trek. Halfway up the hill, there was a passageway which led to some derelict building. Turning swiftly on his heels, Laurence pushed the tramp into the passage with great force. The man gave a soft grunt of surprise and almost lost his footing. His reactions were painfully slow and it took a little while for him regain a secure balance. He leaned against the wall, his little eyes flickering wildly with uncertainty. With a smile, Laurence stepped forward and smashed him hard in the face with his fist. He felt the bones in the man's nose break and blood exploded from the nostrils. Before the creature had a chance to collapse to the floor, Laurence hit him again. Harder this time.

The man gave a muffled gurgle of pain and collapsed to the ground unconscious.

Laurence stood over him, breathing heavily, full of passion and hatred. He gazed down at the pathetic bundle of rags, the bloodied face, twisted and immobile. With a cry of anger, Laurence brought his foot down with great force onto the man's head. The body shifted slightly and the mouth opened slackly. 'Want the price of a cup of tea, do you,' he snarled and stamped hard on the tramp a second time. He heard the skull crack and the head twisted awkwardly as though the neck was broken.

Laurence stood for some time breathing heavily staring down at the contorted corpse before him, a steady stream of red blood seeping from the back of the man's head forming a thin scarlet rivulet in the dirt of the passageway.

Suddenly he found himself smiling and then laughing in a suppressed fashion, so much so that his body shuddered with the effort to contain his amusement. God, that was good, he thought.

Really good. Killing for no real purpose, no underlying motive, randomly, on a whim. That was good. That's what made him happy. And what harm had he done? This piece of human shit was better off dead. Killing him was tidying up society a little.

He could barely tear himself away from the sight of the grubby tramp's dead body. He found great pleasure in admiring his own handiwork, but a pang of self preservation persuaded him that it was imprudent to hang around too long. Quickly wiping the blood from his hands and shoe with his handkerchief and checking his clothing, he withdrew and within ten minutes was in one of the newer bars in the centre of Huddersfield – all chrome and plastic facia – having a celebratory drink. He had first gone to the lavatory to cast an eye over his appearance and wash his hands thoroughly to swill away any traces of blood.

'A little water clears us of this deed,' he grinned at himself in the mirror above the washbasin.

He ordered a malt whisky in the bar and slumped back in one of the faux leather armchairs. He was happy again. The real Laurence had returned. One simple act had allowed him to slough off the grim shackles that had been in danger of imprisoning him. He realised now that ever since the Matt Wilkinson fiasco, he had felt trapped into scenarios not of his own making. He had been obliged. And that was not for him. He was far too much of a free agent. A free spirit. He must be allowed to pick and choose whom he wanted to kill. And most of all, it must be done without ...

what was that legal term? – ah, yes, without just cause.

Laurence raised his glass of single malt in a toast.

## THIRTY-NINE

After stepping out of the station, Paul Snow was immediately seduced by the beauty of York: the honey coloured stonework, the gentle rise and fall of the ancient wall as it hugs the contours of the city, the broad and tranquil expanse of the river which threads its quiet way through the heart of the metropolis and the beautiful Minster tower rising high into the pale blue autumn sky. He was sorely tempted to abandon his mission and revisit the Minster to recapture memories of his visits there with his parents when he was at junior school: those halcyon, innocent days when worries were simple things and pleasures likewise. Still, ever the realist, he knew that he had neither the time nor the stomach to indulge in such nostalgia. In the end memories only brought you pain.

Nevertheless, he wandered off his planned route to stand outside the magnificent church and gaze up at its grandeur. What passion, what skill, what dedication, what determination and hard work had gone into creating such a magnificent edifice. He stood quietly amid a whirl of jabbering, camera-snapping tourists of various nationalities, drinking in the spiritual beauty of the building. It was calming, therapeutic and strangely uplifting. Snow wasn't at all religious but he was susceptible to beauty.

After five minutes or so, reluctantly he returned to reality and with a sigh set off with a purpose to York University. It was here in a little office crammed from floor to ceiling with books that he met Professor Peter Richardson, a squat bearded fellow, with bright darting eyes forever peering out beneath heavy overgrown eyebrows. All the time he was talking to Snow, he was sifting through the maelstrom of papers in his desk – notes, essays, letters and various lists. It was as though he had lost something – something, Snow thought, he would never find.

'Oh, yes, yes, I remember Laurence. Fascinating chap. A bit autistic in some ways. Although I've no medical qualifications to justify that judgement, you understand. It was just my feeling.'

'In what way "autistic"?'

'Well, he had great ability to read a text, to emote a character's feelings. He found it easy to get under the skin of a character and bring him to life ... but in the real world he failed to connect with people. It was as though...' Richardson paused as he reached for the right expression. 'It was as though he couldn't get under his own skin. He didn't know how to play himself.'

Richardson grinned beneath his hairy beard, pleased with his analogy.

'Was he ever cruel or vindictive?'

Richardson's eyebrows fluttered towards his hairline.

'Funny you should say that. It was going to be my next point. He could, indeed, be very cruel. He had an acid tongue but you know I don't think he fully realised the pain and hurt that he inflicted because of this...' he flapped his hands '...lack of connection that I mentioned. However, he had a superficial charm and a lot of the girls liked him. Well, he was good looking and had the confidence that a privileged upbringing provides.'

'Any serious girlfriend?'

Richardson shook his head. 'Uh, uh. The connection problem again. Whatever the girls were after, all Laurence was after was sexual gratification. He hadn't the means to entertain notions of love, affection and all that. There was a series of girls – but not girlfriends, if you get my point. All quick flings as far as I was able to ascertain. No serious relationship at all. That wasn't his scene.'

'What happened to him?'

'He got an agent in his final year and went into acting. Changed his name.'

'Did he? What to?'

Richardson grinned. 'Laurence Barker became Laurence Dane. Get it?'

Snow shook his head.

'What's the greatest part an actor can be offered? The most difficult, the most challenging of all Shakespeare's roles?'

'Hamlet, I suppose. Or Lear.'

'Hamlet it is. Hamlet the Dane. Well Laurence could hardly call himself Hamlet Barker, so he settled for...' Richardson's hands did another windmill motion... 'Laurence Dane.'

After his interview with Professor Richardson, Snow allowed himself the luxury of a stroll by the river to collect his thoughts and do a little creative thinking. He now had a mountain of information connected with the Matt Wilkinson murders and associated events, odd pieces of the jigsaw that frustratingly almost fitted but didn't and so the overall picture was still incomplete. There was nothing else for it: he would have to push and shove these recalcitrant pieces together with brute force and hope some image came into focus. He was now convinced that the three men who had invaded Matt Wikinson's house and killed him and his two cronies were Russell Blake, Alex Marshall and Laurence Barker/Dane. And these three men had been playing a game of murder – motiveless but premeditated murder for over ten years. For sport. For fun. For the sheer pleasure and power of destroying life. They had picked on vulnerable strangers in a variety of locations, ensuring there were no clues and no connections.

How clever.

How sick.

And now Blake and Marshall themselves had been killed. Either there was a fourth mysterious figure in the game, or Laurence Barker/Dane was his man.

Surely?

When he finally returned to the railway station, he had achieved his goal, after a fashion. He held in his mind a picture of events as he imagined them. It was, he thought with a tight smile, his Picasso canvas: it was clear, dramatic and com-

301

plete if a little incredible and bizarre but he was not sure it would make sense to many people. Still it was something and it gave him a course of action to pursue.

It was just after 3 p.m. when he arrived back at his office and before he had time to sit at his desk, there was a brusque tap at his door and Michael Armitage entered. Snow's heart sank. What now? he thought.

'There's been a murder in town,' Armitage announced without ceremony. 'An alkie has been beaten to death.'

Snow nodded and waited for Armitage to continue.

'I'd like to handle the case. It's time I had a crack at being in charge of an investigation. With your recommendation, I could act up. We're stretched as it is and it would be a good way of easing things. I want you to get me this.'

There was a strange vulnerable desperation in Armitage's demeanour.

'What makes you think I can do this ... even if I wanted to?'

Suddenly Armitage's stance changed and with it his mood. 'You can ... and you will,' he intoned. The warning was implicit in his tone.

'So this is another of your threats is it?'

'You can do it for me. I deserve it.' Surprisingly there was almost a pleading note in Armitage's voice.

'I probably could do it, but you certainly don't deserve it,' said Snow with deliberate slowness. He was not about to list the various reasons – such as Armitage's laziness, his slovenly attitude

302

to detail and his lack of real intelligence – why he would never recommend Michael Armitage for any kind of promotion or position of real responsibility He would never recommend him under normal circumstances, that is. But these were not 'normal circumstances' and if he needed confirming evidence of this fact he only had to look at the man's countenance. His features now had darkened, the jaw line tightened and the eyes suddenly blazed with anger.

'I don't think you've a choice in the matter, sweetie. I say you do it and by hell, you do it.'

'Or else?'

Armitage nodded. 'Or else.'

'Leave it with me.'

Armitage was about to say something in reply but he refrained. He gave Snow a sarcastic grin, a grin of triumph. 'Don't leave it too long ... sweetie,' he growled before making a swift exit.

Snow did not stir from his chair. His only movement was the clenching of his hands on the desk top. This would go on until the crack of doom, he told himself.

But no ... it couldn't go on. Something must be done.

Something.

But what?

# FORTY

A couple of weeks later, Snow sat with a can of lager watching the television. Well, at least he was seated before the box and it was on. His eyes scanned the pictures before him but his mind was elsewhere. It was mired in the dilemma of what to do about Michael Armitage. Slipping him some cash on demand was one thing but pushing the bastard up the promotion ladder was another.

He groaned and took a large swig from the can of lager. As he did so, his eyes caught something on the television screen. It was the cast list of *Emmerdale Farm*, the programme that he had not been watching.

There it was. The name: Laurence Dane. He had been playing a character called Sebastian Barnes. Before he knew it, there was the Yorkshire Television logo and the adverts had started, 'Now hands that do dishes can feel soft as your face...'

Snow switched off the set and reached for the *TV Times*. He checked the cast list of *Emmerdale Farm*. There it was:

*Sebastian Barnes* ............*Laurence Dane*

He flicked through the pages of the magazine and found the next episode of the soap opera with a little picture of 'Sebastian Barnes posing a threat to Sophie Warren'.

Sebastian Barnes was tall, thin, good looking in an arrogant sort of way and he seemed to do menacing very well.

This – or rather he – was the missing piece in the puzzle.

## FORTY-ONE

Snow was about to leave the house the following morning when the telephone rang. He stared at it jangling on the hall table as though it was an unexploded bomb. He rarely received calls at home and when he did, they tended to be unpleasant ones connected with work. His day was planned and he didn't want those plans disrupted by demands on his time. He was sorely tempted not to answer the thing. Five minutes later and he would have been out of the house anyway.

The more he stared with the squat plastic casing, the louder the ringing seemed to get. His curiosity and his professionalism got the better of him and with reluctance he picked up the receiver.

As soon as he heard the voice at the other end, he wished that he hadn't.

'I hope I didn't get you out of bed, sir.'

It was Michael Armitage.

'What do you want?'

'Just a little reminder about the conversation we had yesterday. I expect you to take action soon. Very soon ... or things could take a nasty turn.'

'Indeed they could,' said Snow replacing the receiver.

When he arrived at his office, there was a package waiting for him on his desk. 'What's all this about?' he asked Bob Fellows.

'Search me, sir. It arrived by special delivery this morning.'

Snow gazed at it suspiciously. It was addressed to him marked personal and private. As he reached out to pick it up, his telephone rang with a ferocity that made him jump. Annoyed at himself, he grabbed the receiver. 'Snow,' he barked, more officiously than he'd meant to.

'Blimey, you got out of the bed the wrong side of the bed this morning, didn't you, lad?'

It was Inspector Ray (Dinosaur) Daniels.

Snow ignored the taunt. 'Morning, what can I do for you, Ray?'

'It's more what I've done for you. Has it arrived?'

'What?'

'The little present I sent you?'

Snow gazed at the package on his desk. 'Well, yes I reckon it has. What is it?'

Daniels gave a throaty chuckle. 'My special gift to you. You'll think Christmas has come early.'

'I'm not good at riddles this early in the morning.'

'After our little chat over a pint the other day, I got to thinking about your case and Russell

306

Blake's murder. So I went back to his house to have another shufty round to see if I could find anything that might throw a bit more light on matters. Found bugger all. That is until I had a look in the garage. Up in the rafters – crafty sod – in a metal tool box, I found it.'

'Found what?'

Another laugh. 'You've not opened it then?'

'No.'

'Well go on. Enjoy. I reckon it'll be a real boon to your investigation. I don't want to act on it myself. I retire in two months' time and I'm not after doing anything strenuous, following up leads and the like to trouble me in my last days on the beat. I reckon you'll do a grand job of chasing things up. Best of luck.'

The line went dead.

Snow made himself a coffee and shut himself away in his office alone with the package. Pulling back the copious wrapping he revealed a note book with a stiff cardboard cover. Snow placed the book on the desk, opened it, took a sip of coffee and then began reading.

Laurence had just finished the brief scene and was about to make his way back to his dressing room when the director. Ted Torrance took him to one side.

'Bad news, I'm afraid. The powers that be have decided to axe your character as originally planned in a few weeks' time. It's their thinking that a sharp-suited, smooth-talking villain would be out of place in a rural setting. I think they're wrong ... but...'

307

Laurence nodded. It came neither as a great surprise nor a great disappointment. He had enjoyed himself on the soap but he could see that it proffered many dangers. It was a fur-lined rut, a place where real acting disappeared and one just adopted the reactions of your permanent alter-ego in repetitious scenes. In many ways you became your character, merging your personality with them, and so in the end no acting skills were required because, in essence, you were playing a version of yourself. It was a conveyor belt for thespians with limited vision or a pension scheme for the older hacks. This was not for him. As a rung up the ladder to more satisfying and financially rewarding work it was fine, but as a long term arrangement ... well for him it had all the charm of a spell in Wormwood Scrubs.

'You'll be told officially, but I thought you'd like to know as soon as poss.' He wrinkled his nose. 'Then you can make plans.'

Laurence squeezed Torrance's arm. 'I appreciate that, mate. Thanks.'

The director nodded, gave a tight smile and wandered off on to the set. Laurence made his way back to his tiny dressing room. He didn't quite know how he felt. Relieved that he hadn't been given an option to stay on the soap but annoyed that it wasn't him who had made the decision to leave. He liked to be in control of his own destiny.

As he passed down the narrow corridor towards his dressing room, one of the production assistants, a girl young enough to be still at school, with the standard prop clip board in hand, stopped him. 'Hi Laurence, you've got a visitor in your dressing room.'

Laurence found his visitor, a thin-faced solemn looking man somewhere in his mid-thirties, sitting casually on one the chairs in the little cell that was grandly referred to as 'his dressing room.' He rose when Laurence entered.

'Mr Dane?'

'That's me.'

'I'm Detective Inspector Snow of the West Yorkshire Police.'

Laurence knew then, knew with a fierce crystal clarity, he knew. He knew that this was the beginning of the end.

'And I thought I'd paid my television licence.' He sat down and took a packet of small cigars from his pocket. 'Would you care for one?'

Snow shook his head. 'No thank you.'

'Not on duty, eh?' Laurence lit up and blew the smoke over his shoulder. 'So what's all this about?'

'Well, let me say at the outset, that I know. I know everything. I know about "The Brotherhood".'

His eyes were steady and cool, unwavering in their stare and Laurence believed him. Other words were not necessary. This man really did know. He could tell that this was not a bluff based on half-formed ideas and guess work. How he had found out, he couldn't fathom. But he had.

He took a long drag on the cigar. Well, charades had to be played.

'I'm sorry, you've lost me. You'd better explain,' said Laurence smoothly, a gentle smile curling his lips.

'Well let's start with your friends Russell Blake

and Alex Marshall and what you three did to Matt Wilkinson, Ronnie Fraser and Dave Johnson the night you visited Wilkinson's house.

Laurence shook his head. 'I'm afraid I don't know what you're talking about.'

'Then to protect yourself,' continued Snow, 'you murdered your two friends, Russell and Alex.'

Laurence laughed and regretted it immediately. It was too theatrical a laugh to be convincing. It was the laugh of denial that a pantomime villain makes. He was a better actor than that and he should have known.

'But you have killed before, haven't you? Several times no doubt. What about Darren Rhodes?'

'Indeed, what about Darren Rhodes? Who's he?'

Snow sat down again and leaned back in his chair. 'I think the time for play acting is over.'

'It's what I do for a living, Inspector. Aren't you a fan of *Emmerdale Farm?*'

'I don't profess to know the full details of your criminal career. I know how it started – the kidnap and killing of Old Mother Black's dog, but I can make informed assumptions and I'm sure you'll tell me the rest.'

At the mention of Old Mother Black's dog, Laurence's face paled, and his eyes widened in surprise. 'I'm afraid I really don't know what you are talking about,' he said but the smooth bluster had faded from his voice.

'Russell Blake began a journal all those years ago when you first met at Greenbank College ... it has recently come into my possession. It makes fascinating reading.'

Laurence opened his mouth to say something

310

but no words came out.

'It's over, Laurence. You've run out of luck.'

'You're still not making sense, Inspector. What have the juvenile ramblings of an old school friend of mine got to do with these murders?'

'You are going to tell me. I want to know. I've tracked you down but for the life in me, I don't understand you. I'd like to give you a chance to explain.'

Laurence gave a sneer. 'To confess, you mean. To talk my way into a prison cell for life.'

'To explain. I'm here on my own aren't I? No note-taking sergeant in tow. No tape recorder. Just a private conversation. To clarify matters. I am intrigued.'

'You are mad.'

'It's possible,' said Snow, aware that he was about to take that dangerous and crazy pathway he had contemplated.

Laurence narrowed his eyes and scrutinised this strange policeman. 'What are you after?'

'The truth.'

Laurence grinned. 'Ah, what was it old Keats said: "Beauty is truth, truth beauty – that is all ye know on earth and all ye need to know."'

'This is just between ourselves.'

The words lingered in the air for some moments.

Laurence reached over to a small cupboard and extracted a bottle of whisky and a couple of mugs.

'Will you join me?' he said, uncorking the bottle.

Snow nodded, aware that he was on the verge of getting what he wanted.

Laurence splashed very generous measures into the mugs and handed one to Snow. 'Well,' he said slowly. 'Where to start... Oh, yes...Well, Inspector, are you sitting comfortably. Then I'll begin. It's all about a grand game.'

It was a bloody tale. And Laurence recounted it with a gripping conciseness, while still managing to keep in the important and the gory details.

Snow sat absolutely still, held by the narrative, both fascinated and appalled by its revelations. He was also conscious that Laurence was treating the occasion like a confessional. He was at last able to unburden himself of all the dark sin that had built up like a heavy outer coating weighing down his soul.

Or was he just boasting?

'Strange fellow, aren't I?' Laurence said with a sour grin when he had finished. 'Of course you won't get me to repeat one scrap of that again at any time or in any place – but I hope I have satisfied your curiosity.'

Snow nodded.

'So, Mr Policeman, what are you going to do now?'

Snow paused. He knew what he was going to do now, but like flying a hang glider, he needed to screw his courage to the sticking place before he leapt off into the scary unknown.

After a pause, he said softly, 'I'm going to make you an offer.'

Laurence's eyes widened in surprise. 'Oh, yes?'

Snow leaned forward. 'Do you take commissions?'

# FORTY-TWO

Snow popped his head around his office door and called across the room. 'Bob, could I have a word?'

Sergeant Fellows looked up from the tedious paperwork which was demanding his attention and failing. Anything rather than this, he thought, but was wise enough not to verbalise the notion.

'Sure,' he said, and joined his boss in his office.

Snow waved him to a seat. 'I've got a tentative lead on the Wilkinson murders. Something that Dinosaur Daniels let me have.'

'That's great,' grinned Fellows.

Snow did not return the grin. 'It's tricky and rather sensitive so ... I'm going to handle it myself for the moment.'

'What do you mean?'

'Look, Bob, I can't explain fully, but if I involve the troops out there the whole thing might go belly up. I need to do this alone.'

'With respect, sir...'

Snow held up his hand. 'I know what you are going to say, so spare your breath. I'll take full responsibility for my actions – but I wanted it known to you that I was working on the case in a solo capacity.'

'Solo capacity. That's a new one. What d'you expect me to do with this information?'

'Nothing. Just store it for further reference – if needed. That's all.'

Fellows shook his head in bewilderment.

'That's all, Bob, you can get back to those fascinating files now.'

With a shrug, he rose and headed for the door. 'Just you take care, sir,' he said quietly as he left the room.

Snow sat back in his chair and sighed. Well, he'd done all he could do. Now it was up to the fates.

Michael Armitage hauled the two carrier bags out of the boot of the car. He had always hated shopping and while he was married he had been very adept at avoiding getting involved in the process. But since his divorce, he really had no option. Every bloody Thursday, down to bloody Sainsbury's like a bloody fishwife. He slammed the car boot down and struggled up the path to his tiny terraced abode: his prize for being kicked out of the family semi up in the posh environs of Fixby. Now he had to find his bloody key. He dropped the two bags on the door mat and sought for his house key in his jacket pocket.

'Michael Armitage,' said a voice in the darkness behind him. Armitage turned awkwardly to face the speaker.

'Who wants to know?' he asked gruffly.

'No one of consequence,' said the stranger, thrusting his hand forward. As he did so Armitage felt a sharp pain in his abdomen. He glanced down as the stranger withdrew his hand and he saw that it was holding a knife: a long vicious-

314

looking knife which had dark stains on it.

Blood.

His blood.

Before he could react, the man plunged again, the blade sinking even deeper this time. Armitage groaned in agony and doubled up after the third blow and slumped to the ground. His vision grew foggy and his attacker now became just a vague shadow. With the fourth blow of the knife, Michael Armitage lost consciousness and any hope of survival. Very quickly life, like the blood around his stomach, gushed out of him, his head resting on one of the shopping bags.

'Brother, hail and farewell,' said Laurence before turning and making his way down the path.

A little way along the road was a man standing in the shadows near a street lamp.

'Mission accomplished,' said Laurence as he approached the man, not noticing the gun he held in his hand.

'Good,' said the man. 'Very good.'

And then he pulled the trigger. Twice.

As Laurence toppled to the ground, Snow gave a grim smile. 'Game over,' he said.

The publishers hope that this book has given you enjoyable reading. Large Print Books are especially designed to be as easy to see and hold as possible. If you wish a complete list of our books please ask at your local library or write directly to:

**Magna Large Print Books**
Magna House, Long Preston,
Skipton, North Yorkshire.
BD23 4ND

This Large Print Book for the partially sighted, who cannot read normal print, is published under the auspices of

## THE ULVERSCROFT FOUNDATION